'I am not, by any means, a ...
observant, always affable, a ...
not going to moralise: I do n.. ....ppointed censor of
the times in which I live. I do .... care a pin what becomes of
society, so long as I succeed in avoiding the arrows of detraction, scorn,
and contempt which it launches against any luckless member who has
the misfortune to be found out. I hardly think it will do so in my case; at
any rate, I take all possible precautions to pursue my silent path of
sensual indulgence in obscurity and peace.'

Thus our heroine Eveline confesses on paper what she is so
careful to conceal in public – throwing caution to the winds in
this frank and detailed account of her adventures in Paris and
London.

Also in this series:

SUBURBAN SOULS, BOOK ONE
SUBURBAN SOULS, BOOK TWO
A MAN WITH A MAID, VOLUME I
A MAN WITH A MAID, VOLUME II
OH WICKED COUNTRY!
THE ROMANCE OF LUST, BOOK ONE
THE ROMANCE OF LUST, BOOK TWO
MORE EVELINE
BEATRICE
THE BOUDOIR
'FRANK' AND I
RANDIANNA
ROSA FIELDING

EVELINE:

The Amorous Adventures of a Victorian Lady

A STAR BOOK

published by

the Paperback Division of
W. H. ALLEN & Co. PLC

A Star Book

Published in 1983
by the Paperback Division of
W. H. Allen & Co. PLC
44 Hill Street, London W1X 8LB
Reprinted 1985
Reprinted 1986
Reprinted 1988

Published by arrangement with Grove Press Inc, New York

Printed and bound in Great Britain by
Cox & Wyman Ltd, Reading

ISBN 0 352 31337 4

Contents

Preface vii

Book One 1

Book Two 91

Book Three 201

Preface *

Among the pornographic effusions which deluged the period approximately between 1790 and 1810, mostly published in the form and after the illiterate fashion of the chap-books, or pamphlets garnished with ill-coloured plates, and embellished with high-sounding titles, sold by itinerant venders who were called "chapmen," there were one or two which, from whatever source they emanated, claimed a literary merit not altogether thrown away on the connoisseur.

---

*This Preface is taken from the 1904 Paris edition of *Eveline*. We do not know the identity of the editor.—Grove Press

In my early memory there were many of these flimsy publications still existing, always to be had, originally *sub rosa* from the enterprising *colporteur;* and within my own experience, as curiosities, from such booksellers as dared to risk the serious penalties attaching to their sale.

Among these numerous catchpennies there figured: *The Amatory Adventures of a Lady's Maid, The Footman, The Adventures of a Quaker*, and *The Modern Eveline*

It is to the last I would call attention. I only know of one notice existing of this very remarkable work.* The original is absolutely lost to the bibliophile, while to my certain knowledge, there are at least two copies accepted, catalogued and preserved in the private library of the British Museum.

As to the book itself, it has always been a puzzle to the bibliophile of the past generation. In its composition and style, while displaying a fair amount of literary ability, it is sketchy and vague, written in

---

* *Eveline, or the Amours and Adventures of a Lady of Fashion.* London: Printed and published by Charles Roberts, Wardour Street. 12mo., 6 badly coloured lithographs. 2 vols. 105 and 85 pp.

This edition appeared about 1840, but it is not the original which was, I believe, entitled *Evelina.* I have two other editions before me.

a) On the title page are four lines of French poetry. London: Printed for the Booksellers, 12mo., 130 pp. This was, I believe, published by Anthony Dyer in, or shortly before, 1843.

b) Title as above. London: Printed for the Bibliophilists, 8vo., 151 pp. This I take to be the edition of W. Dugdale, about 1860, in spite of his cataloguing it as "Evelina, with fine plates (probably eight in number; they are wanting in the copy before me) price two guineas." "Catena Librorum Tacendorum." London, 1885, 4to.

short jerky sentences and very unsatisfactory as to the development of the story. It breaks off with long lines of asterisks, without explanation or attempt at completion, and the average reader resigns it with hopeless indifference. It seems to have failed in its intention of presenting the heroine as she was meant to be by the original author.

Behind all this are two hypotheses from which, in my opinion, to choose. Either the author, whoever he was—evidently a writer of no small ability—contented himself with writing for his own gratification, and subsequently consigned his manuscript to a publisher with certain portions expurgated, or the original publisher, imbued with the ignorance and rapacity of the period in such matters, cut out all which did not conduce to the vulgar taste of his time. Be it as it may, I never saw or heard of any other edition of *Eveline* than the mutilated one to which I allude, and I was personally acquainted with the publisher who produced the only edition extant, and preserved, as already stated, in the secret library of the British Museum.

Eveline has been described as any ordinary nymphomaniac; and as such the book has been dismissed in a short notice in the bibliographical work to which I have already referred. It is to be regretted that a more careful analysis was not made by the talented compiler. Had he done so, he could not have failed to perceive that the heroine was nothing of the sort.

Eveline, as portrayed by the original author, is a young woman of acute sensual instincts. There is, in her case, strong evidence of congenital aberration of certain cerebral organs. In other words, she inherits on the father's side a trace of a certain brain centre obliterated, that of the moral perception so far as it relates to the sexual instinct and no further. This does not prevent her from possessing much intelligence and quick intuition. She sees her opportunities, and with her own vitiated appreciation of ordinary life, applies them to her own indulgence.

What mere nymphomaniac could be all this? I have known, in the full blaze of modern London society, at least twenty women who could emulate her vices, but neither her audacity, her surprising resource, nor her inductive perception and ingenuity.

Many years ago, being struck with the unusual quality of the original, I undertook to supply as nearly as possible, the numerous omissions marked by half pages of asterisks throughout the book, following what I conceived to be the intention of the author to make his story a succinct narration. Unfortunately, my publisher, in a sudden access of folly, sold to a passing stranger the copy from which I worked. I still retained many extracts and notes which enable me to remember the general tenor of the story, and as such I give it herein.

So much for the history of the work which I have thought so well worth perpetuating that I have embodied as much of the original as my memory and my notes supply for the delectation of the curious. If I have wandered from the original, it will be in the power of the authorities who guard the only known copies in existence to correct me.

It has been my design to adapt the subject to the present time, not only because of the difficulties in supplying the omissions of the story in the original style, and fitted to the period in which the author wrote, but because whatever may have been the condition of society when first *Eveline* found its way to the compositor's hand—probably in the days of the third George—it could hardly have been published at a period of society corruption more appropriately illustrative of its meretricious incidents than the present.

In conclusion, while carrying out my original intention of filling up the missing passages, the additions are in no way allowed to subvert or alter the main incidents. In revising this book and rescuing the work from its deformity, I have endeavoured to insert only such matter as serves to make the story succinct, and to develop the character of the heroine as the author intended to portray it. I have followed closely throughout the style of the original composition, and now present this revised edition of a very singular old work to the curious in such literature.

—THE EDITOR.

Book One

Chapter I

I am considered by those who have the honour of my acquaintance to be a pattern of propriety. I am pointed out by anxious mothers as an excellent example of careful training, combined with the advantages of a Continental finishing course at a most select *pensionnat de demoiselles* in the environs of Paris. I am the invited of very strict old maids, because I affect to enter into their schemes for the conversion of untold savages, am liberal of purse and reticent of tongue. The latter quality runs in my family. Our history demands an extraordinary amount of it. It is quite as well it should have been so treated. There are at least two families of high and ancient aristocratic pretentions, whose loud-tongued, drinking, gambling male descendants openly boast that they have never allowed a maiden of their noble line to pass, as such, out of the family and into the arms of her spouse. Ours is a third, only we are not so simple as to publish the fact.

I am not, by any means, a saint in outward seeming. In my appearance and ordinary habits I am not so straightlaced as I am represented. I do not set up for particular formality in my daily pursuits. I am only quiet, observant, always affable, amiable and sometimes a trifle volatile. The men call me dull, and say, "a pretty girl, but you know, dear boy there is no fun in her. No use to try it on, dear old chappie, you'll only come off second best."

"Fun," in the mind of the society man of the present day, means immorality. They adopt the word because it is a light and gay style of describing the loose conditions which bind together all that they care for in the nature of modern society. At present, society is content to parade itself with a superficial and very flimsy disguise over its naked deformity. In a few years' time, at its present rate of progress, it will work barefaced in the open light of day.

I am not going to moralise; I do not even wish to be a self-appointed censor of the times in which I live. I do not personally care a pin what becomes of society, so long as I succeed in avoiding the arrows of detraction, scorn, and contempt which it launches against any luckless member who has the misfortune to be found out. I hardly think it will do so in my case; at any rate, I take all possible precautions to pursue my silent path of sensual indulgence in obscurity and peace.

My father, Sir Edward L——, Baronet, started life a rich man—rich, even in these days of treble millionaires, American heiresses, and other innovations too numerous to mention. He entered the army, served with his regiment in India, and returning to that empire after a short furlough, met and married a nobody with whom he was shut up for a month or more on his voyage out. She was good-looking, tall, and coarse. He soon tired of her. After dragging her about for three months with his regiment, he sent her home to England. I do not know that I inherit any single trait of my mother's personality, and I rejoice to think so. She never cared for me or took any particular notice of me. I had two brothers older than myself. Of the elder, I may speak later, I knew little of him in my childhood. As to Percy, we were companions until I was sent to school and he to Rugby. He was fifteen and I thirteen when these important events happened.

I suppose I was always curious and enquiring as a child. I have been told so. Personally I only remember a few prominent incidents of my early childhood. It was not a joyous or even a happy one. My brother and I were thrown much together. He was curious also. Together we secretly investigated the remarkable differences in our physiological structure. We came to the natural conclusion that such opposite developments must be designed for some purpose which at present we did not understand. The tree of knowledge being denied to us, we set about making our own investigations. The result was that we discovered a certain indefinite gratification, even when on being at each end of a large marble bath, our toes encountered certain exposed portions of each other's persons which at all other times we were told we must hide and never talk about. Secretly, also, we mutually inspected these remarkably different developments; it was a new field of investigation and insensibly we enjoyed it. We pursued our studies at such intervals as our privacy and our opportunities permitted. We slept in the same room, and we would steal furtively into each other's beds to whisper and wonder at the delight which the feeling and the caressing of these dissimilarities afforded us. In short, we masturbated each other, until my brother Percy, at the age of fifteen, attained a precocious development of his private parts quite sufficient to destroy all vestige of maidenhood in his young sister, two years his junior.

Arrived at this age we were separated as I have already related. A couple of years at a Brighton seminary exclusively for "the daughters of gentlemen" did not eradicate the lessons in physiology I had already learnt. Quite the contrary—I listened while my companions compared notes, and I found most of the girls were equally well informed.

Indeed, one or two of the elder "daughters of gentlemen" informed us of the junior classes, while we listened to the absorbing topic with wrapt attention, what a naked man was like with curly hair on his belly, and a thing dangling between his legs which they described as twice the size of my brother Percy's. They went further, and one averred that she had seen and handled one. That they grow quite stiff and stood upright. In that condition men endeavoured to thrust them into girls.

I listened and said nothing, and for my pains they called me a little fool and an innocent. Even at that early period of my existence, I had imbibed the instinct of reticence, so generally absent in young women.

Two years of study on all the subjects conventional and impractical to which "the daughters of gentlemen" are subjugated at my age and in such establishments, afforded me ample opportunities of acquiring the rudiments of a society education. How much longer I might have remained at the Brighton seminary I know not, but an untoward accident put an end to my career there, as also to the "select establishment" itself.

It happened thus. Among the domestics was a page, who had commenced his duties there as a small boy. As he was a very quiet, well-conducted lad, he remained a long time, and in fact grew up to puberty in the house. Nobody seemed to notice the change. The lad waited at table, in gorgeous buttons and claret-coloured cloth, and did other useful duties, quite unrestricted, about the premises. One of the elder girls however, whose inquisitive genius had discovered the interesting fact that he had hair on his belly and a thing which stood upright, essayed in secret to take advantage of this development; induced him to put it in her on more than one occasion, with the result that she was discovered to be *enceinte*. The fact could not be concealed; the Brighton press took it up, and the "select establishment" was closed forever.

My father was at this time on military service in India. Through interest, although comparatively a young man, ever active, he had risen to the command of his regiment. I was not allowed to remain at home. My prayer for a governess was peremptorily refused; my mother could not endure my presence. I was packed off to a *pensionnat de demoiselles* near Paris. One which had been specially recommended by the lady mother of two promising and "honourable" young members of a noble house.

It was at this place that I was destined to be initiated into the more practical knowledge of mankind, so far as their sexual instincts and aptitudes are concerned. The house was large, and stood in its own grounds, with a short garden in front leading to the *loge du concierge* and the great iron gates which closed the establishment to the public road. The lodge was tenanted by a singular individual, a hunchback, who had held the office of janitor for some years. He was a man of some forty-five years of age and stood about four feet and a few inches in his boots. His hump was a sufficient disfigurement, but his ungainly ugliness, his long hair and his huge hands and feet added greatly to his weird appearance. With all this, however, his face was not repulsive, and his manner the reverse of brutal. He was considered a perfectly harmless unfortunate, bore an excellent character, and had the entire confidence of Madame St. C——, proprietress and directress of the *pensionnat*.

When I became intimate with my fellow pupils, I learned that they were quite as well acquainted with natural phenomena as my old friends at Brighton, indeed more than one of the French girls made no scruple of boasting of her exploits. One in particular spoke openly of her acquaintance with a certain playfellow of the other sex, who had obtained from her such favours as only lovers are permitted. The *concierge* was allowed to eke out his small revenue by the harmless privilege of retailing sweets, chocolate, etc., to the *pensionnaires*. The girls, during the hours of recreation, would return from his little den in the lodge with red cheeks, and their mouths full of sugar-plums.

I never had the child's weakness for *bonbons*. I was not fond of them. The *concierge* and myself remained strangers for a considerable time after my arrival. I often noticed that the man took extra trouble to salute me in passing. He offered such civilities as were decorous and polite. The girls spoke sometimes of little commissions which they had given him to perform for them. I soon found he was considered a sort of safe intermediary between the world at large and the elder girls.

When I crossed from Dover to Calais, *en route* for Paris in charge of a governess who collected the English pupils, I chanced to sit next to two gentlemen who conversed together of Voltaire and his works. I possessed a girl's natural curiosity—I listened. They mentioned his allusions to Charlemagne. One exclaimed how he recognised the biting sarcasm of his style. He quoted the account given of the great king's private vices. The other cited Addison to show how little concern the great Frenchman had for virtue in itself. It was a pretty dispute. They raised their voices. I made notes, and determined to read Voltaire and judge for myself. I did not want *bonbons*—I wanted Voltaire.

One afternoon, I passed the door of the lodge. It was not closed. The *concierge* had an inner room. There was a curtain across the door between the two. I had seen one of the older girls, about sixteen years old, go in a few minutes before. I entered after her. All being silent, I peeped through a corner of the heavy curtain. The hunchback was standing sideways to me, inclined a little towards the curtain. She was sitting in his big chair before him. Her clothes were disarranged and her legs and her white belly uncovered. The man's big paw was between her thighs. He was fingering her pretty slit.

What struck me most was that he had in front a huge and naked limb. It was quite twice the size of Percy's. It was very straight and stiff. The young lass was sucking the big lead-coloured knob which was rolling in and out of her mouth. He was wriggling backwards and forwards, so that sometimes almost all of the knob appeared. Then he bore forward, so that nearly the whole of it went in between her red lips. Both her little hands were clasped round his long thing. She bent her head forward in little bobs. She met his movements. Both were too much occupied to think of the curtain. They thought themselves safe. His eyes were half shut. He had a satanic expression of enjoyment on his face. His lips were apart. His breath came in loud hissing sobs. On the table was a packet of *bonbons*.

There are certain trifling things one hears when young which make a long and lasting impression. They remain for quite a lifetime. Such was the Brighton girl's description: "A man with curly hair on his belly, and a thing twice the size of my brother Henry's, which got stiff and stood up straight." Here was one at last. The very thing of which that Brighton girl had told us.

I remained still and looked on. They were only some ten feet from me. They had no idea of my presence. He breathed hard and fast. The pretty girl seemed to like the tickling of the paw which moved crab-like about her thighs. Presently she stopped. She drew back from the shiny thing which stood smoking in front of her young face. He said something which I could not catch. The hunchback's limb was quite nine inches long and very thick; it was as much as the girl could do to clasp it in her delicate hands. He pushed it towards her lips again and pointed to the packet of sweets. She took the terrible morsel once more into her pretty mouth. He continued his touches. He put his right hand upon the back of her head and pressed her to him. The whole of the big knob was now covered by her moist lips. Suddenly he struck her little hands from their hold and took his limb between his finger and thumb. He drew forward her head with one hand and held her close. He pushed forward. The lass tried to extricate herself. In vain she struggled. The man's thing was firmly held in place in her mouth. He began gasping and stamping on the tiled floor. The pretty girl choked and struggled. He gradually stopped all movement. He looked ready to drop. Slowly he withdrew his limb, which now drooped like a dying flower. It was dripping with a white froth. The lass began spitting and coughing. I thought she would have been sick. I turned away, and stealing out, ran up to the house.

That night I dreamed of a man's belly covered with hair, and a long thick limb which dangled between his legs, and could on occasion stand upright, quite twice as big as my brother Percy's.

Chapter II

The third day after was a *fête*. Most of the girls
went out to the Bois de Boulogne with the gov-
ernesses. I pleaded a headache and remained within
the precincts of the *pensionnat*. In the afternoon I
strolled down to the lodge. The *concierge* had a
window which looked up the avenue towards the
house. He saw me coming, and was at the door.

He asked me why I had not gone with the others.
Then he asked me if I liked *bonbons*. He said I
never came to him for them.

"I have no taste for sweets. But you can do me a
little favour. I want a book to read. Do you think
you could get me one?"

A wicked look came over his face.

"One with pictures, *mademoiselle*, one of those
elegant little books about the amorous fancies of
young ladies and gentlemen?"

I laughed. I told him I wanted Voltaire. He
promised to try and find me a copy. He would make
enquiry. Would I come in, and he would take down
the title? He looked up and down the drive, and
then led the way into his lodge. On a table lay his
assortment of sweets.

"It is a thousand pities you do not like sweets."

"Does little de Belvaux like sweets? She offered me some yesterday. She must be a good customer. Is it always for sweets she visits you?"

I laughed again. The little man laughed also. He looked a little uncertain. Then his face cleared. He saw I knew more than I cared to say. No doubt there were confidences among the *pensionnaires*. Doubtless I possessed a knowledge of what went on there.

He offered me a chair. He leant over me while I sat and wrote the word "Voltaire." His breath came hot on my neck. The situation was novel. A strange excitement possessed me. He took the pen from my hand. As he did so, he seized my wrist and pressed it.

"What will you give me, if I get the book?"

"Whatever you like, if I am not found out."

"All right, come in here, *mademoiselle*. You are the most beautiful girl in the *pension*. I would do all for you for nothing. Why do you laugh? *Eh bien*, nearly for nothing. At any rate for something you would like."

He led the way into the inner room; the window which looked up towards the house was covered with a muslin blind. He closed the curtain behind us. I had seen him shut the outer door. There was another door at the back of the lodge which led into the shrubbery. He stood in front of me. He took me round the waist. Encouraged by my submission, he drew me to him. He pressed his stunted body to mine. He quite took my breath away.

"You darling! You beauty! You are not afraid.

You shall know all—you shall see all. Look at this!"

He quickly unfastened his trousers. I was horribly afraid we might be interrupted.

"Don't be uneasy. There is no chance that anyone can disturb us. Here, my divine little beauty! Give me your pretty hand."

He seized it. He conveyed it to his person. He placed it upon a monstrous limb half swollen with desire. It lolled in my immodest grasp. My fingers clutched it and closed upon it. It was my initiation to a man's parts. He uncovered his belly and fully exposed all. He was covered with short, curly, dark hair. The limb throbbed and lengthened in my hand.

"Rub it like that—so—that's lovely! Oh! That's exquisite! How nicely you do it, *mademoiselle*."

His member swelled and stiffened till it was more than half the length of his stunted thighs. The red and blue knob looked like a shiny ripe plum.

"Do you like that, *ma belle*?"

"Yes, I like it—are you quite sure we are safe?"

"Quite safe—go on, *ma petite belle*, I will tickle you too, presently."

I continued my gentle friction, looking all the while at the strange thing I held in my hand. There was a large hairy purse below, which wagged about as I worked. I rubbed the limb up and down as he told me. It grew as hard as a piece of wood. I grasped the loose skin which could no longer cover the big plum. I pressed it back at each movement. His pleasure seemed to increase—my strokes grew quicker.

"I shall come soon. *Je vais jouir!* Oh! Oh! Go

on—go on! Faster—do not let go—*mon dieu!*
What pleasure! Hold tight—oh!"

With my right hand, I moved up and down as the
girls milk the cows. I looked down at his naked
limb. He uttered some inarticulate words. Suddenly, as I looked, a stream of thick hot stuff shot
out and fell in a shower all over my hand and arm.
I worked away until the thing, covered with froth,
slipped out of my hand.

"Now you must promise me that book as soon as
you can get it, or I shall not come again to visit
you."

"I am going tomorrow to the *quais* on purpose.
No doubt I can get it there."

"*Bonjour, alors.* I will come for it the day after
tomorrow."

"Ah, my sweet dove, then you shall learn something more; something very nice that all young
ladies like very much."

"But I must have my book."

"*Sans faute, au revoir!*"

You—Eveline—the girl they all call so delicately
beautiful, so refined that they say your noble and
ancient blood stands out in your face and figure—
you associate with such a being as this! A hunchback, whose ugly head lies deep between his shoulders, whose dwarfed stature barely exceeds four
English feet, whose ungainly legs bow apart like
the opposite staves of a barrel!

Yes—Eveline pleads guilty. In art it is the rule
that all should be in good proportion; all must unite
to form a pleasing similarity. In lust it is the reverse. Lust is fed by disparity. By incongruity and
perversity. The tall man loves the little woman.

The old man's senile passion is stimulated by the immature girl. The elderly lady takes a boy of twenty to her arms, and lavishes presents upon him so that his interest, if not his desire, should be involved. Endless requirements arise out of these anomalies. Then why should the gentle, the graceful, the elegant and the delicately bred and nurtured Eveline not find a similar stimulus in dalliance with a deformed but interesting hunchback? Eveline is perverse. If you do not believe it, please close these memoirs. They are not for you.

But at the same time the hunchback is a strong man with a large limb. Eveline, even at that early age, had conceived a desire for strong men with large limbs.

Two days later I found an opportunity during the recreation time to wander down to the porter's lodge—not for sweets.

All was quiet. The *concierge* was at the little window. It commanded the straight avenue to the main building. He had evidently seen me coming.

"I have come to know about my book—my Voltaire. Have you got it for me?"

"Ah, *mademoiselle*, as if I could forget such a sweet and beautiful being as you. Of course I have it. Behold it here!"

He held up in both hands several small volumes bound in rusty leather and waved them triumphantly over his ugly head. He deposited them on the table. I looked at the title, *Essai sur les Mœurs et l'Esprit des Nations*; *Voltaire*. I picked up Volume I—Charlemagne.

"You are very good. It is what I want. Tell me the price?"

"You beautiful *chérie*, you have already paid me for anything I can do for you all my life long. Afterwards we will talk of the price."

He struck his great hollow chest a sounding blow. He actually bowed. Then he struck an attitude.

Had I not felt he was assuming a part, I might have believed in his vehemence. As it was, I knew well enough his vicious designs upon myself. I was on my guard. I put the little volume in my pocket.

"Well, and now, my pretty one, you will give me my reward."

He pressed his long arm round my waist. He gave a side-glance up the avenue, then with his left hand he coolly undid his nether garment and shamelessly produced his big yard.

"I am a man of few words, dear *mademoiselle*, but only just feel the weight of that!"

I looked upon his nakedness. He took my hand as he spoke. He laid it upon his member. Even as my fingers closed on his exposed nudity his request had become impossible. Snake-like, the huge thing straightened and lengthened itself. It rose with strong muscular jerks. It stood proudly up by itself at a small angle with his hairy belly. I looked at it, and at the man himself, with a strong inclination to laugh.

The little fellow was evidently in no humour for jesting. His face, inflamed with the coarsest lust, was opposed to my own. His bandy legs, his squat body, his long ungainly arms appeared to me irresistibly comic. As he stood in front of me, his left arm resting on his hip, his right close to his side, and his long and vigorous limb stretched disproportionately before him, he seemed to me to resemble nothing so much as an exaggerated teapot with a straight spout.

Then a strange sensation of abandonment came over me. I felt excited beyond all self-restraint with the strangeness of the situation. I put my little hand again upon the huge spout. I felt it throb. The man's lust extended its influence to me. I was quite ready to meet his salacious advances. I seated myself in his armchair. He placed himself in front of me. I examined the big limb. I caressed it with my hand. I shook it and played with it, wondering at its size and elasticity.

"Now it is my turn. I must find where all your pretty charms hide themselves, *ma belle*."

He suited the action to the word. He thrust his hand up my skirts. He reached my thighs unopposed. I was not in a humour to resist his audacious proceedings. Suddenly, he threw up my clothes. He saw the most private portion of my person fully exposed to his eager view. Instantly his face approached me, and sinking on his knees, he glued his lips to my orbit. I felt his hot tongue licking me like that of a dog, as he darted it backwards and forwards. Presently a sensation of voluptuous pleasure overpowered me. I shivered, and was conscious of having experienced the climax of sensual delight. The hunchback, however, continued his employment with evident relish. Very soon I found the same tingling spasms of pleasure pervading me, and my head fell back against the soft cushion while I lay in a sort of dreamy faint.

I was aroused by finding the *concierge* standing

close before me, his long stiff member pressed
against my cheek.

"*Ma chérie*, how you have come! You have had
pleasure; tell me, was it nice? Now you will do for
me what I have done for you, *ma belle*, will you
not? Kiss it."

He pressed the knob of his thing against my
lips. I kissed it just upon the small opening which
showed on the end. I opened my mouth to speak.
Instantly he pushed the big member forward. The
knob passed in between my moist lips. It tasted nice.
I liked it. I let him have his way. I did not care, I
wanted to enjoy. So did he. I clasped the broad
shaft with both hands, there was space and to spare
for both. I sucked it. I thought it was delicious. He
writhed about. He worked up and down. He was
plainly enjoying the liveliest sensations of pleasure.
I tickled all round the little hole with my tongue. I
withdrew my wet lips. I could look down it a little
way. The big knob grew more purple and tasted like
hot cheese. I held tight to his member. I worked my
hands up and down it.

"Oh! Oh! Oh! It's delicious—go on, *ma belle!*
Oh! Oh!"

I determined to go on. I suspected what he
wanted to do. I did not mind. I would let him have
his will, I continued sucking. Sometimes he almost
withdrew the red nut from my lips and sometimes
he thrust it as far as it could go into my mouth. His
features worked with convulsive enjoyment. I also
experienced a distinct and undefined pleasure in the
act I was committing. Presently some slippery
drops came from his limb. I felt half inclined to
draw back. Before I could do so, however, he

pushed forward. A perfect flood of hot stuff flew from the orifice and filled my mouth. I pumped with both hands, and sucked with my lips. I only desisted when he became calm. He groaned with ecstasy while he was discharging. He seemed a very long time about it. I received it all in my mouth. It ran from my lips in a stream.

I found an opportunity a few days later to visit the *concierge*. Madame St. C—— was never tired of sounding his praises. He was such a conscientious little man. He strictly observed his religious duties. He so well knew how to drive away the people who tried to gain admittance with begging letters and other means of practising upon the unwary. In short, he was inestimable. I only found him useful, and his singular passion excited my precocious lust for a knowledge of the male sex. He was an embodiment of very ordinary erotic desire and as such I made use of him.

He was as usual in his lodge. He welcomed me with a snort of obscene triumph. After seeing that all was secure, he invited me into his sanctum and pulling open his blouse and trousers produced his truncheon. I loved to grasp the long thing in my little hand. Before it could swell to its full size and be stiff and self-supporting, I put my lips to it and sucked it. I thought it delicious. Evidently he was of my opinion. It quickly—too quickly for my fancy —swelled and stiffened till I could hardly close my lips over the whole of the big knob.

He was plainly enchanted with my willingness.

He had no idea how lewd a well-educated, well-bred young girl can be when she is absolved from all fear of the consequences of her indiscretions.

I revelled in my discovery of the male organ in all its strength and virility. We were utterly alone. We both knew it. The fact supplied the confidence necessary for the full development of our lasciviousness. He had never found so free and capable a pupil. I had never discovered a chance so favourable to the gratification of my precocious instincts.

I have given our dialogue in English, but of course it was carried on in French. I was accounted one of the best of the English girls as to my fluency; and I was told frequently by my masters that my accent was exceptionally un-English and good.

It was early in the afternoon. There was a long interval from study. We felt ourselves safe. I hardly remember all that passed. The hunchback held himself in reserve. I allowed him to visit my person to greater advantage than before. He tried to profit by my simplicity to make me a real victim to his lust. I repelled all such attempts, not entirely because I feared either the consequences or the violence of the aggressor. I had my own views. What those were will appear later. Finding me obdurate and that I would not consent to the admission of his monstrous truncheon between my thighs, he fell again to sucking my parts. He revelled in this exercise. He reduced me to a condition of exhaustion. Then he presented his huge limb to my lips. The previous scene was repeated. I acquired the remaining volumes of Voltaire. I stole through the shrubbery to the house, my little volumes in my pocket.

Chapter III

My sojourn at the *pensionnat* was drawing to an
end, when an event happened which I had foreseen
must sooner or later take place. One day the lodge
door remained closed; the window shutters un-
opened. A woman did temporary duty at the great
iron gates. The pupils were restricted to the lawn
in front of the house in the hours of recreation. The
whole establishment wore an air of melancholy res-
ignation.

Then the mystery leaked out. First, of course,
from the servants. The teapot had disappeared—
spout and all! My friend the *concierge* had at last
been "found out."

But this was not all. Two of the elder girls with
whom I had not formed a very close association
were gone also. Another was locked up in her room.
Gradually the whole truth unrolled itself bit by bit.
Mademoiselle L—— and Mademoiselle B——
had been sent back to their parents, each bearing
increasing evidence of the efficacy of the teapot's
long straight spout in their domestic arrangements,
Mademoiselle X—— having no parents, and her
uncle being abroad, had been retained to await the

ultimate issue, but it fortunately turned out, in her case, that the spout had not injected its prolific essence to the detriment of her pretty figure!

Of course, there was a scandal. As in the Brighton case the public got hold of it. *Ruy Blas*, and other smart newspapers published racy details, and more or less beyond the facts, which were strong enough in all their naked simplicity.

It was from this girl, Mademoiselle X——, I finally learnt the real facts. It seems they were all three in the swim. The ugly *concierge* must have had a good time, for the girls, especially the latter, were all good-looking and well-made. I was lucky to be out of the trouble. My conduct had always been quoted as exemplary. It was held up as a pattern to the rest. The *concierge* had the merit at least of not talking of his *amours*. I remained unsuspected.

That he had managed to penetrate the private parts of these girls was evident. I was anxious to know all about it. I could not understand how so gigantic a member of a man could enter them. I wormed the whole story out of Mademoiselle X——, being selected as the only companion permitted to visit her.

It appeared they had actually discovered a means of escaping from their bed-chamber, where all three were supposed to sleep in separate little beds. They waited for dark nights. They took it in turn to go down to the lodge. The hunchback had always some trifling trinket or some *bonbons* to bestow on his nocturnal visitors. Soon, however, their senses awoke to a reciprocation of his lascivious sensations. They relished his embraces. My unlucky companion described all that had passed in terms which did not exhibit much repentance for her indiscretion. She discovered very soon I was by no means an unsympathetic listener.

It was delicious; she would do it again had she the chance. He possessed a thing which was delightful. It was also very long and very thick. Did I know that the little girls were, some of them, in the habit of sucking it for *bonbons*? But it was true. She had sucked it. He enjoyed that very much. She also enjoyed that. He would then suck her parts. In the daytime they were very guarded. At night they were free. They did as they pleased. They used to take it in turns. He was always ready for them. He induced her to take off her *peignoir*, under that was only a skirt and a *chemise de nuit*. He made her quite naked. He produced his big limb. She caressed it and sucked it. Then he visited her body all over. One day he laid her on his bed. He was much excited. He had only his *chemise* on. He pressed her and kissed her everywhere. On the mouth. He would not let her finish him off as usual. He was fond of finishing his enjoyment as she had already told me—in her mouth. A quantity of thick white stuff came from him. It was nice. His member was oh, so long. Oh, so thick, too! It was like that— and thick like that. It was too terrible—so big—so strong! "*Eh bien!* This time I was on my back. He was on my belly. His member was between my thighs. He made me open them. He pressed, he rubbed the big member in between the lips down there. He hurt me more. I cried out. He called me *petite imbécile*. He was furious. I put my hand down to stop him. I caught hold of his big member. I found quite half of it was inside my parts. Oh! It

was so stiff, so strong! He continued to thrust—to
force into me this enormous thing. It would enter
no further. He cried, 'Now I discharge!' I seized
the member again in my hand to pull it out. I felt
throbs pass along its sides. Then he sank down on
my body. I knew that the thick stuff was spouting
into my belly. After he had quite done, he got off
me. He made me rise also. I was all covered with
his discharge. My legs were slippery, so were my
parts. They ached dreadfully. But what do I care?
My good uncle will not be angry. He will love me
very much himself. He is always good to me. One
day when I was little, he made me feel his member.
It is not so large as that of our *concierge*, not nearly
so large. I will love him. He will put it in where
that enormous *concierge* could not enter. I shall enjoy. My uncle will enjoy—we shall be happy."

Once more the train to Calais, once more the
dreadful sea sickness. I am free. No more school;
no more *pensionnat* for Eveline! My father had returned from India. His term of service had ex-
pired. He had received his C.B. He was now retiring as a Major General. His breast was covered
with the medals he had won, yet except some mere
scratches, he had never received a wound. He was
still a young and vigorous man in the prime of life.
He was also the lineal descendant of an ancient
family, and a Baronet.

I was seventeen. I was considered to have arrived at an age when I might bid *adieu* to educa-
tional routine. I was to spend a few months at home

in Mayfair, to improve the occasion in the reception of music and singing lessons from the first professors. Not that my mother desired my return; she had her own reasons for her unwilling assent. Lady L—— had never overcome her antipathy for her only daughter. Sir Edward, however, had a distinct desire to have me at home. It was to him I owed my emancipation. We had not met since I was a child of eight. My sympathy was all for him. I shared his desire to meet again after so long an absence.

Sir Edward was absent shooting in the North when I arrived. My mother was suffering, so she informed me, from rheumatism. She kept to her room. My time did not hang too heavily on my hands for all that. I had plenty of liberty. The carriage was at my disposal. We were rich. The house was commodious. The servants were numerous and well paid. They were evidently overjoyed to welcome me to my home, and have someone to break the monotony of their existence.

I very soon began to discriminate among them. There was the senior footman, John Parker, who was particularly polite and attentive to me. My mother preferred to take her meals in her own room upstairs. I dined all alone, save when I invited a young friend of my own age to share my meal. On the occasions when I was quite by myself, John would venture to suggest various choice portions from the dishes set before me. He cut and arranged them on my plate. He interested me. He was a man of some eight and thirty, not very tall for a footman, but stout and broad. I thought in my ignorance he was magnificent in his handsome livery, with his gold garters, black silk stockings, and his crimson plush breeches. He made a great impression on me. I suppose I showed my interest in him too plainly. He soon became more attentive, more subservient—more familiar.

"How long have you been here, John?"

From the first I could never bring myself to call him Parker.

"Three years, miss, come Christmas."

"You must find it very dull now Sir Edward is away and Mr. Percy in Canada. I expect you have gay times downstairs, when your work is over in here."

"Well, miss, not so much. The others are not a very gay lot and the cook goes out when the work is done. The girls both sit upstairs with my lady's own maid. Now you're here, miss, if I may be allowed to say so, the house is not at all the same. It seems quite lively—at least to me, miss."

"Where is my maid, John? She has not brought my shoes. I cannot bear these boots any longer, I am tired."

"Mary is upstairs, miss, shall I call her?"

"No, John, if you will be so good as to undo these laces, I can sit more comfortably at the table."

I pushed out my foot. I placed it on a stool. John stooped over it. He began to fumble at the knot. His hand trembled.

"I am afraid, John, you are not quite a lady's maid, but I think you are very nice all the same."

John chuckled. I gave a little kick out with my foot. It touched his plush breeches.

"Oh, you hurt me, John—no—not your knuckles —it's the lace at the back of the instep—see here—"

He took my foot in his hand. He touched my ankle.

"It's just there, John, please rub it a little."

John set to work to rub the ankle. As he rubbed, so I swayed my foot backwards and forwards upon his plush breeches. Something hard seemed to grow up under my foot.

"What have you got in your pocket, John? Is it a flute?"

"No, miss, I am not musical. I don't play any instrument."

The man blushed scarlet as his breeches, and seemed quite confused.

"It feels exactly like one, John, and it gets bigger and bigger."

I pushed my little kid boot into closer contact with the thing. John's hand was now on my calf, and my black silk stocking evidently delighted him, for he made pretence to linger where he was.

I put on my most innocent and childish air.

"Do all the men have those things there, John? The girls at school told me lots about them."

"I don't know, miss, I suppose so. I—really! Miss! I'm afraid someone may come."

"Don't be alarmed, John, no one will come. I want to feel it."

"Good Lord! Miss—if they should know—if I am found out I shall lose my place."

"But you won't tell, John, will you?"

"Oh dear, no, miss! But you might let it out unawares-like."

I sprang forward. I seized the object in his red plush breeches with my hand. John stood quite still and breathed hard.

"Good Lord, miss! If they come, if we're found out!"

"They are all upstairs—we are alone. I must feel it. I know what it is, John. My goodness! How it throbs—how big it is getting now—let me feel it."

The footman submitted with a good grace. It was clear he was by no means unwilling. He evidently enjoyed my fingering. I slyly undid the corner button of his flap. I audaciously slipped my hand in. I ran it quickly down his belly. I encountered his nice clean shirt all warm. Then my hand fastened on his limb. I pulled away his shirt. I grasped his naked member. It felt very fat and thick. It was still stiffening. I gave it a sudden twist. It stood up now against his belly.

"Is that nice, John?"

"Good Lord! Yes, miss, it's heavenly, but I'm afraid we may be caught at it."

He appeared to have an enormous limb, not so long as the horrid *concierge*, but very thick and strong. I managed to pull back the skin. I felt a big, soft, beautiful knob on the end. He turned towards me. He favoured my toying, but the space was too confined to enable me to finger it as I liked.

Just then the front door bell rang.

I withdrew my hand. John buttoned up. The next minute he was opening the door with the grand air of a butler who could crush the comer with a glance.

I set to work to scheme a way to arrive at the sum of my desires. There are some things one must do for oneself. I nerved myself for the occasion. I went to a quiet street in Soho. I had noted a second-rate shop which was fitted up as an apothecary's—as we say in London, chemist and druggist. I entered. I had chosen the quiet time in the early afternoon. No one was in the shop. A good-looking, fair-haired young man advanced from the back room.

"Good morning. I want a syringe—a female syringe; show me some of your best."

"Certainly, miss, please to step this way."

He led me to the further end of the counter. He produced from a drawer a number of the articles in question.

"These are all good, but this pattern is the one we specially recommend. It is of vulcanite. It cannot break, or do any mischief."

I looked them over with a professional air.

"Yes, you are right. I will take the one you recommend."

Probably he saw I was a little awkward in handling the thing. I looked him in the face with a smile. His eyes sparkled.

"Do you understand how it should be applied, miss?"

"Well, not properly, perhaps."

He smiled this time. I laughed softly.

"How do you fill it, and with what?"

"We have a detergent always made up, miss. If you will wait a moment, I will get some water and explain the action."

I nodded gently. He went into the back room. In a few moments he returned.

"Please come in here, I can show you how it works."

I followed the good-looking, fair young man. He filled the syringe with water, and squirted it out again into a basin.

"You should always wipe it after use and return it nicely to its case—thus."

I laughed again softly.

The young man laughed also. I was wicked enough to encourage his hilarity. He evidently took me for a representative member of a class to which I had not the honour to belong. I determined to humour him. He grew more familiar.

"After all, it is not at all equal to the real thing. Would you like me to try it for you? I shall be delighted to serve you, miss."

"Thank you, but I should prefer *the real thing,* if it acts at all like the imitation. Probably you have none in stock?"

He laughed outright this time. He glanced around. We understood one another in a moment. He caught me round the waist.

"You beautiful little devil! Where do you come from?"

"Are we quite sure to be alone? Suppose someone enters the shop?"

"They must wait. I can shut the door. See, there is a muslin curtain. We can see out. They cannot see in."

"Then try the real thing—if you have one!"

He had roused my lust. He was very good-looking. He locked the door. He pushed me towards a leather sofa.

"You really mean you will let me do the job for you, eh? You are awfully pretty, you know. I never saw such a beautiful girl. You are so beautifully dressed. I am not rich, you know, you will not want to bother me afterwards?"

"I ask nothing. I should not like to disappoint you."

"Oh, my God! What fun! I never had such a chance. How sweet your kisses are! Let me feel."

"Where is your syringe? Oh, my goodness! What a beauty! It is much larger, though, than the imitation. Kiss me!"

"Yes, much larger and almost as stiff. It holds nearly as much also, as you will soon find. Oh, your kisses are sweet."

I held his limb in my gloved hand. His fingers were in the moisture of my slit. He was beautifully made—not nearly so large as the *concierge*. I was dreadfully excited. I longed for him to "do the job," as he called it. He was stiffly erect.

I had not long to wait. I was utterly devoid of modesty. I fancied I knew how best to please him. I played my part.

"Be quick—I want it! Come!"

I pulled up all my clothes. He saw all my nudity.

"My God, what lovely legs! What fine stockings! What exquisite little boots! My God! Oh—what a chance!"

The young man mounted quickly upon me. In an instant I felt him penetrating my orbit. My slit was all on fire with longing.

"My God, how tight you are—keep still—it's going in now. Oh, my God, how nice! I'm right into you now!"

It was true. I tasted the pleasure of coition for the first time with a full-grown man. I could not speak—I could only sob and moan in the ecstasy of that encounter. I clutched him by the shoulders. I felt the light hair of his belly rub on my flesh. He thrust vigorously. His limb grew stiffer and harder. It seemed to push to the extremity of my capacity. The pleasure was divine.

"Oh, Christ! I'm coming! I'm—coming! Ugh! Ugh! Ugh!"

"The syringe! The syringe! Give it me all!"

The young man discharged—gush after gush. He had spoken the truth. His syringe was ample. His sperm squirted into me in a flood.

"You beautiful little devil! How deliciously nice you are. Now you must make use of the imitation. I will get you some water."

"Thanks. Remember to wipe your syringe and return it carefully to its box."

I walked home. I was no longer afraid of John now.

Chapter IV

I had been at home three weeks. Lady L—— kept
to her own apartment upstairs. I saw very little of
her, except only when I paid my dutiful morning
visit. Sunday is not a lively or convivial day in London. Not in a general way. I lunched alone on this
Sunday. Sir Edward was to return in a week's time.
I was thinking his advent would be a change for me
and a relief. I sat before my empty plate.

"Will you take some more sweetbread, miss?"

"No, thank you, John. You may take it away,
and bring me some seed cake. Who is Lady L——
entertaining upstairs, John?"

"The Reverend Mr. Doubletree, miss. He is the
Honourable and Reverend Trestleton-Doubletree.
He belongs to the church they call the Sepulchre,
miss, round in the square."

"Was that he who arrived an hour and a half
ago in our carriage, John?"

"Yes, miss, my lady always sends it after the
service on Sunday mornings to bring him round
from the Sepulchre."

"He does not look as if he required much bring-

ing round; he does not strike me in any way as re-
sembling a ghost."

"Oh, no, miss, he's in very good condition. He
knows how to keep it up too; I never knew such a
particular gent. He can't eat any soup but real tur-
tle, miss—except on Fridays when he says he tries
to digest mock. He must have his grouse with a nice
bit of red in the breast. He says there's only one
cook in London who can do quail proper, miss, and
that's ours. Yes, he's a funny gentleman for a parson. He's so particular about his stomach—says
common food doesn't agree with him. Can't digest
it, miss—comical stomach, very. He's funny in
other ways too, miss, when he likes."

"How so, John?"

"Why, one day he caught my lady's own maid,
Sippett, on the stairs, miss, and chucked her under
the chin, quite familiar-like."

"Dear me, John! And what did Sippett do?"

"Oh, she just did nothing, miss, till he was gone.
Then she up and told my lady. Not that she got
much by that, for my lady told her not to mind.
That it was only his kindness; for he was like a
good pastor to his flock, and he considered her like
one of his lambs."

"What did she say to that, John?"

"Oh, she kept her mouth shut, as was her duty,
miss, but when she came downstairs, she let out. She
said that if he tried on any more of his pastoral
tricks, he would find she was no lamb, but a ravenin'
wolf, miss—there's the drawing-room bell, miss!"

"The Honourable and Reverend Trestleton-
Doubletree would like to know, miss, if you will see
him in the drawing room."

"Say I will follow you immediately, John."

I took just one look in the glass. I tripped lightly upstairs. John opened the door. The reverend gentleman came forward with an air of ineffable tenderness and condescension. I took him in at a glance. I mistrusted those roving dark eyes; that anxious smile on the broad sensual lips of a man about forty years of age.

"So glad, my dear Miss Eveline, to make your acquaintance. They told me you were at home; your lady mother has commissioned me, my dear girl—"

My baptismal name! My dear girl! What did he take me for? I cut him short.

"Have you lunched? I trust they have taken care of you? I fear Lady L—— is too great an invalid to receive you properly."

"Oh, yes, a thousand thanks, we lunched together. Had I known—"

"Oh, thank you, I took my little meal alone. It is a very simple one—a cutlet, or a sweetbread—a slice of seed cake—that usually comprises all I care for alone."

"*Côtelettes à la Nesselrode—riz de veau à la sauce blanche* are things not to be lightly denied; or perhaps you prefer them *à la sauce financière*?"

"How did you find Lady L—— today?"

"She is suffering. She confided to me her wish that we should meet, that we should confer—ahem, that I should endeavour to impress upon you the advantages of attending divine service at our church of St. Sepulchre at least once on the Sunday."

"My mother is very considerate towards me. She has never yet mentioned the subject to me herself."

"Oh! Possibly not—possibly not. Oh, no—no—

quite likely! She is so nervous, you know, such an invalid—still, if you will allow me to suggest—"

He began to see it might be dangerous to persist.

"It is a subject on which I have formed my own judgment."

"What? Already? So young too! Well, well; we will not pursue the subject further now. The young nowadays desire a large degree of latitude—a very large degree of latitude. I am always disposed to grant it them. I approve of freedom of thought; of individual responsibility. There are those who in their weakness require spiritual guidance. You are not one of those, my dear—my dear young friend. But you are too young, and permit me, too beautiful —far too superbly beautiful to altogether emerge from the cocoon of childhood into the full-blown perfection of womanhood without advice, without some sort of tuition. The world is deceitful—very much so."

I listened with patient wonder. I saw at once that my reverend visitor had lunched perhaps not wisely, but too well. As he spoke, he drew his chair towards mine quite confidentially. His breath was redolent of wine. He leered into my face with an expression that reminded me of my old friend the teapot.

"But you forget that before I can emerge as a moth to flutter round the candles of society, I must have been a grub!"

"A grub—but what a grub! And now a butterfly. Ah! Ah!"

The whole manner of the man had undergone a change. He was no longer the reverend incumbent of St. Sepulchre endeavouring in his choicest inflection of pulpit eloquence to win a lamb to his fold. He was the man of the world—the would-be lover of one he took for an inexperienced schoolgirl. One who in her ignorance would be flattered by the gross and too palpable insinuations of his honeyed words.

"A butterfly—ah! Such a beautiful, beautiful butterfly, whose golden wings, softly perfumed with the choicest scents of Araby, waft their sweet fragrance to the inmost follicles of my manly heart!"

He spoke in a purring whisper. I felt that his eyes were fixed upon my face. My own gaze rested on the pattern of the carpet. I waited for what was to come next. He moved nearer. His arm passed behind me. It dropped from the back of the chair in a half unconscious way upon my dress.

"You will not deny me the delight and the privilege of being your friend—your guide—your protector in this mad society of London?"

I made him no reply. My foot beat a warning tattoo, and my breath came in an angry flutter from my lungs.

He misinterpreted my agitation. He altogether delighted in my emotion. He counted already on his easy victory. He drew his arm closely round my waist. He advanced his thick and sensual lips. He actually imprinted a kiss upon my right cheek.

"Thus, my dear child, do we seal our compact!"

I snatched myself away. The blood of my ancient race rushed furiously through every vein.

"Then take *that* from the butterfly!"

A sounding crack like the sharp report of a pistol. A moment's silence. The reverend incumbent of the Sepulchre had risen from his seat with a savage glare in his dark eyes. His hand covered a very distinct outline of my palm upon his left cheek. A study in red and white.

The door opened. It was John.

"Did you ring, miss?"

"No—yes, John. Show this—this *gentleman* to the front door."

I ran upstairs. I entered my lady's room. I found her in her easy chair. She was apparently asleep or unconscious. Sippett was agitating a Japanese fan before her flushed face. I took in the situation at a glance. On the table were the remains of the luncheon; two empty champagne bottles among them.

"Quick, Sippett, open her stays—give her air."

I rushed to the window. I threw it open. As I passed behind the heavy curtain to do so, I kicked over another empty champagne bottle. A second, half full, stood beside it. Two or three empty soda-water bottles rolled upon the floor.

Sippet had opened the front of Lady L——'s morning wrapper. She was fumbling over the laces of her corset.

"Scissors! Sippett—cut them! Let her breathe freely."

I remained just long enough to see that Lady L—— was recovering.

"Sippett, you will not leave your mistress for a moment on any account."

I had been only just in time. She had been as near an attack of apoplexy as a stout and inebriated woman of her age could be without incurring the full penalty of her conduct. Then I left the room.

Vexed, humiliated, degraded, all the angry contempt which had culminated within me during the past twenty minutes gave way to a feeling of passionate despair.

I felt at that moment the "little devil" my friend the fair young man of Soho had called me. I slowly descended the broad stairs. John was in the dining room. He was employed in clearing away the lunch things.

"Where are the maids, John?"

"Sippett is upstairs, miss, the others are both gone out. It is their turn out, Sunday afternoon."

"Where is the butler—and the cook?"

"Cook is preparing for the dinner in the kitchen, miss. The butler is asleep before the kitchen fire."

"Make haste. Clear the things away. I want you, John."

"Yes, miss."

I threw myself into an easy chair. I waited. Presently John returned.

"Oh, Miss Eveline! How you did give it to him!"

"No more than he deserved, John."

"Anyway he got it very hot, miss. I doubt if he'll ever come back."

"I have hurt my hand very much. It aches, John."

I held it up. My little palm was all red, and tingled dreadfully.

"So you have, miss. You're still all of a tremble."

"Only wait, John, until Sir Edward comes home."

"Well, miss, of course it is not my place to say so, but if I was you, miss, I should say nothing about it. My lady has been going on for nearly a year now like that. Sir Edward knows it, miss. But he can't stop it. No one can stop a woman, miss, once she takes to *that*."

I held up my hand to show him. It stung and burnt. John took it respectfully in his big paw. He carried it to his lips as if I was a child.

"Poor little hand! Kiss it to make it well!"

It only wanted that. I broke into a flood of tears. One touch of sympathy is worth a sack of gold sometimes. How lonely I was! Why was I thrown into this man's arms?

I leant my head on his shoulder. John's attention was divided. A great part no doubt was full of sympathy for me. The rest was centred in an effort to protect his best livery.

"Don't take on, missy. It's all right—I knew how it would be. I was near by. When I heard the sound of that smack, miss, why—I was in it too. I would have knocked him silly, if you hadn't."

I kissed John on the mouth. John kissed me back. I dried my tears and saved his Sunday livery.

"Are you sure the butler is fast asleep, John?"

"Well, miss, he always takes an hour after his dinner, Sundays, and he's only begun snoring about five minutes ago."

"John, you're a good fellow and I like you very much."

I smiled up at him through my tears. I put on the air of a spoilt child.

"I want to feel that thing again, John."

He looked right and left—then he listened.

"There's no one about now, miss."

I had suited the action to the word. My hand was on his plush breeches.

"Oh, John! How stiff it is! My hand can't get round it."

His eyes glistened. He got more at home.

"Put it in here, miss."

He undid a couple of buttons. I plunged my hand down. I grasped his huge limb. Only his shirt covered it now. It was hot and throbbing. I pressed it. I pinched it. I tried to get my hand under the shirt.

"Wait a minute, miss. If you must, you know, you must."

He undid the other buttons. His limb was now free with only his linen over it. It stuck up in front of him like a great peg to hang dresses on.

"What a beauty he looks, John!"

"He is that, miss. My mother found that out when I was a little 'un, miss. She used to show him to the neighbours. One old single lady used to bring him bicuits."

"Biscuits—John—why? How could he swallow biscuits?"

"I ate 'em for him, miss. They went down to him that way, I suppose. They was ginger nuts, miss. Anyhow, he got fine and large."

"You ought to give him a name, John. I shall call him Robin, because of his red breast. Come here, Robin."

I had released the prisoner from his confinement. I beheld the man's nudity erect in all its glorious proportions. How shall I describe the thing which reared its noble crest close under my nose as I sat in the low chair, its huge white shaft standing out against the curling black hair of John's belly? The blue veins coursing over the pale waxy surface; the big bell-shaped top—dark, menacing, its knob de-

scending until a little slit-like aperture terminated
its broad surface, which pouted on either side like
ripe cherries.

"What a beauty he looks, John, my Robin!"

The man's lust, however, was rising furiously all
this time. It was no child's play for him. I had excited the lion. It wanted flesh. He lost much of his
subservient manner—his respect. He knelt down
and pushed his hand up under my clothes. His cheek
flushed and his breath came hot and fast.

"My good Lord, miss, how beautifully made
your legs are! What lovely stockings—oh, what a
soft thigh! Ah! Oh! How delicious it is! It's like
so much velvet!"

The last exclamation was called forth by his
touching a certain central portion of my person, the
moist and hot reception with which his finger was
regaled giving him evidently the liveliest pleasure.

"That's where Robin wants to go. That's where
he'd like to hide his head, miss. Just in there!"

He slipped his finger in and tickled my button
acutely—deliciously. I retained my hold of his thing.
I gently moved the loose skin up and down.

"I am afraid he would not be content only to hide
his head there, John."

"He can be very soft and gentle when he likes,
miss."

"He may go wherever he likes, John. Only be
careful and quiet."

He now lost what little self-restraint was left to
him. He caught me in his strong arms. He rubbed
his body against mine. He kissed me on the mouth.
Our tongues met—my eyes looked into his. He read
desire—hot, voluptuous desire, there. We both

groaned to indulge it—to enjoy—to satisfy it. We were mad, but there was method in our madness. John glanced all round. The armchairs and sofa were tempting, but then it was just possible we might be interrupted. Suddenly an inspiration came to him. By the door he could hear all approaching footsteps. The case was desperate. There was no time to be lost. He pushed me roughly with my back against the door. His breeches' flap was already unbuttoned. His nakedness was in full evidence. I assisted him to raise my clothes in front. He pressed his belly against me. He stooped. He thrust his hot, long limb between my legs. I opened them to make way.

"You must be quick, John. Listen! Do you hear anything?"

"No, no, all is quiet. It is the only chance. Let me do it. I am bound to get into you now, miss."

With my own hand I guided the red head to my slit. I rubbed it between the lips of my orbit. He bore forward. It slipped in. In and up me half its length at least. I put my hands on his broad shoulders. I raised myself to meet his fierce thrusts. With each strong effort he almost lifted me off my legs. I moaned faintly. The pleasure mounted quickly. John hissed his ecstasy in short gasps.

"Good Lord! I'm in now—it's—it's—oh! Oh! I'm nearly coming!"

He gripped me round the haunches with an iron hold. He moved in quick, short jerks. His limb grew hard and even stiffer. He pressed me to him. I felt his discharge. I knew he was flooding my interior with his sperm. I cared for nothing but to receive all, *all*. He withdrew in haste. My parts were swimming. My thighs were slippery with the thick warm seed. A pool of it lay on the carpet between my feet.

"Oh, John, you have nearly killed me. You must never do that again."

I ran upstairs to my own chamber. I made liberal use of my toilet appliances. I neither cared, nor feared, for the results of my imprudence.

Twenty minutes later, John came to announce the carriage at the door. He assisted me into it with the most respectful and matter-of-fact air in the world.

Chapter V

The following Thursday witnessed the return of Sir Edward L——.

As to the condition of Lady L——, all concealment was in vain. He questioned me, and I made a clean breast of it, so far as related to her conduct and condition. One detail led to another. The incident between myself and the Reverend Mr. Doubletree was obliged to be included. In fact John had forestalled my confession by giving my father a glowing account of that famous interview.

The first acts of Sir Edward after his arrival were to engage a housekeeper, and send for the family physician.

I had not seen my father since I was a child of nine years of age. His long service in India and my absence at school had been the cause of his knowing little or nothing of the subsequent development of his little and only daughter.

I had arrived from Paris during his absence in the North. It was therefore with much trepidation that I met him on his return.

All my fears on beholding him vanished into thin air. He held me at arms' length; his handsome face beaming with admiration and delight. He kissed me again and again. His look, full of surprise and pleasure, melted into an expression of the tenderest sympathy as his keen, soldierly eye surveyed my girlish figure from head to foot. It was evident he had not expected to find me so entirely to his satisfaction. From what I know now, I am inclined to think he had not been in the habit of receiving either a kind, or a true report of my youthful progress towards womanhood.

"My beautiful—my darling child! And so this is the little one I have come back to find! Well, my eyes are opened! So you are the brave little champion that defeated the clerical dragon? By Jove, Eveline, you should have commanded the regiment! You would have made the Pathans run even faster than we did!"

"I have no wish to emulate Joan of Arc, papa, but I am sure you will remember I am a L——."

"Indeed I do, my little paladin! Why, this is really charming—as the youngsters say—most awfully jolly!"

We became friends at once—close friends. The first thing to do was to set the house in order. That was soon accomplished. At the end of a fortnight, Lady L—— was able to take carriage exercise again. The London season was approaching. There were all sorts of gaieties in preparation. There were invitations to balls and receptions. Entertainments of all sorts were commencing to occupy the attention of that large and influential circle within whose sacred precincts none but the privileged can enter.

The old Duchess of M—— was to give her long

projected and splendid costume ball. It had been the talk of the town all last season, but court mourning had postponed it. It was to surpass anything and everything her Grace had ever done. That was by no means trifling, for she was celebrated for her lavish hospitality.

Then there was the ever varying charm of the Opera—of the theatres. In fact, I was in fairyland.

Papa and I sat much together. He appeared to take great delight in my society. I made it my study to please him. The house had received a new impetus; a new life, since his return. Mrs. Lockett, the new housekeeper, was assiduous and painstaking. Her eye was everywhere. Even John had to be on his guard lest by word or look he should betray some incautious instance of familiarity. Needless to say no chance existed any longer for a renewal of our secret intercourse.

Nevertheless, I suffered. I chafed at the restraint.

"Good night, dear child, good night and pleasant dreams. You seem dull and out of spirits today."

"No, dear papa, I was only thinking perhaps that I should take more exercise on foot. Walking is always sure to improve the appetite."

I did dream that night—not altogether unpleasantly. I dreamt of the great Charlemagne—and of my papa.

"Shall I call a cab, miss?"

"No, thank you. I will walk. The exercise will refresh me. Your shop is rather warm. Please send my purchases without fail tomorrow."

It was already getting dark. I noticed a man who persistently passed me. Then he would let me overtake him. On doing so he looked each time pointedly in my face. At last he touched my elbow in going by. I was approaching a quiet street, which led me home by a short cut. I began to regret I had not brought the footman. The man kept now a little in front. I saw him furtively take note of me in the windows as we walked on. He was short and broad. He wore a long overcoat. Suddenly the man quickened his pace. He turned into the entrance to a yard upon the left. I wondered at his movements. I was in doubt as to his object in acting so strangely. I looked down the yard as I passed. He was standing opposite me in the full light of a gas lamp. No one else was near. His coat was open. Without the least attempt at concealment—in fact, he was holding his dress open—he exposed to me his naked person.

The strangeness of the thing bewildered me. I had been thinking of John as I walked. I was at first horribly startled and shocked. In a flash later the absurdity of the affair irresistibly possessed me. I wavered and opened my eyes wide, I suppose, at the sight. Then I passed on. As I did so, the man smiled. He looked down at his nakedness. There was no mistake. He held in my full view a long and stout limb, stiffly erect.

All this had only taken a second. The blood rushed to my head. I walked past. I paused again. The thing excited me. I was in a state to receive such an impression. My curiosity was aroused. I retraced the few steps I had taken. The stranger half turned so that I should lose nothing of his exhibition.

"Come here, I won't hurt you."

"What are you doing that for? You will catch cold."

The impulse was irresistible. I moved nearer. I seized the limb in my hand.

"Not while your hand is so warm. Come down here. I will show you why I did it."

It was now quite dark. The poor street was dimly lighted. The man led the way. Instinctively I followed. I trembled a little, but not from fear.

"This is a timber yard. There is no one about at this hour. I know the people. It's all right."

The timber was on every side. Between it there were lanes. A sharp turn put us out of the direction of the gas lamp. My companion turned. He put his limb again in my hand. He kissed me before I well knew what he was about.

"What a pretty girl you are! Do you like that? Isn't it a fine one? We are quite safe here."

He took me round the waist. I could not resist squeezing the thick limb I held in my grasp. I actually pressed it with delight and desire. He might well be proud of it, I thought. He kissed me again. Overcome with a sensation of diabolical lust, I kissed him back. He took all sorts of liberties with me. It was too late to resist, even had I possessed the means, or the desire. He held me tight with his left arm while with his right hand he lifted my clothes. He passed his wanton hand underneath. What he found only increased his libidinous instincts. His fingers touched my legs—mounted slowly my plump thighs. They inserted their tips in my moist and excited parts. I could not resist the throbbing, tickling sensation with which they inspired me. He seemed to subdue me by his influence.

"Oh, please be careful of my dress! My clothes! You must not. Really you are too rough! Be more gentle. I will let you feel. Oh!"

All this time he was making use of filthy and disgusting language. His intention was obvious.

"We can do it here, my dear, hold up your clothes."

It was quite dark now. We were round a corner out of the radius of the gas-lamp. He pressed close to me in front. I felt him slip his long, stiff, hairy thing upwards against my naked belly. He was fumbling about to adjust it to his liking. I was now overcome with desire. The indelicacy of the thing never seemed to occur to me. Lust for enjoyment took possession of me. I put my hand on his limb again. I placed the tip between the hot lips of my slit.

"Put your foot up on this piece of wood, my dear. Stop, here is a place will suit us nicely."

As he spoke, he moved me to one side. He lifted me bodily on to a projecting plank which formed a convenient seat. I opened my thighs. He held me round the hips. I again assisted him. One thrust sent half the length of his member into my body.

"Oh, my dear life! But it's in now. How delicious! How tight it is! Hold up! Catch me on the shoulders. Sit forward, my dear."

He seized me tight as I sat. He pulled me closely to him. He commenced the act with frenzy. He worked up and down, withdrawing the thick shaft to the knob. Then he thrust it up again. I held tight with both hands. I partook of the pleasure. My brain reeled. I gasped. I moaned. He worked harder than ever. My parts were in a churn of liquid ecstasy. I feared to let him see how I enjoyed. Presently the end came. I felt his limb harden suddenly throughout its length. He discharged copiously. A deluge of seed spouted into me.

"Oh! Oh! You must have it all! It's coming still. It's, it's—oh! My dear life! What a treat!"

He withdrew quickly. He lost no time in readjusting his clothes. In another second he was gone.

I hastened along that quiet street. Of course there were no vacant cabs in view. I turned a corner. I found myself in a better thoroughfare. I stopped before a well-lighted pastrycook's shop. I read an announcement, "Afternoon Tea." I entered, overjoyed to find myself safe. Behind the shop was the tea-room. Behind that again a smaller room, also with small tables for tea. I traversed all. I sat down. A nice-looking woman, in a rustling silk dress and white apron, followed me. I ordered tea.

"Will you wait a little, or shall I serve you now?"

I wondered why she asked. I did not immediately reply. I demanded the ladies' retiring room. There I rearranged all my disorder. On my return, the tea had been served. There were two cups on the tray.

"Please bring me tea-cake and some ginger nuts."

The nice-looking woman appeared disconcerted.

"Are you quite alone? Is it tea for one, miss?"

Suddenly the explanation came to me. I had heard of these little "Afternoon Tea" shops. This

was one. I glanced around. In one corner was a
tiny iron spiral staircase. A small door, which closed
with a spring, led from this room towards the side
of the house. I took all in directly.

"Yes, I am alone, as you see. I fear there has
been some mistake. My friend will not come now."

The kind-looking woman smiled. She evidently
thought I was disappointed.

"Never mind, he has probably mistaken the
time."

"No doubt. Where does that staircase lead to?"

The shopwoman smiled again. She evidently did
not believe in the sincerity of my ignorance. She
leant forward and whispered:

"You have been here before, miss. I saw you
knew all our little ways, all our little arrangements.
You ought to know where it goes."

"Still, you see, it is pleasant to revisit old scenes."

"No doubt, when one has been well amused
among them, miss. Pray come up. You are welcome.
Mind the high steps and the sharp turn."

We mounted the iron ladder, for such almost it
was. To my surprise, I found myself in a small, but
beautifully furnished room, half boudoir, half bed-
chamber.

There was a somewhat narrow bed in a corner,
a cosy sofa, a toilet table, marble washstand, etc.,
several pretty chairs, and some framed oleographs
from the illustrated papers on the walls. One discreetly curtained window afforded the necessary
light.

"Looks comfortable, does it not, miss? If you
could send me a line another time beforehand, it
would be better, and I could have all prepared. We

are obliged to be very particular, as you know."

We descended. My new friend let me out by the little side door into a passage which led into the street again. I had had my tea. I had also a bag of ginger nuts. I reached home. Good Heavens, what risks to have run! What ruin may I not have courted!

Chapter VI

"Where is Sir Edward?"

"He is already in the brougham at the door waiting for you, Miss Eveline."

"Thank you, John. Here are some ginger nuts for Robin. Where is my maid? Fanny, I will wear my seal jacket. Thank you, Fanny. Open the door, John. I am ready."

"Dear papa, how well you look today! Shall we go to the park, or have you any calls to make?"

"No, my darling, we will go first to the park."

I had dressed myself with particular care on purpose to please him. I saw him taking note of all. His delight in my society appeared to increase. When we were alone he assumed quite a different air towards me. It was not artificially assumed, but evidently real. He lowered his voice; its intonation became more tender—more sympathetic. He would sit in the brougham with my hand in his, gently stroking the soft kid of my gloves, and leaning towards me until his moustache almost brushed my cheek. He would tell me of his Indian experiences, of the battles, his narrow escapes, his troubles and triumphs.

On this occasion it was nearly dark before we returned. We had enjoyed a very snug and confidential drive. His arm was passed round my waist and his right hand toyed as usual with mine. I leant my head on his shoulder. My warm breath fanned his cheek. His eyes looked into mine. They were fine eyes on ordinary occasions. I fancied now they were full of passion. He kissed me hotly on the lips.

"My darling Eveline, you are cold. Your neck is uncovered."

He essayed to clasp my seal jacket closer. His hand wandered to my bosom. There it stopped.

"Poor little girl, she is too good, too beautiful to be cold when I am by to warm her. I will not drive to the club. I will return with you."

He tightened his grasp of my figure. He renewed his caresses.

"Dearest papa! If you knew all that your little Eveline thinks of you! How she values your love, and your kisses. She has never known much affection before. Now you are with me, all is changed—all is happy."

He turned still more. His breast beat upon mine. Our lips met in a long delicious kiss. He was half beside himself with passionate desire. I was fully as much entranced. The utmost disorder reigned in our embrace—in our posture. His hand trembled violently as he thrust it within my dress and grasped my bosom.

"Oh, my child, how beautiful are you! How magnificent already is your development! What a lovely bust!"

Our faces would have betrayed us had anyone suddenly appeared. They were scarlet with the wildest desire. I dare not give it another name. I noticed we were nearing home. I cautioned Sir Edward. He recovered himself with precipitancy.

We understood each other now. A silent confidence had been sown which would bear its fruits hereafter.

I dressed for dinner with care. No low dress, but a close-fitting bodice which showed my youthful figure to the utmost advantage.

I took especial care to study my papa's tastes. He had excellent taste in dress. Young as I was, I had already acquired among my friends a character for correct taste in all matters relating to feminine attire. It seemed to come natural to me. A woman dresses to please others, and in her success or failure she has her reward. It may be that, in some cases, she may dress to spite her own sex, but the ultimate result is the same——she triumphs with the male sex to her dear friends' discomfiture.

Most men have idiosyncrasies in some small matters which in sensual temperaments are sometimes exaggerated to the extent of manias.

Sir Edward was sensual to the centre of his being, only you had to find him out. He had a habit of disguising it under qualities of a rougher nature. I knew already his little weak points. They were no manias, but they were there. I traced them. My quick woman's wit, my habit of close observation, a restless spirit of inductive reasoning all combined, enabled me quickly to arrive at a thorough knowledge of his inner character. I detected the sensuous eyes, the evident pleasure with which he fondled my soft gloves, or allowed his gaze to linger upon my daintily fitting little boots.

After dinner, papa went to his club. Lady L—— had kept her room all day. Champagne and soda were doing their work again. Somehow, in spite of Mrs. Lockett's caution, she had got a supply by means of Sippett, her maid. I went up to my own room. Thence I turned into the corridor which led up to Lady L——'s suite. Halfway up, I espied Sippett sampling the beef-tea, which, by the doctor's orders, she was taking to her mistress. I felt uneasy. My senses had been roused. I was on fire in my longing for gratification. I hated this restraint. I went back to the dining room. I rang the bell.

"I want some tea, John. What time is it?"

"It's not ten yet, miss."

"Where is the butler?"

"Sir Edward has sent him out, miss, to see the painter. He is not to send his men in the morning unless it is quite fine."

"How is poor Robin, John? I am afraid he is drooping."

The footman came closer. He bent cautiously down to me.

"Drooping? Miss Eveline, I wish he was! Why he stands up in the mornings and looks me in the face. It's shocking how he suffers. I'm quite ashamed to look at him, miss."

"So am I, John. All the same, let me see the poor thing. I might be able to do him some good."

The door was shut. John looked all round. He listened. All seemed in order and quiet. He saw his chance. In another instant, he had opened his flap. He twisted his big limb out from under his shirt.

My hand closed on it. It was already stretching itself out, and half erect. I loved to feel it thus—so warm, so soft!

I bent my head over it as I sat. I kissed the red tip. The impulse was too strong for my resistance in the condition in which I was. I opened my moist lips. I let the big nut pass in. I sucked it. It swelled and stiffened. John involuntarily moved himself backwards and forwards. It very quickly attained its extreme stiffness and dimensions. I withdrew my face a little to look at it. The big round top shone as if it had been varnished.

"Take care what you do, miss. He's not to be trusted. He's in such a condition. What you have just done has made him more rampageous than ever."

I rubbed his member up and down quickly. He put down his hand and stopped me.

"Oh, Miss Eveline, mind your dress, miss."

"Is it so near, John? Poor Robin! He must have all the pleasure I can give him to make him more tractable."

I put down my head. I applied my lips again. I only released his limb to whisper:

"Let it come so, John! I want it!"

The idea made him mad. He pushed forward, breathing hard. He moved his loins again. I took into my mouth the whole of the big nut. I tickled it with my tongue. I moved both hands in little jerks upon the white shaft.

"Oh, Miss Eveline! Oh, my good Lord! I shall come! Oh!"

He discharged. My mouth was instantly filled with a torrent of his sperm. I swallowed as much as

I could. It flew from him in little jets. It must have given him immense pleasure. Soon all was over.

"Now fetch the tea, John. I hope Robin will be better. If it had not been a cock—your Robin—I should have said it had laid an egg and broken it."

"Hansom? Here you are, miss!"

"Go to P—— Street, Soho. Stop at the corner."

I alighted. I paid the fare. I walked on. I could not recognise the house. There was a chemist there, however. The usual coloured bottles in the window which still adorn those establishments in indifferent neighbourhoods. I walked in. The fair young man was behind the counter. He did not know me through my thick veil. I waited until he had served his customer, and then I said:

"I have come for another syringe, please."

He looked hard at me. I lifted my veil. His face brightened with pleasure.

"Oh, it's you! My dearest girl, how delighted I am!"

"Yes! I did not know the house again—surely you have altered the outside."

"Yes, I have had it all done up. When you came before, I was only the assistant. Now the place is mine. I have purchased the lease and taken over the business. But really now, I am so glad to see you. Come into my back room. It is now my consulting room."

"You are a surgeon, then?"

"Yes, my pet. I have taken out my diploma now.

Things have been looking better for me. A relation left me a legacy."

"I congratulate you. I am really pleased at what you tell me."

He sat down. He took both my hands in his as I stood before him. He inspected me from head to foot.

"Why do you look at me like that?"

"I am trying to make out who and what you **are**."

"You had better not do that."

"But I have been thinking so much of you, **and** wondering if ever I should see you again. You don't know how much I have thought of you. You are **not** an ordinary girl, you see. You seem quite different from others."

"Perhaps I am not. I should not like you to interest yourself too much in me."

He observed me attentively. He seemed suddenly to grasp the situation.

"I knew it! You are not of that class at all. But you know you are running a great risk. You must have a position to lose."

I felt annoyed. He saw it, I thought. I was the more angry, because he was quite right.

"You must not suppose I am always so easily assailed as by you on the last occasion. I assure you I know very well how to protect myself."

"Yes, yes, I am sure you do, dear girl, but there are many dangers of which you, at your age, can know little or nothing."

"That may be. Before I go any further, you must promise me one thing: not to attempt, in any way, to know more of me than I choose to disclose. Can you not be content with that, and promise me?"

I read disappointment in his eyes.

"Well then, so be it! But I have let my memory dwell on you so long since I saw you—you—are so beautiful that I felt fond of you. Some day, possibly, you will trust me further."

We sat on the sofa. He put his arm round my waist and kissed me.

"You have forgiven me then. I know you will respect my incognito."

"Of course I will! Who could refuse anything to such a beauty as you? Look here! It is Saturday, and just time to close. We can remain here undisturbed. My boy puts up the shutters. You make me feel worse than ever."

He began to whisper indecencies which made my cheeks burn, and not wholly from shame. He got excited. His expressions grew coarse.

"Did I do it nicely last time? Would you like it again? I am longing for it! So are you, I can feel. Oh, how sweet you smell! How soft your beautiful legs are!"

Meanwhile the boy had put the shutters up and closed the shop.

"Shall we do it on the sofa? Put your dear little feet up. So! Never mind the boy, he's gone out to get his tea. We are quite alone. We can amuse ourselves all the afternoon in here, now. See, here's the syringe! It's awfully stiff. You shall feel it work, too. I know how to please you. I'm awfully randy."

"So am I. What fun! What a fine syringe! Is it loaded? You'll syringe me nicely, won't you? Tell me, did you like me last time? Was it very, very nice? You're awfully large and stiff."

He undressed. I grew impatient. He assisted me

to remove my walking dress. I slipped out of my skirts. I was now an easy prey to a man. He felt me all over. I was as excited as himself. Our lips met. Our tongues fondled each other. He bore me back to the sofa. I fell on my back. He toppled onto my belly.

"Open your legs! You're longing for it! How wet your pretty slit is! Let me put it in for you, darling. There it goes! It's in! Oh, God! How tight you are!"

He got right up me at the first lunge. Then he raised himself on his hands. He seemed to be contemplating his victory.

"It feels so nice—it's lovely! You're so stiff and strong."

He went to work. He churned up and down. I closed my eyes. I panted with the feeling of luxury which was fast increasing. He drove his limb into me up to the balls, and then withdrew it to the nut. My spasms came suddenly upon me. I kicked about with my legs, I heaved up my body. I squeaked aloud like a rabbit. I was not ashamed to return him his indecencies. I implored him not to spare me —to push as hard as he liked. The old sofa trembled and groaned. His thrusts were lovely. He held on to me tighter than ever.

"Oh, Christ! I am just about spending!"

"Give it me, dear, I want it—all of it!"

"Now! Take that then!"

His weight fell on me. I felt a warm jet of his nectar come from him. It filled my slit. Then he lay still.

After the storm—a calm. My friend produced some tea and bread and butter. The tea refreshed me. He commenced to talk professionally. He asked me many questions. Some I answered, others I avoided. He seemed a sensible young man. He was evidently much attached to his profession.

"I have had lots of experience with women. When I was at Guy's, I was for some time dresser to Sir William ———. I liked my work. He would trust me, when the others were not to be counted on. Do you know, you are most splendidly made? I never met any girl so young, and yet so wonderfully developed. I have a great fancy to see you stripped."

He fondled me in a wanton manner, as we sat together. His fingers were between my thighs. I did not care to restrain him. Suddenly, without any warning, he slipped his second finger into me as far as he could go.

"Goodness me! My dear girl, really you are wonderful! You have an abnormally long vagina. I cannot even arrive at the matrix."

"Do let me be! Oh! I say! This is too much—really!"

"But what I say is true. You must remember, I am your doctor now. Will you only let me examine you properly? I might tell you something more than you know already. Something to your own benefit—trust in me!"

The appeal was not in vain. He rose and went to a drawer. He produced a small instrument. At his request I lay down. He examined me professionally.

' It is as I thought. There is nothing to alarm you. Nothing even to distress you. But, may I tell you? Well, I do not remember so distinct a case.

Everything is perfect, except one little thing. That slight impediment is quite sufficient, unless it is removed, to prevent you from ever becoming *enceinte*."

"But how is that? You take my breath away!"

"It is quite true, nevertheless. A little thing—a membrane to divide, a very slight operation to undergo, and you can be the mother of a family. Without it, as you are—never!"

I was thunderstruck. His air was now that of the skilled physician. I felt he was speaking the truth.

"You are quite sure of what you tell me?"

"As sure as that I am kissing your sweet lips. More than that, it is most curious in a young woman of your build, but let me tell you, you have the longest—I mean the deepest—vagina I have ever examined. Still more curious: I have good reason to know that the elasticity is perfect and the diameter very narrow."

It was already late in the afternoon as I passed the entrance to the mews by our house. A thought occurred to me. I had not ridden my beautiful horse which papa had just bought for me. I would try him tomorrow. I turned towards our stables.

I put my hand on the latch of the door. As I did so, I heard the sound of conversation. A woman's voice—a low and smothered exclamation. I am a woman. I am endowed, I suppose, with the curiosity natural to my sex. I dropped the latch noiselessly. I looked around. There was one window. Under it stood an empty barrow. The piece of mus-

lin that served for a sort of blind had come off the
nail. One end hung down. I mounted into the barrow. I looked into the stable. There was just sufficient light for me to see the groom standing at the
foot of an empty stall. With him was Mary, the
under-housemaid. They were close together. His
arm was round her waist, while she held in her right
hand—yes, I was right—the man's privates! A
huge, erect, and solid male organ! Such as one
dreams of, as large, or even larger and longer, than
that of my first friend, "Teapot."

I continued to gaze, fascinated by the lewd sight,
for fully a minute. Then, fearful of discovery, I
stole back to the house trembling in every limb,
with a mad desire to be in Mary's place—a fearfully jealous longing to get her out of the way.

Chapter VII

"Eveline, will you go to the opera tonight? There is *Lohengrin* at Covent Garden. Your mother declines to go."

"I shall be delighted, dear papa. I have just time to dress before dinner. We can even dine half an hour earlier."

Papa was pleased. He looked young and handsome that day. He was really young for his years. Hale and stout—vigorous, active, he commanded respect. He had the air and carriage of a great soldier. I was as charmed in his society as he evidently was in mine. When we were quite alone he would sit with my hand in his. Frequently he would slip a new ring furtively on my finger. When I discovered the little device, he would ask me to kiss him for it. At such times his voice would sink almost to a whisper; his eyes suffused with sudden passion. His breath would come in great sobs of delight.

I knew well enough why my mother had refused to go. She had been indulging again in champagne and soda all the afternoon.

The spirit of jealousy and mischief possessed me. I dressed with extraordinary care. I put on exactly what I knew papa liked best. Beautiful long white gloves fitting like my own skin, softly glowing in the sparkling light from the huge chandelier. My low dress, the bodice covered with the finest Brussels lace. My jewels, selected for their simplicity and their rarity, were confined to bracelets and earrings. A small bouquet of the choicest flowers rested on my corsage. He gazed upon me with an admiration which was only given to myself to understand. His inordinate sensual instincts were aroused. Like the bloodhound who scents the vital fluid, so he, in his innate sensibility, scented the perfume of my being. Desire shone in his large eyes. He was in a condition of extreme excitement. It was my purpose and my intention to fan the flame.

I know I am beautiful. Do you suppose that any woman does not know the exact merit of her own attractions? I know a beautiful face when I behold one. I am capable of the same artistic admiration for a beautiful statue, a lovely picture, which is shared by all who are even novices in art. I am not usually taken for a fool. I look in my glass. I see there reflected a face, a bust, a figure and a personality which is not only beautiful—unusually beautiful—but graceful and elegant, endowed with such power to please—when I choose—gifted with such rare possession of a power to charm—when I desire to put it forth—that Eveline could have the world at her feet—did she desire it.

I am not going to indulge you with a vulgar list of my perfections—you must take the fact from me. Or, if you prefer it, close these pages. I do not want your admiration. I am not open to your flattery. Every woman, young even to childhood, or matronly enough to be the mother of a family, can readily dissect your mere flattery, if they have only the sense to pause—to think; you want something, if only to gain the attention of her you flatter. In flattering me you are flattering yourself—*voilà tout!*

"My darling Eveline, you never looked more beautiful than you do tonight."

It was no flattery. He felt it. It came straight from his inner consciousness. From his brain to mine.

"I am always happy when I please my dear papa. You are inclined to enjoy yourself tonight. You are free, and alone with your little Eveline beside you."

I leant towards him. I caressed his hand in mine. Under pretext that his white dress tie required arrangement, I put my gloved fingers under his nose. I could see his nostrils dilate as he sucked in the perfume of my glove.

"Darling girl!"

"I do not care much for the music tonight, papa. The instrumentation is too much for me. It gets on my brain. It makes me nervous. Let us sit back in the box. My head aches."

"Dear child! Let me kiss it—so—on the temples —on the cheek. Now say if it is not better? Give me again your dear little hand to hold in mine."

"Kiss me again, papa. I love your kisses."

In the shadow of the box he kissed me long and voluptuously on the lips. He took my hand. He pressed it. He laid it on his left thigh. He must surely have counted on my inclination for pleasure. I felt a something which throbbed beneath the soft impression of my hand.

"You are not quite in spirits tonight, Eveline. I think the music, as you say, is too much for you."

"It is too bad to blame Wagner for my nervousness, dear papa, yet I know I am a little distraught."

I leant my head on his shoulder. I pressed more firmly on his thigh. I felt the throbbing mass increase in volume. I turned my eyes up to his. We read each other's thoughts.

I felt his hand, trembling with passion, pass round my satin-robed bust. I even moved that the action might be facilitated. He sighed with pleasure—with longing—undeveloped, but to become realised.

"Poor papa! You are out of sorts also."

"No, Eveline, not out of sorts, but this atmosphere is not agreeable. I am half suffocated. I want air. Suppose we leave, and go to a restaurant and have some supper? You hardly dined at all."

"Oh, papa, that would be lovely!"

We descended—called a cab. Sir Edward ordered the driver to go to a certain well-known but somewhat retired restaurant.

We were easily installed. A little charming boudoir on the first floor—what they would call in Paris a *cabinet particulier*.

The obsequious waiter, having deposited a sumptuous supper on the table with champagne of approved mark, left us to ourselves.

"How good of you, papa! This is fun!"

I perched myself upon his knee. My seat was not altogether a comfortable one. He shifted about. There was something terribly hard and unyielding beneath me.

We supped well. I had an appetite. The champagne warmed our blood. I laughed. I was gay.

"Oh, my garter is coming down!"

I put a daintily booted little foot upon a chair. In so doing, I let him see well up my calf to my knee.

"How clumsy I am! I must have had too much champagne."

"My darling, let me try. See, I can fasten it at once."

"Oh, but you tickle, you naughty, dear papa! It has come undone again!"

His hand trembled with excitement. He was in no mood to draw back. His fine eyes looked imploringly upon me, alternately fierce and loving.

I nestled close to him.

"Poor papa! Eveline loves to please her darling papa!"

My dress was well open in front. His hand still lingered on my knee, on the silk stocking around which I sought to clasp my garter. I kissed him warmly on the lips He returned my kiss with interest. He pressed his left hand on the back of my neck. He pushed the tip of his hot tongue into my mouth. My tongue met his. We remained thus. Our tongues played lovingly together. His right hand stole forward towards my thighs.

"Dear papa! Your little Eveline loves you dearly."

I laid my hand again upon his thigh quite by accident. It encountered the same bulky mass.

"Oh! Eveline!"

"Oh, my darling papa!"

His hand went further. I squeezed that which I felt beneath my fingers in his trousers. There could no longer be dissimulation between us.

He renewed his kisses. His tongue again sought mine. He was beside himself with passionate longing. I maddened him still further. It gave me exquisite delight. My hand moved gently up and down his thigh. My eyes looked into his. He read consent there.

"Dear papa! Your Eveline is your own little girl!"

"My sweet! I love you beyond all in the world!"

He sank down at my feet. He attempted to raise my clothes. I did not yield, yet I offered so faint a resistance that I spurred him on.

"You have all the right to love me, darling, for I am your girl."

He bent forward over me. His face was close to mine. His passion appeared to have reached its climax. As his fingers touched the centre of sensation, I felt myself dissolving in a furious sense of longing for what was to come.

I pushed my hand impudently inside the opening of his trousers. He assisted the movement, which was sufficiently suggestive. I turned aside the fine cambric shirt he wore. I grasped that which I had determined from the first to possess.

It was indeed beautiful. To my disordered imagination it appeared the perfection of man's sexual power. He pressed me down upon the lounge on which we had been sitting. He threw up my clothes. He implored my pardon for what he said he could not resist. I rendered the attitude more propitious. I was on fire. His excitement even exceeded mine. His salacious rage was pitiable. I endeavoured to adjust the parts. He approached his impatient member to the orifice. The hot head even sought the well-moistened lips. To my surprise—to my utter dismay at that moment he sank forward on my prostrate body. With a groan of disappointment, he discharged a volume of seed all over my belly and my thighs.

"Cab! Drive to H——— Street. Here, Eveline, take my key! Or stay, I will drive you to the door, dear girl!"

I noticed the cabman had a hare-lip. He was a sulky-looking fellow. I got out. Papa said good night. He wanted, he declared, a turn in the street before going to bed. He took my hand, kissed me affectionately. I had just time to whisper the one word, "Courage!" He turned and walked away. It was John who opened the door. He had been sitting up for our return. He lighted a candle. He preceded me upstairs.

"Are they all in bed, John? Do nothing to awaken them."

"Everyone, miss. You are late home tonight, miss."

I was in an indescribable condition. My vitals appeared to be throbbing and pulsating. I could not remain still.

"Sir Edward is only taking a turn in the fresh air. You will hear him come in, John. He will go straight, no doubt, to his chamber. Whisper, John!"

"Yes, miss. I understand."

I could not resist. I looked with eyes full of lust

and longing on the strong fellow who preceded me up the softly carpeted stairs. I reached my chamber door. I took the candle from him.

"Shall I turn out the lights on this floor, miss?"

"Yes, John. In twenty minutes come quietly up to my door. I want to speak to you."

"Good night, miss."

There was no other reply, but a gleam of delight danced for an instant in his eyes as he turned and disappeared in the darkened corridor.

I had told my maid not to wait up for me. I expected we might return late. I am accustomed to manage for myself. I pity the young women who are slaves to their waiting maids. In ten minutes I had slipped out of my bodice—out of my skirts. In a few more, my hair was down—my toilet made. Under the time specified, I stood in my satin *peignoir*, a picture for the gods. Nothing but my *chemise* of fine batiste intervened.

I listened. Sir Edward had let himself in and retired to his room. My door was ajar! The house was quiet. I heard a faint scratching on the woodwork.

It was John. He entered on tip-toe. I put my finger to my lips. I closed and locked the door.

In the meantime I had arranged everything.

"John, you are not to speak at all. Listen to me. If anyone should, by any chance, come to my door, remember you must slip into my morning room through that door. You will take everything you have brought with you. You will watch your chance to gain the corridor by that way while I am occupied in replying here. Take off those things."

I was running a risk. I could not help it. I could

not withstand it. I had weighed all the chances. This man had nothing to gain by troubling me. He was selfishly anxious, on the other hand, about his character and his place. He knew well enough the fatal consequences to himself in case of any untoward event. He was a London servant in a first-class position. He had acquired the confidence and respect of his employers. He would retire—a nothing, a castaway, without resource, without employment. Yes, he was a safe medium. I risked it.

He removed his coat, his waistcoat and his breeches. He placed all on a chair by the inner door. Then he came to me; his white shirt sticking out in front.

"Let me look at it, John. I want to see Robin!"

He raised his shirt. He exposed his huge limb naked to my gaze, stiff and ready, red-topped and distended already with the sense of the pleasure to come. His belly was covered with short curly black hair. I took his thing in my hand and rubbed it softly up and down. Our lips met in a moist kiss.

"What a lovely thing you have, John! But it is much too big."

His delight was intense. He was ready for anything. I kissed his limb. I put my tongue to the top of the purple knob and tickled it. I opened my moist lips and sucked it. The faint taste and smell were delightful to me.

John fairly snorted with lustful longing. I was equally impatient.

"Won't it be nice, John? You shall do it to me at your ease this time."

"Yes, miss, we'll do it properly this time. Only look at my tool!"

I thought I had never seen such a thing. It was so stiff that the head bent almost on to his navel. He pressed me back against the bed. He played with my breasts. I played with his "tool," as he called it. I threw open my *peignoir*. He raised my *chemise*, and looked on my naked body.

"How lovely you are, Miss Eveline!"

John bent forward, his hot kisses covered me. He descended. I felt him licking the centre button of my orbit. It was shockingly voluptuous.

"Oh, John! Oh, that's lovely!"

I raised myself on to the soft bed. I lay across it. John opened my thighs and stood between. I put his big limb against the moist lips of my slit. I guided it in. In a second it went right up me. I felt it stretching open my vagina. It was dreadfully hard and throbbed with spasmodic pulsations as it entered gradually to its utmost length.

"Go gently—very gently, my dear John, you are so big. Oh, goodness, how you push!"

He thrust more carefully. My sensations rose to boiling point. I clutched right and left at the bed-clothes. He did it slowly, working deliciously up and down.

"Oh, John, dear John, it's nice, so nice now! You may push now—push! Oh! Oh! My goodness! Push me hard, John—I'm coming—John!"

The man could only breathe hard and gasp in the intensity of his pleasure. He had never had such a chance, and a real young lady was such a treat to the sensual fellow that he was beside himself with passion. He wanted no incentive, but drove up and down my little belly in an ecstasy.

I delighted to watch him; to feel the big, strong

tool throbbing inside my parts. My spasms came again and again while he was having me.

"Oh, miss! I shall have to come directly! I'm coming now—there—there—oh!"

John gave me a convulsive clutch; he pushed in his limb to the balls. I buried my face in the pillow to prevent sighs from being audible, as he discharged. He inundated me with a torrent of hot sperm. I threw open my legs to receive it. It entered my womb in gushes. He withdrew with reluctance; he dragged out his big limb red and smoking. I wiped it for him. I rushed to my toilet and neglected no precaution.

We sat together on the little sofa. John was never tired of feeling my legs, my buttocks, and my slit. His fingers roved everywhere and his limb very soon showed evidence of his returning virility. I stooped down, played with it and sucked it, and it very soon stood again fiercely erect. We neither of us spoke, but I motioned him towards the bed. I laid myself upon it and put a pillow under my buttocks. John laid himself upon my naked body. I guided his huge thing into me and took it in up to his delicious balls. He lay a long time in me, doing it slowly. Then he got near his crisis and soon after spent in a gush of seed that sent me into the seventh heaven.

I handed the man his clothes; he dressed silently and rapidly. I watched a moment at the open door. Only the ticking of the hall clock. I waited till it struck three, and then, while the vibrations were still in the air, I closed my door upon him.

I enjoyed a sweet unbroken sleep till past nine o'clock.

Chapter VIII

I have already told you I am beautiful. I am dearly fond of the beautiful in art. What can be the difference then between the beautiful in the glass and the beauty in the picture? Rely upon it, every woman is certain to know the exact measure of her good looks—if she possesses any. She is sure to be reminded of her defects. Her inner consciousness will, whatever may be her natural vanity, infallibly lead her to a correct appreciation of her charms. She may think she can impose on others by her beauty. It is only by the flattery, or the honest opinions she obtains, that her vanity is touched, that comparisons are made. When she goes home and in privacy she sees, she knows the naked truth for better—or, for worse.

When a man tells me he thinks me the most beautiful girl in the world, I know he is talking nonsense. When he simply and obviously admires me for my comeliness, I may believe him. If he goes further, if he ventures to speak of love to me, I know I have excited his desires. I can see it in his eyes. It is evident in the parted lips, the ardent, furtive, searching glances with which I feel he is striving to pierce the thin veils in which modesty—save the mark!—robes the nude form of woman. He is gloating secretly on all his fancy pictures hidden beneath. He is forming his ideas on the subject of my nudity—of the extent of my fabricated personality. Poor man, if he could only look in reality below, he would find there was nothing there but Nature unadorned. In fancy, he gives his ideal full swing. He sees me as his lust would have me. He sees the perfect bust—the panting bosom which no fashionable corset could "improve"—the waist and ample haunch—the buttocks which no dressmaker ever pads with wretched cotton wool. The man, after all, is only a society satyr. His lust, subject as it must be to the decencies of ordinary life, lifts him, for the nonce, from the commonplace, knockabout man of average intelligence, into a being which interests me. In fancy he beholds me stripped—at his mercy—small mercy I should receive at his hands! He rages in private. He snorts like a stallion over a young mare. I have no contempt for this poor creature. Shall I confess the truth?

I feel intensely for him. That confession does not prevent me from displaying to him such attractions as my beauty—my knowledge of mankind—enable me to excite him with. His agony of lust is to me a selfish gratification. It is joy to me to watch his hardly concealed emotion. I know him. I treat him simply as he would me. I am, in his shortsighted view, too innocent and too young—altogether too inexperienced—to understand anything connected with the realities of sensual instincts. He does not scruple to let loose, for my benefit, his lust of the flesh. It has extended to my flesh. He figures to himself, in his licentiousness, all the delights he would enjoy in my possession. In his bestial concupiscence he revels in the ideal enjoyment of my innocent young charms.

Could the man who struts in society only know how his glances at Eveline are noted and enjoyed, he might indeed be more bold, but he would none the less meet with the failure he merits. She is not the girl, young and innocent as he deems her, to play the puppet while he pulls the strings, and boasts loud-tongued at his club of his society successes!

A fine morning. Actual sunlight, and in London! I spring out of bed. Just eight o'clock. My cold tub is there ready. How refreshing it is! How I glow all fresh and red as I stand and rub myself down! The act reminds me of Jim—of grooming a horse. I should like Jim to groom me. Well, should I really? Yes, that I should, when I remember the sight which for a moment met my gaze through the stable window. I commenced my morning toilet. I gradually matured at the same time an idea which became more and more fixed in my mind. My passions, I fear, are not always made subservient to my higher perceptions. It is my nature to give them a flight sometimes. To indulge them against—sometimes— my cooler judgment. How can I, with my temperament, stop to think of risks—of results? So my fancy ran free now. In fancy I was again at the stable window. That did not prevent me from completing my morning toilet. I descended to breakfast

in the dining room. Papa was there already, his
newspaper and his letters before him.

"Good morning, Eveline; here is a letter which
will interest you."

A large envelope enclosing a card. The arms of
the late Duke of M——. The invitation at last to
the costume ball.

"It will be magnificent, my darling. You must
make a sensation. All the guests are to represent
some particular personality. How will you go? You
would look adorable as Anne Boleyn."

"And my papa would look defiantly inscrutable
as Charlemagne. Oh papa, it is fixed. You must go
as Charlemagne!"

"And you, Eveline?"

"I shall represent my great-grandmother—your
grandmother, papa. I have already considered all.
We have her jewels. We even have in the great
wardrobe the dresses she wore at my age. You told
me yourself how like I was to her in the picture in
your study. I can imitate the pose—the look—
everything. It is fixed, papa—you will not deny your
own little girl?"

He never denied me anything. He would go to
the Duchess's ball as Charlemagne, if practicable. I,
as my own *great-grandmother*!

"Do not forget we dine tonight at Lady Lessleton's. There will be some nice people there who
are always worth meeting. She is very erratic in
her assemblage of guests at these little dinners. You
may depend on it you have been asked to meet
someone in particular; such very young ladies are
not always selected for these affairs."

"I will not forget. I shall try to look as bright as

possible to please my dear papa first, and the somebody in particular next."

"Naughty girl! Kiss me!"

The dinner passed pleasantly enough. Lady Lessleton laid herself out to be very nice to me. Papa
was right. I was coupled with a delightful old gentleman—the magistrate at Bow Street. Sir Langham Beamer was a bachelor, a gentleman and a man
of taste. I like old people. I took particular pains to
be agreeable to him. He was a very smart, gay old
gentleman of the old school. He loved the society
of the young. He was evidently delighted to find
that his hostess had not forgotten his foible. I
heard him express his gratification in no measured
language to her after dinner. I found him full of
anecdote and information, with a distinct and irrad-
icable tendency in his conversation to revert to his
own profession. I thought him charming. He made
me promise to come round with papa and see him
administer his functions in his Police Court.

At quite an early hour we returned home. It was
the brougham they sent for us. Sir Langham
Beamer put me in himself. Papa received me in his
arms. We rolled away, our lips sealed together—
our hearts beating against each other—our hands—
ah me, our hands . . . The restraint was dreadful—the longing terrible. Between the two I was
nearly mad. Papa, I could see, was not much better.

"Covent Garden—opera—oh, here it is. *Faust*
tonight. Look, what a splendid cast! Will you go,
Eveline? The music of Gounod always delights you.
Will you go?"

"Yes, dear papa. It will cheer me up. I feel I want to hear something sympathetic. I love Gounod. I am not tired of *Faust*."

"Agreed then, we will order the dinner and the carriage in good time."

For some days he had withdrawn himself a great deal from my society. Only on such occasions as were unavoidable did he come to me, or venture himself within my influence. I was certain he had been forming resolutions to restrain his passion.

I had been absent and abroad during three years. I went from England and from what most children look on as home—my mother's house—a child. I returned a blown woman—very young, it is true— but still a woman physically and mentally, with such experience as only a debauched French *institution de demoiselles* can supply to colour the life of a young girl. My sensations as I prepared myself for the evening were of the wildest anticipation. On this occasion I determined to go straight through with my intrigue. I was infatuated. I had nursed this passion a long time. I had built up all the most captivating and extraordinary theories and fancies respecting it. I imagined the pleasure—the sensuous gratification to be derived from it, to be supreme. The lines of Voltaire haunted me. *We had already gone too far to draw back.* He knew it as well as I did. It was that which induced the present visit to the Opera.

I dressed myself to please him. I decked myself out in just that dainty and coquettish style which I knew would swell his lust. The corsage just showed enough to make the observer wish to see more. My whole toilette was of that ephemeral character which could serve only to heighten the unruly passion which burned to fever heat in his veins. I was armed. I had no regrets. I only dreaded a failure.

The great theatre was crowded. The atmosphere was oppressive. Sir Edward leant over the back of my chair.

"My darling Eveline, you look more beautiful than ever tonight."

"I am always glad when I can please my dear papa."

"Your dress is perfection, it leaves nothing to be desired."

"Absolutely nothing, papa? Poor Eveline!"

"Why do you say that, my dear child?"

I took his hand and held it. I leant back in my seat, and put my face close to his. His eyes shot flames of passion. I had shut mine and sighed. He kissed the nape of my neck just under my hair. I squeezed his hand and patted it with my softly gloved fingers. I put my right hand on his thigh. My breath came fast. I trembled. His agitation became extreme.

"My beautiful—my darling Eveline!"

We had heard the last of the beautiful serenade. We sat silent. It was the *entr'acte*. His arm was round my waist, my hand wandered slowly and caressingly upon his left thigh.

"My sweet Eveline, you excite me dreadfully!"

"Why not, my darling papa? Your Eveline loves you so dearly; you alone are my ideal."

He pressed me closer, but in silence. His passion rose hot, furious, it showed in his bated breath, his swimming eyes, his every movement. His nostrils were dilated like those of a stallion with the intensity of his lust.

We were well behind the curtain and in the recess

of the box. I threw my head back. He kissed me on the lips. A long, lingering embrace which spoke volumes of his desire.

"Shall we go to the restaurant and sup there again, my sweet?"

"Yes, papa. It is most oppressive here tonight. The opera is too long. The instrumentation makes my head ache. Let us go at once."

The supper was exquisite. The wine warmed our blood. Sir Edward drank freely. I read a fixed purpose in his eyes. He could not keep his hands off me. He helped me to all the choicest morsels. By his desire I retained my gloves. He watched the exit of the waiter and tipped him handsomely. Then he locked the door.

We sat side by side upon the sofa. His arm was round me; with his right hand he caressed by bosom. We exchanged burning kisses. I boldly laid my hand on his limb. It was hard and stiff and seemed half as long as his thigh.

"Does that give you pleasure, dear papa?"

"It is delicious, my darling Eveline."

"May I undo the buttons?" I whispered.

He saved me the trouble; my daintily gloved hand was pushed inside, I held his limb in my grasp. Meanwhile he was busy with my legs and his touches penetrated quickly to my naked thighs. I wore no drawers. His limb seemed larger than ever. My skirts had been arranged for the occasion. He gasped in his eager lust.

"How happy you make me, dear papa!"

He embraced me rapturously.

"Your touches are more intoxicating than wine, my sweet Eveline."

He gloated over my shoes, my silk stockings. He

passed his trembling hand softly up and down over all. I had rightly gauged his fancy.

A sudden movement released the noble limb. I saw it standing up stiffly. I seized on it again. I beheld the long white shaft, the mottled blue veins, the purple head—all, all for me at last!

I gently moved my hand up and down, covering and uncovering the big nut.

"Does that hurt, papa?"

"No, my darling, you give me delicious sensations."

"I am so glad, papa! What a sweet thing this is!"

"I rejoice in possessing your love, my child. You may continue to feel it. Do you also really enjoy the excitement you experience in handling it?"

"Yes, certainly I do! I am never so happy as when my hand is round it."

"Dear girl! What lovely soft gloves you have! I love to see them daintily clasped round the impudent fellow. See how he raises his red head! My Eveline, you must not deny him; you must let him have his way tonight."

"I am yours only, dear papa! Do with me what you wish!"

"We will intoxicate ourselves with pleasure, Eveline, but we must be careful and take all possible precautions against any mischance.

He pushed me back gently upon the sofa. He loosened his clothes to be more at his ease. He raised my legs upon the couch and knelt between them. Then he sank softly down towards my bust and I felt him endeavouring to adjust his limb to the lips of my slit. He set his teeth hard and pushed his loins forward. I opened my legs for him.

"Oh, papa! Dear papa! You hurt me—you do hurt me so! Oh! Oh!"

He thrust again. There was no mistake this time, and at least half his long limb was in me. I felt it throbbing in my vagina. Then came more thrusting against a contraction I well knew how to apply.

"Papa! Papa! You are killing me! Oh, it is too much! I cannot bear it—indeed you hurt dreadfully! Good Heavens! I shall die! Take it away—oh!"

He had done his worst. I felt my parts dilate; his limb passed up me. He was at last in the full enjoyment of my person. The whole length of his delicious thing was in me to his balls which I felt bang against me underneath.

The pleasure was celestial.

He worked up and down, evidently intent on the delight he experienced. I resigned myself—I even assisted him with a gentle undulation of my loins.

"My Eveline, my sweet girl, the pain has passed; there is nothing but pleasure left now. There! There! Feel how it throbs, the poor thing! Let it go in. There now, open your dear thighs—so!"

I lay gasping in an agony of spasmodic convulsions. At length I felt he was approaching the climax. With a sob of rapture, he discharged right into me. I felt his hot sperm spouting up me. It was too much ecstasy. At length, he slowly withdrew. I quickly snatched a steel pin from my hair and pricked myself on the edge of my parts. Seeing I was unable to move and apparently faint, he promptly applied his handkerchief, even before I could find mine.

"My darling Eveline—you have indeed suffered!

You have bled, my child, my kerchief is stained with blood."

"Cruel papa! But I love you!"

Sir Edward opened a door—a dressing room with toilet arrangements was disclosed. He led me there.

"Quick, Eveline, wash well and with cold water. Here, put a few drops of this brandy in the basin. My darling, be sure you are thorough in your present *petite toilette*."

In a few minutes I felt myself again. The thing was done. I had gained my end. My theories were correct; nothing could ever equal the pleasure he had given me.

We sat together on the sofa, our hands linked, his arm round my waist.

He looked at the clock. It was yet early.

"We came away from the Opera in good time, we need not hurry. I want to enjoy my sweet Eveline again. Does she regret what we have done?"

"No, papa. Great men are excused faults which in ordinary people are crimes. In my eyes you are a great man. You remember that Charlemagne enjoyed two of his own daughters? He was only a great soldier like my papa."

"Yes, indeed, but how did you come to know that?"

"I read it in Voltaire—when I was in Paris."

"But how come they to let you read Voltaire at school?"

"Oh, with a little of one's pocket money there is no difficulty in getting the *concierge* to do one so trifling a favour as to buy a book. I had four little volumes from him which he bought for me expressly and kept in his lodge. I had a great fancy to read Voltaire's account of Charlemagne. Was it wrong to do so, papa?"

"No, my child—only you seem to have run a risk of being detected."

"There is no pleasure without risk. Are you intoxicated already with yours, dear papa?"

"No, my darling Eveline, let us have more. Let us do it again!"

I put my hand on his limb. He released it for me to caress. It rose stiffly under my touches. It regained all its grand dimensions. I bent down my head and kissed it. I opened my lips, took the big knob into my mouth and sucked it. It was delicious. Papa groaned with rapture.

We were mutually excited. He took me in his arms. He laid me again upon the sofa, raised my clothes and lay again on my body. He entered my parts and had me again deliciously. He discharged copiously. I sucked in every drop of his sperm. I could have screamed with the pleasure, had I dared.

A little later we descended to the private entrance of the restaurant. Papa called the cab which stood opposite. As he closed the doors of the hansom, I recognised the man with the hare-lip.

END OF BOOK ONE

Book Two

Chapter I

Papa is absent fishing about Maidenhead somewhere. He loves the art. As far as I can see he
never catches anything. Lady L—— is taking advantage of the opportunity as usual to go in for any
extra quantity of champagne and soda. Sippett is,
also as usual, assiduous of her mistress's interests
regulated in diminutive proportion to her own.
Mrs. Lockett is the only active person on the establishment and she is about to visit some friends at
Croydon this afternoon. The carriage has gone to
Kensington to meet papa, and will not return till
six p.m. It is now exactly ten minutes to five.

I was all alone. I was not "at home" to callers. I
was lazy and idle. There is an old saying about idle
hands and the devil. I suppose that was why he
prompted me. Or was it some lesser imp endowed
with the power of knowing exactly what Eveline
demanded? I had on my walking dress. I had just
come in. No one had seen me, or heard me. I went
out again and closed the door with my latchkey. I
would go round myself and see how my horse was
and give my orders myself for the morning. Possibly Jim would be there. I met no one in the mews.

I entered our stable. My horse was comfortable in his stall. Jim was making the beds ready for the carriage horses on their return.

"Good afternoon, Jim. I see you look well after my new horse."

"Yes, miss. But he must not have too much corn. He gets too frisky. He hasn't work enough. He's too fond of his play."

"Is he indeed, Jim? I suppose there's lots of play round here. What was Mary playing with the other evening when she was here?"

"Mary, miss? Why—how do you know Mary was here, miss?"

"How do you know I am here now, Jim?"

"Cos I can see you myself, miss."

"Well then, Jim, it is because I saw Mary."

The young groom looked confused and rather silly. I put on my most childish air. My eye held his, while a sort of fluttering smile beamed out on my rosy cheek. I put my finger across my lips. I glanced half fearfully, half poutingly towards the door. Jim rested his fork against the manger and stood staring at me doubtfully.

"I hope, miss, you won't be hard on us. We were only having a little talk together. We might have had a minute's play to pass the time."

"I know what she was playing with, Jim."

Jim caught my expression. He was evidently alarmed and perplexed.

"Would you like a little play with me, Jim?"

His face changed suddenly. It was if he had caught up his stage cue and could go on. My eye wandered again to the door.

"Oh, Miss Eveline— if you were only in earnest!"

"Lock the door, Jim."

He went promptly and passed the bolt.

"You seemed to like Mary very much. Is she your sweetheart, Jim?"

"Lord, no, miss. I rather wish she wouldn't come slipping in here when I'm at work. I'm not over fond of her, I can tell you, miss. She'll be getting me into trouble with her tricks. I was only having a bit of fun with her."

"Would you like to have a bit of fun with me, Jim?"

He had come back, and stood close to me.

"Oh, miss, that would not be for the likes of me! You are such a beautiful young lady—so thorough-bred. The servants all say you're an angel."

His face flushed. He stood the image of doubt and timidity.

"You may play with me, if you like, Jim. I am only flesh and blood like Mary, but you must not kiss and tell."

I extended my gloved hand. He caught it up, squeezed it, and kissed it.

We both listened. All was absolutely still at that hour. We were alone. My desire rose stronger and stronger.

"Is the door locked, Jim? Then kiss me!"

His eyes sparkled. I put up my face to his. He put his rough big hands around my waist. He drew me to him and covered my face with kisses. His confidence seemed to come back to him. He was no longer afraid to venture; in fact he showed evident symptoms of quickly rising passion. The young man was transformed. I watched with surprise the effects of my childish nonsense. His eyes glistened lewdly

as he kissed me. His lips grew hot and shot his
warm sweet breath in my face. I grew excited as I
noted the result of my indulgence. There is no
pleasure for a woman equal to the delight of witnessing the sexual transports of which she is the
cause. He put his hands on my bosom. He pressed
me rapturously in his arms. I felt a hard thing
against my belly.

"Oh, Jim! How rough and strong you are! You
must not do that!"

I put down my right hand. It encountered his
limb, over which the thin stable breeches he wore
were tightly stretched.

"Oh, Jim! Is this what Mary was playing with?"

The young fellow had no better reply than a grin.
He had one hand round my waist, but with the
other he quickly unbuttoned his flap. He released
his shirt. It stuck out horribly in front. Under it
was something I meant to investigate. I pushed the
shirt aside. My hand closed on his limb—a monstrous affair quite as large as that of the "Teapot"
and much nicer to feel. It was at least nine inches
long and awfully thick! I laughed and pointed at it.
He had lost all reserve now. I took a good look at
his big thing. He had two large balls below. He
was very hairy, much more so than John. He became dreadfully excited—quite mad with mere animal desire. He seized me again in his powerful
arms.

"Jim! For shame—you must not do that! You
are lifting me off my feet!"

He had his hand up my clothes. I struggled in
vain to keep my balance. I had sown the wind—I
was about to reap the whirlwind.

There were some trusses of straw in an empty stall. He lifted me bodily, turned me round, and threw me upon them. I fell on my back. Jim pressed down over me.

"Let me get up! Do you hear, Jim? I am frightened! Oh, it is too bad!"

He ruthlessly pulled up all my clothes. I wore no drawers. Everything was at his mercy. He was like a lion in his rage.

My thighs were exposed as I lay. He felt me all about—my legs, even my buttocks. He bent over me and held me forcibly down. He knelt between my legs. His monstrous limb stood stiff—impatient —fiercely erect, almost against his hairy belly.

"Oh, Jim, do you want to kill me? Let me go, I say!"

He dragged me towards himself. He opened my thighs. I thought it best to lie still. His intention was only too plain.

"No, but I mean to stroke you, if I swing for it. It will be nicey nicey presently. Only let me put it in."

"To stroke me, Jim?"

"Well, anyhow, to have you."

"What do you mean, Jim? Dear Jim! Do let me go!"

"Well, damn it, to roger you! It's too late to stop now. You're such a lovely little treat, you know, Miss Eveline! Who'd have thought you would have come in here just as I was feeling so randy?"

"What do you mean by 'randy,' Jim?"

All this time he was making awkward attempts with the huge knob of his weapon against my parts.

I put down my hand as if to defend myself. No wonder he could not get it in! The head of his limb was the size of a large egg-plum! I intended to brave all. In reality I was as lewdly inclined as he was. Secretly I enjoyed his brutality. My excitement rose to erotic fury. I made as though to divert his attack. He continued his cruel thrusts. I suddenly placed the tip of the knob between the humid lips. I clenched my teeth. So far from flinching, I bore up to him. I felt he was in the right place; but oh, the stretching, the striving, the pushing! At last the thing went in—in—up my vagina—opening it as it had never been opened. He went to work—to "stroke" me, as he called it. He pushed furiously. The straw was elastic. We bounded up and down. Soon the pleasure was awful. I rolled in an agony of lecherous frenzy.

"Oh, my goodness! Oh! Oh! It's getting nicey nicey! Oh, Jim! You're stroking me now, Jim, ain't you?"

The man could only grunt and thrust. He was in ecstasy. While he was having me, he kept stopping to grip me tighter—to push in closer. He gasped—he snorted with the pleasure. I kept on coming. My spasms never ceased all the time he was in me.

"Oh, Jim, don't push so hard! You are so dreadfully big. You're too far in. Oh! My goodness, how you are thrusting! It's all wet! How lovely it feels now! Push! Push now, Jim!"

"Good Lord, miss! I'm coming—oh!"

He gave some thrusts the like of which were new to me. They caused me to come again. They were short, hard jerks. I felt him discharge right into me. The hot seed came from him in jets. I closed my eyes—my limbs quivered in the luxury of wallowing in this common fellow's sperm. I received every drop in my belly. He seemed a deliciously long time in spending. At last he lay still.

"You must never stroke me again, Jim."

"Not until next time, I hope, miss."

He assisted me to rise. I could hardly stand. I regained the house. I entered with my own key. I regained my chamber unobserved. My face in the glass was more like that of a ghost. Jim's spendings were running down my legs and all over my silk stockings.

🌺 🌺 🌺

"Please, Miss Eveline, there's a cabman at the door says he wants to see you. He would not tell me his business. He's a sulky-looking chap, miss. Shall I send him off?"

"No, John, I am going out. I will see him myself."

I chanced to be in the hall. I was ready for my morning walk. John watched me with glistening eyes and moist lips as I drew on and fitted my beautiful new gloves. I gave my dress a shake and a twirl, I put my dainty little foot up on the hall chair. John pretended to dust it with his pocket handkerchief. Robin was making himself evident.

"Open the door, John, please—I am ready now."

I knew the man at once—the hansom driver with the hare-lip. He turned from his horse towards me as I emerged from the house.

"It's all right, thank you! You can close the door, John, and go in."

"Well, you want to see me. What do you want?"

"Look here, miss! You left this here in my cab t'other night when I druv yer 'ome from the restaurant."

"No—I am sure I left nothing. Besides, that is not my property."

I knew that if he had really found a purse in his cab, it was his duty to take it to Scotland Yard. I said nothing more. I waited.

"If it isn't yours then it must be somebody else's. It doesn't alter the case though. The other night *it was you* as I druv here from the Up-to-Date Supper Rooms. Everybody knows what goes on there. When I sees a young lady comin' down from them there cabinet party ticklers to the private way out at twelve o'clock at night, I knows it's not for nuffin."

"What do you mean? Don't speak so loud, my good man!"

"I mean wot I ses: when I sees a gent—a reglar toff, old enough to know better—handing a vartuous young lady into my hansom from them rooms —a young lady livin' here, and 'as parents as is proud of her, as knows nuffin of these goin's on— then I ses, ses I to myself—it's a shame, it's a blot as oughter be cleaned out, and the sooner them parents is made acquainted with 'em the better."

"What does all this mean?"

"Wot does it mean? It means a tenner if as how I'm to 'old my tongue. I can't have my time wasted. I've 'ad two days' 'unt about the family and the 'ouse. I knows now who you are, miss. If you take my honest advice—you'll square it. I've druv yer twice from there."

"What's a 'tenner'?"

The fellow had lowered his voice. He stooped, pretending to be arranging the India-rubber mat in his cab. I began to grasp the situation. My last question was only a *ruse* to gain time. Meanwhile I had made up my mind.

"Wot's a tenner? Why a ten pun' note to be sure, and it's nuffin when you consider it. S'pose I rings the bell, and axes your flunkey to see his missus, Lady L——, werry partic'lar? I oughter do it—it's only my dooty."

"But, my good man, it's a large sum of money. I haven't got so much here. I should have to go to the banker's for it and cash a cheque."

"That's only reasonable. You can go now, and I can drive you. I don't want to make no trouble if I can 'elp it, and you're such a nice quiet sorter young lady. Only I tells yer—you'll 'ave to pay the fare there and back—nobody does nuffin for nuffin."

"You promise me if I give you this money that you will keep the secret?"

"In course I will! It's only between us two—at present. Jump in, missy! Where to?"

"Drive me to Temple Bar. Go by Leicester Square and Long Acre. I want to stop at the Floral Hall by Covent Garden theatre as we go along."

"Right yer are, miss!"

As I sat back in the cab, I thought quietly over this business. Certainly it would never do to drive the man to extremities and let him communicate with Lady L——. Neither could I think of worrying papa, or of dragging him into the affair. It would set all my mother's worst suspicions at work. She would never stop till she had wormed out something damaging to us both. It would cause endless trouble. It was not to be thought of. Eveline was in a somewhat tight place now, if ever she was.

The cab went gaily along through the square, up Long Acre until it arrived at the corner of Bow Street. There the traffic was more congested. The hansom went at a walking pace. Exactly as I arrived opposite the Police Station, I saw a constable by the kerb. I beckoned him.

"Come here, please—stop this cab immediately. I must see Sir Langham Beamer—don't lose sight of the driver!"

The policeman went to the horse's head. He called another man from the doorway. He spoke to the man with the hare-lip. The cab drew up to the kerb exactly before the stone doorway over which was written "Police." The policeman politely opened the doors of the hansom. He handed me out.

"We have his number, the man can't go away."

"You will find the Inspector in the office, miss. The Court is up."

I went in. I handed my card to the Inspector. I asked to see Sir Langham Beamer.

"Is it private business? Sir Langham's in his room—but I'll take the card in with pleasure, miss."

He had a good look at me. Evidently he admired me. He was a very fine man, tall and powerfully built—exactly the sort of man to suit Eveline—to be also the terror of the evildoer. I flashed a glance at him before he disappeared.

"Sir Langham will see you at once, miss. Will you please to walk this way?"

It was quite easy to stumble on the thick door-mat—so very natural that Inspector Walker should catch me by the hand. It was also even necessary for us to hold on, so that he could squeeze my soft kid glove in his strong palm, because I might have fallen.

"So you have found your way already? So very glad you did not forget the old man of the lock up. Ha, ha!"

"Oh, Sir Langham! How could I so soon forget you and your kind invitation. But I must not make that my excuse even for venturing to trouble you now."

The dear old gentleman was seated at a large table. Before him was a luncheon tray with a cover for one. He had risen with the air of an old beau as I entered. He pressed me into a chair and re-seated himself.

"Well, what can I do for you, my dear young lady? By the way, how charming you look to-day! You will not object to the presence of my lunch. If you permit me, I will commence my chop. Nothing in all the universe so good after all as a real London mutton chop—mind!—a loin chop—none of your chump chops!—but a *loin* chop like this— ha, ha!"

The cheery old gentleman raised the tempting morsel on his fork for my inspection. I duly admired it. In fact I had no appetite just then for chops.

"I wish I had another to offer you. How's Sir Edward? Grand man, Sir Edward! Why did you not bring him too? Not but that I am naturally charmed to have a *tête-à-tête* with—permit an old boy like me the privilege—with so beautiful a young lady as you, Miss L——."

"It's about a cabman. The man is here."

"Ah! Disputed fare, no doubt. These fellows like to get hold of an inexperienced young creature like you, my dear child."

"No, no, it's more serious than that, Sir Langham. The man thinks he has a secret, and demands a large sum of money to keep it."

The police magistrate put down his knife and fork. All his professional instincts immediately awoke.

"Ah! Why that must be strange! *You* can have no secrets worth the fellow's keeping—it sounds like blackmail. Are you sure there is no mistake? You say the man is here?"

"Yes, I came here in his cab. The policemen have taken his number."

Sir Langham touched his little silver gong. Inspector Walker appeared. Sir Langham gave an order in an undertone. Then the Inspector vanished, but not before our glances had crossed.

"Now tell me all about it."

"A few nights ago I went to the Opera with papa. I had not been feeling well all day and had foolishly gone without any dinner. At the Opera I felt the heat, and the noise of the music seemed to stun me. Papa guessed the cause. He proposed we should leave. As it was late and the servants had orders not to await our return on such occasions, Sir Edward suggested going for some supper to a restaurant. We went to one they call the "Up-to-Date." There we supped. Afterwards papa called a cab—this man's cab—which was at the door, and we drove home direct. I went in with my latchkey. Papa went away along the street for some fresh air before 'turning in,' as he calls it."

"Well, my dear young lady—I'm as wise as ever."

"But please wait a moment, Sir Langham. On another occasion papa and I arranged to sup there again. This cabman was there once more. Sir Edward put me into the hansom and gave the driver our address. Then he said good night, and kissed me as I sat in the cab. He walked straight off to his club, having an appointment."

"I confess I do not see how any trouble could come out of all that, my child. With Sir Edward, your father, you were quite safe anywhere. Besides you have already so perfect a character among your friends for prudence—I hear it everywhere."

"But here is where the trouble is. You are perfectly aware my mother is an invalid. She has no sympathy for poor papa. Of course, Sir Langham, I am speaking to you in all confidence. My mother is not affectionate to me, her only daughter. Strange as it may appear, she more than dislikes me. Her illness is to a great extent self-caused. She has a habit which we fear is rooted."

"Yes, yes, I have heard that before. Well?"

"If my mother were to hear that my papa had taken me to such a place to supper, she would be furious. She would make his life more wretched and unbearable than it is. She would never rest until she had fastened on him a character for frequenting fast places, and even worse—for permitting his daughter to accompany him! You know how good and noble he is? It would kill him. She must not know."

The tears stood in my eyes. I am told I am at such moments more seraphically beautiful than usual.

"Now I understand. Confound the fellow! He has taken your companion for a friend. He thinks he has a pull out of the affair. Putting it all together, with my knowledge of the world, I can see his drift. You are right, your mother must not know. Leave it to me. You have done quite right to come to me."

The magistrate touched his gong. The Inspector entered. He laid a sheet of parchment and an oval badge with a strap on the table. He stood waiting orders.

"Walker, please bring that cabman in here and leave us together."

A few seconds later the driver with the hare-lip stood before the police magistrate. His old air of insolent triumph had given place to a pallid and dejected look which plainly told his tale of apprehension and alarm.

Sir Langham glanced at the parchment.

"This is your license is it, my man? I see it has one endorsement already. You have been here before."

"It wasn't my fault, please your worship."

"Of course not. The present business is, however, likely to have considerably more serious consequences for you. This young lady charges you with demanding a sum of ten pounds from her under a threat. Now, do you know where that takes you, my man? If proved, it means under the new act six months if I have the case before me, but—stop! Listen—don't interrupt—but if I send you for trial at the Old Bailey, as I certainly should, it would mean five years penal servitude."

A still more significant change came over the cabman. He actually trembled. I thought he was going to faint. He steadied himself by leaning his arm against the doorpost.

"I hope the young lady will not go on with it. I hope you will forgive me, miss—I promise—"

"Never mind about your promises, my man. If this young lady, whom you have mistaken and insulted, decides not to prosecute you, you may think yourself sufficiently lucky. You can go. There are your badge and your license. I shall not put on another endorsement, but I shall make a note of this affair, and if ever you come here again, you shall lose your license altogether, for it will be cancelled."

As soon as we were alone, Sir Langham laughed a quiet little chuckling laugh.

"You will never have any more trouble from that fellow. But, how in the world did you get him here?"

When I had told the magistrate my little *ruse* he nearly choked himself with hilarity.

"'Pon my honour you are a clever girl! Sir Edward may well be proud of you. They ought to have you in the force."

"I am so very much indebted to you, Sir Langham, for all you have done. I hardly know how to thank you sufficiently. I dared not tell poor papa. He would have been so upset. He would probably never have taken me out with him again."

"Well, well, never mind. You have extricated

yourself most properly. The matter was not at all simple. I shall keep the silly little secret of yours, my child, and promise not to blackmail you save for one chaste salute on that charming little hand."

He rose and gallantly raised my hand to his lips.

"Mind and bring papa next time. This interview will remain dark and between ourselves. Now good bye. We have got through all the summonses today in good time, but there are some applications to which I must attend in person. Next time you come I will have a chop for you—a loin chop, mind, not a chump!"

As I passed out, Inspector Walker was waiting in the passage. I gave him my hand to say *adieu*. He asked me if he should call a cab. I told him I preferred to walk across to the Floral Hall. He asked if he might accompany me to be quite sure my friend the man with the hare-lip was not in the neighbourhood. I gave him permission in a burning glance. He was certainly a fine man.

"I suppose you are always engaged at this branch?"

"Oh, dear no, miss, my duties take me everywhere. Sometimes I have plenty of leisure time at my disposal. It depends."

"Does your leisure ever lead you to the park? I am generally there for my morning stroll at ten, principally in the walk behind the statue of Achilles."

"How odd! So am I—is it just possible I may have the happiness to see you again, Miss L——?"

"Quite possible—even tomorrow, if the weather is fine. But I cannot be seen, you know, under such circumstances."

"Of course not. I understand that." He looked down into my face. "I may then hope to see you again. I shall be in plain clothes."

"Yes. Good bye!"

Chapter II

"Here is news for us all, Eveline. I have a letter from Percy. He is likely to be home soon on leave."

"Oh, papa! What fun! I am so glad. It is so long since I have seen him. How he will be altered! He was only a boy of fourteen or fifteen when last I saw him and bid him *adieu*. Now he is a man and a soldier!"

"There is his letter. He has got several steps too. He thinks it likely he will be moved into the other battalion of his regiment."

The letter was full of joy at the prospect of coming home soon. He was very young for the service. He was clever, however. Interest was pushing him along. I wondered what he would think of me. He had only been in Canada a year, but I had been abroad when he joined his regiment.

It was breakfast time. Papa and I sat alone. Lady L—— was indisposed. Dr. Proctor was in attendance. I heard his step descending the stairs. Papa advanced to meet him. They shook hands.

"Much about the same. Yes, these cases are extremely difficult and delicate. You must do all you can to keep down the stimulants. Plenty of beef-tea —exercise—fresh air. We have a very delicate duty to perform, Sir Edward. We doctors, of course, cannot enter into the domestic difficulties of our patients. We must keep aloof—my sympathy, however, I may tell you, is entirely devoted to this case."

"It is not so much your sympathy which I would invoke, Dr. Proctor, as your practical suggestions—your deliberate opinion on the course I should pursue. I am much perplexed—very much distressed."

"Very difficult—very delicate. Better let me know if any recurrence of the excitement supervenes. Meanwhile sedatives—bromide of— Ah, how do you do?"

He had caught sight of little me in the doorway. I bowed. He had been speaking in a low confidential tone intended for papa's ear. There was a callous, selfish ring in his voice, which never left the pompous professional key—never sounded the true ring of brotherly sympathy as from man to man. Dr. Proctor seemed glad to change the subject.

"*You* do not appear as if you required my services, Miss L——, if I may judge by your looks."

"Looks may be yet deceptive, Dr. Proctor. I do not feel any fresher or better for the fatigues of the London season so far. Some of your bromide might not be wasted on me."

He was too stupid, or too much engrossed by the consideration of his own professional importance to notice the ironical tone of my voice.

"Take her into the country—give her bracing air —a few days change to the East coast would set her up. Good bye, Sir Edward, good bye. I have a long round today—and royalty to visit at noon."

"That's rather a good idea. I wonder if Mrs. Lockett could be trusted to look after our invalid. We might run off to C——, or B——, for a couple of days. It would bring back all your roses, Eveline."

"What a hideous thing!" I thought as I stood behind the great statue of Achilles in the park. It was misty, not to say foggy. The air of the murky London atmosphere had not yet been moved by the breeze. It stood in yellow patches about the green glades and spoilt the fresh fragrance of the flower beds. I walked slowly on. A solitary figure came slowly out of the haze. Nearer and nearer. It took the shape of a tall man, broad-shouldered, upright, a military air and independent stride which argued decision and self-confidence. It was Inspector Walker.

"Ah, Miss L——, how fortunate I am to find you out already! Not a very promising morning either. You look frightened. I trust——"

"No, I am not frightened. I am only a little nervous. I am anxious no one should recognise me. You recall too often my individuality. I run a great risk. In fact I have been wrong, I fear, to come here."

"Do not say that. I will not repeat the imprudence. You know I am quite safe in any case to keep a confidence. I am only too grateful to you for permitting me to see you again."

"Can you keep a secret?"

"It is my business to keep secrets. I am a member of the detective force."

"I suppose I may trust you, Mr. Walker?"

"Indeed you may. Let me caution you to lower your veil."

"Are you afraid to look at me?"

My eyes spoke mischief. I smiled, but did not blush.

"Indeed I am. You are too beautiful for a man to look at safely."

"Was that the reason I was to put my veil down?"

"Oh, no! It was for your own protection. You are now quite safe from recognition."

We sat down on one of the seats by the side of the path. No one was about. The nurse-maids and the soldiers had not yet arrived, nor was the morning propitious. The Inspector became very loving, especially when he found I was not offended by his little familiarities. We laughed and chatted. I soon learnt the sort of man with whom I had to deal. He was quite my ideal. I brought him quickly to the point.

"You say you want to be my friend—my secret eye on all around. You should be—if I was sure I could trust you."

I listened to his explanations. I determined to go on with my intrigue. In ten minutes we completely understood each other.

"You would have me treat you so, then, little lady?"

"Yes! Exactly in all respects as if I was one of the class to which I have referred."

"Be it so. You shall find me loyal and true. I am a lucky man!"

"I like you, Mr. Walker. Henceforth you are my dragon—my watchful, protecting dragon."

A look of strong animal passion passed over his features. He had caught the infection from my eyes. I gave him my hand. He pressed the pretty tight-fitting kid glove to his lips.

"At four o'clock we will swim in pleasure. *Au revoir*, my dragon."

"John, where is Mary? I did not see her at work on the stairs this morning."

"No, Miss Eveline. Mary is gone, Mrs. Lockett sent her off yesterday. Shall I bring you a glass of wine, miss?"

Mrs. Lockett had received Sir Edward's orders to discharge the under-housemaid. She gave her a month's wages, one hour's notice, and an excellent character extending over eighteen months. She had known her exactly two. Jim was away exercising the horses when she left with her tears and her box. John brought the wine on a salver.

"Shall I pour it out, miss?"

"Yes. How is Robin, John? He has not had any ginger nuts lately."

"No, he hasn't. He's had no fun either, poor chap. He's overloaded, miss, that's what he is— puffed up with his own importance, like too many folks. He wants taking down a peg."

"Shut the door. Bring him here—quick, let me feel his pulse!"

I had his big limb in my grasp. All was quiet. Papa was down at the Horse Guards, where he had an appointment now. I found the footman's member irresistible. I kissed it. I moistened the willing tip. I rubbed the long shaft well up and down with both hands.

"Oh! That's heaven! It's—it's doing him good already!"

The thing swelled stiffly up. I let it enter my mouth. I sucked it. I tickled it. I worked so quickly that he grew livid with excitement.

"Oh! My God! I shall spend! Oh! Oh! I shall come!"

I continued. John discharged. I received all. Not a drop of his delicious sperm was lost. I had infinite pleasure thus. This form of libidinous gratification was growing on me. From that day I seldom missed my morning dose. Robin took to it very willingly.

At four o'clock I was at the appointed *rendez-vous*. My "dragon" was there. He was overjoyed at my punctuality.

My veil was down. We took a short run. He made sure we were unobserved. Then he hailed a four wheel cab. He put me inside after giving a direction to the driver. He stopped at the corner of a street. I followed him a few paces after he had seen the man drive off. We then crossed the road. My dragon led the way. I followed a dozen paces behind. Presently he entered a large house the door of which he opened by turning a big brass handle. I found him ready to receive me in the hall. No one else had appeared. He led me to a back room upon the entrance floor. To my surprise I found the window shutters fast, and curtains closed against the daylight. A good fire burnt brightly on the hearth. Electric lights shed a golden lustre on a beautifully furnished bedroom. My companion closed and locked the door. Some particularly "risky" engravings hung from the walls.

"We are secure here. We can be absolutely at our ease."

I felt he was to be trusted. He evidently knew his ground.

"Yes, we are alone. We are at our ease."

The words were hardly out of my lips before I was folded in his arms.

"You beautiful girl! This is too much happiness!"

"Do you really like me, my dragon?"

"Like you? It is not safe for man to look upon you, you beautiful little lady. I shall call you 'Beauty.' Come, I want you—Beauty! You know what you promised me this morning? You said we should swim in pleasure. Was it not so?"

"I will do more than that. I will intoxicate you with delight. I will try to make you revel in—in lust. Your pleasure will be mine also!"

I had sunk my voice to a whisper. All was otherwise silent, save the splutter of the burning wood in the newly lighted fire. My companion held me in his arms. I sat on his knee. Our faces touched—our lips met in a delicious embrace. Our tongues rolled together.

I can imagine no finer sensation of refined sensuality than for a woman of salacious temperament to be the instrument of a strong man's pleasure. I love to encourage the gradual approach of such a one. To receive his ardent kisses—his lewd caresses all

expressive of his delight, his passion, and his desire
—to succumb to his strong will, to feel his naked
form pressed roughly, brutally, upon my tender
bosom, my satin skin—his big trembling hands
clasped around my swelling buttocks, as he draws
me nearer, closer, in the lascivious movements of
his passionate enjoyment—to know that I am the
instrument of his supreme delight—that it is I who
am about to receive the essence of his manhood, the
outpourings of his nature, in the satiety of that ecstasy of which I am the cause—all this is joy to Eveline, and in that act of self-abandonment consists
her own moist poignant pleasure.

The next few minutes were devoted to an almost
silent delicious anticipation of pleasure. We looked
in each others' eyes—our lips joined. Then he gently put me off his knee. I guessed his intention. He
opened the front of my dress. I took the hint. He
threw off his coat and waistcoat. He kicked his trousers away from him. He stood in his shirt. I slipped
off my dress and my skirts. I had no drawers. We
both trembled with desire unquenched, as yet to be
assuaged. Then with an animal cry of triumph he
seized on me.

Oh, good Heavens! What do I touch? What is
this object on which my little hand closes convulsively? Oh, what a delicious limb the man possesses! As large as John's—as stiff—almost as long.
Hard and standing fiercely with expectant, impatient lust. I had nothing on me but my fine *chemise*.
He raised it and devoured my white body with his
eyes. I lifted his shirt. I looked on all his hirsute
nakedness.

"Ah! Oh! My beautiful—my delicious little

lady! How I will have you! You are mine! Mine to
enjoy—come!"

He lifted me roughly upon the great springy bed.
He threw himself upon me. I opened my thighs only
too willingly. He thrust. He experienced a difficulty.
He tried again. Then he sprang from the bed. He
took a small white parcel from his coat pocket.
Cold cream—the best in the whole world—from
Bond street. He anointed my little parts. He again
essayed. The big, stiff limb penetrated my vagina. It
bore up me—up—up! He thrust into me to the
balls. The slippery unguent had done its work. It
was delicious to feel how easily—how lusciously the
intruding instrument of pleasure moved and glided
up and down my belly. We neither of us spoke. We
groaned—we sobbed—we panted in the perpetra-
tion of love's seraphic act. The heavy bedstead
fairly trembled under our salacious movements. His
thrusts were terrible in his strength. I heaved up
my loins to receive them. It was too ecstatic to last.
We each tried to prolong the act. The end came all
too soon. He discharged copiously. He flooded me
in his excitement. I joined in the delicious climax. I
squealed like a rabbit as I felt the hot ejection. He
lay still on my bosom at last.

It was over! Shall I admit that I experienced a
revulsion of feeling? Hardly that. It was a touch
of remorse. A feeling that I was committing an in-
justice to someone. I felt uneasy. I knew not why.
This man was no common person to serve my purpose—to gratify my passion and then disappear. I
thought I had lost my prudence. I had committed, I
thought, a great indiscretion. I was no longer *incognito*. This man knew me—knew my family—

knew, moreover, Sir Langham Beamer—was in
daily communication with him. A sickly fear stole
over me. I was only a woman after all. I burst into
tears. My companion saw my distress. He partly divined the cause. It was not possible he could read all
—know all. He set himself to comfort me—to reassure me. I should never regret what I had permitted him. He would always be my friend. My secret
was safe—nay, inviolate—with him. I must dry my
tears, or he must share my trouble. He would not
see me suffer.

Gradually I recovered my composure. "Dragon"
wasted no time in long protestations—in passionate
assurances and vows of secrecy. Gradually he
brought me to see through my own unaided judgment that I ought to have no cause for apprehension. It is curious how quickly the brain resolves
when outer influences are withdrawn. A few moments' calm reflection with a kerchief over my face
and Eveline was herself again.

Gradually too—but without reluctance on my
part—the strong man drew me to him. He covered
my soft white belly with his own, insensibly, yet
with infinite tenderness he gradually inserted his
rampant weapon into my body. I realised the potent argument. I reconciled myself to the position
in which I had placed myself. I gathered force and
power of sensuous enjoyment as he proceeded in his
own wild gratification; until my body vibrated, my
arms enfolded him, and my senses reeled in the full
ecstasy of his manly embrace.

By gradations also we returned to the land of realities. My previous humour perhaps still haunted
me. I turned to my new friend.

"You must think me a strange wild instance of perversity."

"Dragon" sat by me as I rested languidly upon the bed. He threw an eider-down quilt over me before he replied. His tenderness touched me. His manly character was never better in evidence than when he let me see that his gallantry for the companion of his pleasure shone out even if his heart remained untouched.

"If you knew as much of society at large as I do, little Beauty, you would not be so much astonished. You do not know how society is made up—all its hollowness—all its rottenness. You only obey a natural impulse. Unknown to yourself you have flung from you the unnatural restraints which society pretends—mind! I say only *pretends*—to cast around you. Without being aware of it, you have returned to that condition of primitive life which is best represented by the topsy-turvy account of Adam and Eve—to that primitive condition of existence when the sons and daughters of mythical Adam and Eve —brothers and sisters—enjoyed each other—coupled and procreated."

"My dragon—do you know you interest me very much? Where did you pick up your philosophy?"

"I have not passed all these years in the detective service for nothing. Shall I tell you, little lady —little Beauty—that I kiss and worship, that but for the accident of the indisposition of a comrade you would never have met me the other day? But so it is. I was only at Bow Street to fill the place of the inspector who was ill. I am employed generally in the secret service of the force, as what is known to the public as a detective in plain clothes. It is my duty to penetrate, if I can, by the aid of my brains, the criminal combinations, the society mysteries, scandals and infamies—aye, and the political intrigues of those against whom I am let loose. I am the sleuth-hound of the London Police, but I should be very incapable for the execution of my duty were I not exceptionally fitted to fulfil its various requirements, and to sustain its constant strain on nerves and brain."

"You make me quite afraid of you, my dragon!"

"On the contrary, little Beauty, you must see that I only want to be your friend. You have nothing to fear from me. Like yourself, I love to indulge my animal instincts. When I am free, I would be a sensualist always if I could. Shall I confess? You have given me a chance I could not have hoped for—a treat of the senses which I could never have imagined in my wildest dreams of sensuous enjoyment."

"Did I give you so much pleasure—my fiery dragon? You little know how your words excite me. I could have no pleasure in the act if you did not demonstrate your own enjoyment also. Every sigh —every little muscular vibration which serves to betray your gratification thrills me with a kindred emotion. Tell me more about yourself."

"What shall I say? Well, you see in me a man of energy with a very shady sort of calling. Is it not so? Yet I would tell you that I have received an excellent education. My father even intended me for the church. Nothing would satisfy my restless spirit. I laugh to scorn the quiet hypocrisy of the conventional clergy. I found one out in his iniquity. I convicted another of gross vice. I hurled the idea of the so-called sacred calling to the devil. I de-

voted my restless energy to the discovery of such
social problems as interested me. I became what I
am from choice—not altogether from necessity—a
detective."

"You must have had a large amount of experience. You must have gained a thorough knowledge
of London life."

"I kept my eyes open. I had access to all sorts and
conditions of society. I studied their ways—I learnt
their habits—I was up early and late to take note
of their iniquities. The result was—at any rate to
me who expected to find purity and refinement—dis-
appointing. I gradually came to the irresistible conviction that society in London was rotten to the core
—that at no period of English history, not even in
the days of the Second Charles, or in those of the
Georgian Regency, was the outward contempt of
everything noble and virtuous and the meanness of
individual indulgence at the expense of others who
should have been trusted and respected, so distinctly marked and openly encouraged. I found the
married lady glorying in her adulterous lust. The
single woman—no less abandoned—advocating
free intercourse as a mere measure of health. I
found a nobleman, old enough to be your grandfather, charged with infamous offences—members
of the clergy in the same predicament, and a whole
troupe of noble lords and ladies who were content
to drag their dirty linen through the divorce court."

"Your experience has certainly been somewhat
varied, dear Dragon!"

"You are right, little lady, very much so! What
wonder that the middle and lower classes go wrong,
when even the highest authorities flaunt their con-

tempt for decency—I will not say: morality—before their eyes. Women, faded and abject in their worn-out attractions strut in public, content to exhibit themselves as the quondam favourites of those in high places—unconscious that their popularity and their vices go hand in hand and are equally stale."

"Your view of modern English society is not encouraging."

"No, certainly it should not be so—but it is true. When you see women well-known and holding recognised positions in life, degrading themselves to the so-called investigations of the kraals at Earl's Court, taking the brutes away in their carriages, prating to their no less demoralised associates of their exquisitely beautiful soft velvet skins, their huge limbs and their dog-like proclivities for bestial indulgence—what is there left to be said of the refinement, the austerity, or even the modesty of modern London society?"

"Is that really true? Is it within your knowledge?"

"All that, and very much more—but I have done. It reminds me of Satan reproving sin. I am a sensualist at heart. I should scorn to creep behind a husband's back and debauch his wife, or take a young girl from the lawful custody of her parents to satisfy my selfish passion. When pleasure is offered I accept it—but it must be so far as my own perceptions go, willingly accorded. It must be, so far as I can see, without detriment to my companion in voluptuousness, or to anyone else."

We rearranged our disordered toilets. We parted. "Dragon" gave me an address at which I could always hear of him. He insisted that I should not write it down. I committed it to memory.

"Tickets, please. Two first class to H——. Thank you, sir. Yes, I can lock the door if you like. Best train this, sir; no stoppage before arriving at C——. The next is H——."

Papa took me on his knee. We were off at last. We chose a Tuesday. We avoided all the week-end people—we were alone.

"How fast the train goes! I feel so happy now. I am sure this trip will do you good, papa. We both seemed to want air."

"It will also benefit you, dear child. London seasons are dearly bought as to their enjoyment, when you consider the wear and tear. What pretty little boots, my darling Eveline! How well they fit! What graceful outline of instep and heel! What delicate kid, and then how soft and flexible! You are so simply, yet so beautifully dressed, you would rouse an anchorite."

"If I can only succeed in pleasing my darling papa, I shall have arrived at the zenith of my desires. Oh, but you are roused already—wicked, naughty papa."

My hand was on his limb. I unbuttoned his trousers.

"Does my dear papa like his little Eveline to comfort this unruly thing? Does he like my soft touches? Do they give him pleasure? How stiff this is!"

He lolled back in his well-cushioned seat as the

train sped along. I seized on his stiff limb and released it from its confinement. Papa closed his eyes
and enjoyed my toying. The sturdy weapon stood
boldly up in the bright sunlight as it streamed in at
the carriage window. I rubbed it up and down. I
closed my softly gloved hand upon it. The head
grew purple with excitement. I stopped my movements.

"Where are we going tonight, papa dear? What
have you arranged?"

"We have tickets for H——. We sleep there. I
know an old-fashioned hotel in the town with an interior garden, and plenty of fresh air. Just the place
in which to repose for a couple of days."

"How delightful! This sweet thing must not be
too impatient. Little Eveline will give it all the
pleasure in her power tonight, but my dear papa
must not overexert himself."

Two bedrooms adjoining—a delicious sitting
room looking into a well-kept garden, in which the
budding flowers already blossomed brightly. A bal-
cony—a pleasant old world, half-forgotten look
about the whole place. The rooms well stuffed with
rich old furniture—everything polished, bright, and
clean.

"My darling! My beautiful Eveline! *Tonight*!"

We dined well. I had the woman's weakness for
sparkling wine. He liked it also. The *cuisine* was
good. We were well served. We strolled in the garden. And by the sea. We came back to our rooms
refreshed. We enjoyed our tea. We sat at the open
window and inhaled the pure fresh air of the country perfumed with the sweetness of the flowers below.

Chapter III

I was already in bed. He came quickly from his room. I extended my arms. I opened the bed-clothes. I showed him my form which only my fine lace-trimmed *chemise* served to cover. He flew into my embrace. Our bodies were in closest contact. I warmed him in my naked arms. He was radiant with lust to enjoy me.

"My Eveline! My darling! My child!"

He toyed with my breasts. He sucked the rosy little nipples. I tickled the big balls and caressed the limb already stiff and swollen with desire.

"Is my dear papa happy now? Does his little Eveline give him pleasure?"

His breath was agitated——his sighs, his kisses, hot and voluptuous, all denoted his condition. He rose on me. His manly body pressed my light young form. I threw my soft arms around his neck. Our tongues met. Mine slipped between his lips. I opened my thighs to him. The stiff limb pressed open my little parts. He bore in——into my belly.

"Oh, my love, my dearest papa! You make me suffer!"

"My beautiful darling! I must—I will!"

His large limb bore upwards. It slipped entirely into me. He was having me to his heart's content. During the act our tongues met again. He writhed on my body. He raised his head. He paused.

"My Eveline! Dearest girl! I am afraid to finish!"

"Have no fear, my dear papa. You are killing your little Eveline with pleasure. Let it come! Give it me all!"

He thrust his limb in to the balls. I felt it at my womb. He discharged violently. I felt the thrill— the spasms, with which his seed flew into me. My own sensations were celestial. He was giving me the essence of my being. I felt bathed in it. At length we slept. It was still early morning when we woke.

"Let us play a little before we get up. Be my stallion, dear papa, and I will be your little mare."

I rose on my hands and knees in the bed. He raised my *chemise*. He passed his palm over my plump posteriors. He toyed a moment with my buttocks. He slapped them. He caressed them.

Then he pressed down on me. I felt the stiff insertion of his parts. The knob passed in. He bore furiously up me. His balls beat against my thighs. I could hardly bear his weight. His thrusts drove me forward. My head was buried in the pillows. At last it came. He seized me round the loins. I felt the hot sperm spurting into me with each vibration of his body. He clasped me tight until he had done. We lay some time motionless in the dull torpor which succeeds gratified desire.

By degrees our spirits revived. We talked in a low voice of the subject of our secret connection.

There were many things on which I wanted information. I asked many questions relating to the conjunction and the functions of the two sexes, which interested me mightily.

"You ask me what is the spasm which you experience and whether women have seed like men—I will tell you. The first is the crisis of a nervous irritation which is set up partly from outside caress and actual friction, and partly from the imagination acting on the orgasm. Both unite to set in motion the nerves which serve the glands containing the fluid. Women have no seed, properly speaking, and that secretion which they produce has no direct effect in the process of generation. These glands closely resemble those of the throat which are called salivary glands. If you observe a ripe peach, a fine pear, or experience a strong desire for any food towards which your attention is directed these glands act instantly and sympathetically. You say your mouth 'waters' for the thing. The cause and the effect are exactly similar in those glands which secrete the fluid you possess."

"But what purpose does it answer then, if it does nothing towards procreation?"

"There you go too fast, my child. I do not say it does nothing. On the contrary it may—and probably does—do more than is supposed. What I mean is that it has no absolute necessity in the act of generation, because it is well known that conception is obtained without it. It operates, however, indirectly in preparing the way for the conjunction of the sexes. It takes exactly the part of the salivary glands which enable you to swallow, only that its influence is employed in another direction. These glands can act upon occasion abnormally and without actual contact as we know in the instance of nocturnal emission while dreaming. I have also shown you how the imagination can excite them to secretion on the part of the female. This is an obvious advantage to the performance of the act of generation. In this sense the glands of the female second materially the success of the operation."

"I own I was very ignorant of all this, dear papa, but you explain it so nicely. When a man spends then, a woman must spend also?"

"By no means. Only too frequently the female may experience no pleasure or gratification at all. Yet conception may take place. It often does so. Professionally loose women lose the ability to enjoy from overindulgence and the prostitution of the act of generation to their everyday routine. The fluid, in such cases, ceases to secrete. Artificial means are employed to replace it. Habit brings satiety—satiety destroys pleasure. The two are inconsistent. There is no longer any yearning for the peach. The saliva ceases to flow. The functions misused are injured and the original purpose of nature rendered abortive."

"That is very interesting to your little Eveline, dear papa. I shall take care that all my functions are in good order whenever we are together. There is one thing more I want to understand. Can you tell me how it is that a woman misses conception in the act?"

"That is too wide a subject for me to explain offhand. It is essentially a physiological one. Many causes may be at work. There is the cause I have already named. The fault may be on the part of the male, or by reason of the condition or the health of the female. The most frequent cause, however, is that already described, or that the female is barren."

"Are many women barren?"

"More probably than are suspected. The present fashionable tendency to turn girls into tomboys; the exercises, athletic and vigorous, which they now patronise is undoubtedly producing that effect, and unfitting the Englishwoman for the softer and more natural duties of life. She is annually becoming taller, slimmer, more angular, more devoid of the marked contrasts of sex. The bust has already gone, and the dressmaker is called in with padding. False breasts occupy prominent places in London shop windows. Devices of all kinds are adopted to hide the deformity. It exists and it is on the increase. The result must be a sensible diminution of the population. Young married people now have become very alert to the conveniences of limiting the number of their offspring. You hear everywhere the society remark, 'a pigeon's pair—so interesting, you know; just two and no more.' Glances are exchanged—smiles exchanged. The dear creatures are perfectly *au courant* as to both cause and effect. There are, of course, other causes why women miss conception. Apart from artificial means purposely employed, there remains the ever increasing condition of barrenness."

"You think that many women are barren then, papa dear?"

"No doubt many are so. Only look at the number of infructuous marriages. If you ask the cause, I have given you one. The effects of unsuitable climate for Europeans may be another, but considering the matter in a society point of view, from one cause or another, no doubt we can entertain that the habits of life nowadays contribute to this condition. The deformity of the body by tight lacing is another cause. A very slight misplacement of the mouth of the womb is sufficient to prevent impregnation. This may be natural or produced as I describe."

"I am not tightlaced, dear papa. You can pass your hand down inside my stays."

"I know, my darling. Your figure is most exceptional for an English girl. You are formed for a Venus, but for all that you may be incapable of procreating by some such impediment as that of which I speak. However, it is most unlikely. Our precautions are sufficient in any case."

"Take me in your arms again, dear papa. Your little Eveline loves you. This dear thing is already stiff again. Let me kiss it. Oh, darling, what pleasure you are giving your little girl. You are sucking my button. It is the centre of my sensations. Your tongue is giving me divine enjoyment. Go on! Oh, pray go on, papa! Shall I turn round?"

"No, my sweet, remain as you are. Take your pet between your red lips also. Suck! Suck it thus. Oh, that is lovely! It is in your mouth."

We continued mutually until nature relieved us. He discharged a shower of seed. I received all. I returned him a dose which he called the nectar of the gods.

Sir Edward L—— was one of the kindest of men, nevertheless he made himself obeyed on occasions. He was not by any means a safe man to trifle with. To me he was all indulgence. I had obtained the secret desire of my heart. I had done all I could to nurture, to develop his passion for myself. Beneath his seemingly calm and rather austere nature, there lay a very furnace of sensuality—of intense and passionate feeling—a real voracity for the indulgence of the most libidinous pleasures. No one who knew him only as the polished gentleman or the urbane military chief, could have supposed his real nature. I knew it intuitively. He was a member of the family. He could not be otherwise than he was. We were all alike. I worked on the fact—that was all. The reading of Charlemagne's incestuous example had fired my lust. It had communicated itself to papa also. It was only natural.

The Duchess of M—— occupied the ancestral mansion in London. It was a fine old house standing in its own grounds—one of those relics of old times which are screened by high walls and solid barriers against the notice of the modern plebeian. It was a truly palatial residence. The late Duke, imbued with the *laisser aller* spirit of the times, had changed the spacious chapel into a magnificent ballroom. It had been originally constructed at the rear of the garden and communicated directly with the main hall by a short marble vestibule. Unusually lofty, it consisted of a nave and side aisles. A fine gallery was allotted to the orchestra. Under it the Duchess stood on a dais to receive her numerous guests on the night of her famous *bal costumé*.

The order had been rigorously imposed. Every

guest was to be either in uniform, official or military, or to assume the dress and character of some special personality.

The Duchess of M—— was a personage not to be lightly ignored. A peer of the realm had essayed to call on her with his trousers turned up at the heels —a stupid habit among men considered to be "the correct thing, you know, dear boy." The stately *majordomo* had stopped his lordship in the hall, with the remark, accompanied by a significant gesture: "I must trouble your lordship to let your trousers down. Her Grace has given express orders on the subject."

"Papa, dear, shall we go straight in with the throng and follow up in turn to the Duchess?"

"Yes, certainly, dear child, it will be best, and we will take our turn."

It was a magnificent sight. The band had only played as yet some introductory *morceaux*. The presentations were going on.

Sir Edward looked splendid in full uniform (we had had to abandon Charlemagne), the broad red ribbon of the Bath supporting the beautiful star— his breast covered with the medals he had received in the wars.

I wore the costume on which I had already decided. It consisted of the dress actually preserved from the wardrobe of my great-grandmother of pious memory (of whose memoirs you may have heard), such as she had worn at, or about, my own age, with a large "coal-scuttle" hat and feathers, from beneath which peeped the saucy face and flowed the luxuriant locks of little Eveline—her namesake and her antitype. To give piquancy to the character, I carried a charming little basket filled with capital imitations of four-leaved shamrocks. Her Grace welcomed papa with marked cordiality and received his gallant salute on her gloved hand with evident delight. She smiled, I thought, with interest at myself.

The dancing commenced. The Duchess led the first quadrille with Royalty. The scene broke into a moving mass of charming colour and life. The music was delicious.

Papa wandered off among his acquaintances. I sat with Lady Lessleton in one of the spaces between the marble columns which separated the nave of the noble hall from the aisles and bore the roof. Each of these spaces were filled with a very forest of flowering shrubs. Seats had been placed with their backs against these plants.

The tall tropical palms and flowering exotics formed a series of delicate arbours under which the lounges had been arranged to afford rest to the dancers, and also a comfortable nook for the lookers-on. The aisles had been kept free for those who desired to promenade therein. Half hidden among the leaves I reclined lazily watching the fast-gliding couples in a dreamy *valse,* having declined the dance myself. Soon my ear caught the sound of voices on the other side of the foliage. Men were standing there to peer over the leafy screen where, here and there, a chance interstice favoured their view. I could not help catching their words.

"Who is that girl in the old-fashioned dress with the big bonnet?"

"Don't you know? She's the only daughter of Sir Edward L——. This is her first season—she's very young—any amount of dibs. She's a pretty girl enough too."

"Pretty is not the word. She is divinely beautiful. I never saw such a perfect face, such eyes, such hair out of a picture."

"Well, there's no accounting for taste, Endy, my boy! Don't go and get spoony if you don't intend to go through with it. They tell me she's got a temper. A bit prudish, too, they say."

"All the better! I hate your namby pamby girls who possess no more spirit than a tame cat."

"Miss L——, the Duchess has sent me to bring you to her. She has taken a great fancy to your costume. She wants to talk to you."

It was her Grace's private secretary, a young man I had previously met. I rather liked him. He was unaffected and did not try to flirt. I took his offered arm to where the Duchess sat. She pointed with her great fan to a chair by her side and smiled very graciously as I seated myself.

"Well! *You are superb!* They told me you were beautiful, but there!—what am I saying?—the girls were vain enough in my day, but now—they are simply unbearable! I ought not to spoil you, my dear."

"I am not likely to be spoilt, your Grace. I hope I am not too vain either. I discount largely all I hear. I am so pleased you like my dress. May I offer your Grace one of my four-leaved shamrocks? They bring good luck."

I rose. I selected a flower from my little basket and presented it to the dear old lady. She was delighted. I saw the keen look of approval with which she watched all my movements.

Her Grace spread her great fan with a sharp snap. She began to talk to me in an undertone behind it. She had been a very handsome woman in her time. Her rather masculine features and high nose still retained much beauty and refinement only marred by a very perceptible moustache, the dark ends of which gave a somewhat saturnine expression to her face.

"I have hardly had a word with your father yet, my dear. It has not been possible. However, you must bring him here later on and between the dances, so we can converse. The music deafens me. Sir Edward is looking magnificent tonight. How young he is for his age! How well he has got on in the service! He deserves all his honours and will receive more."

Down went the big fan with a miniature crash!

"Can you keep a secret? I suppose not. Girls are so altered nowadays! But, however, I will trust you."

"You may indeed, ma'am. I have only to know that it is your wish, to make anything you tell me sacred."

"You are a dear, good girl, and I'm sure you are no gossip. What I am going to tell you relates to your father—Sir Edward, my dear. I hear from a very direct source that his name is in the next list of honours for the coming Birthday. He is to be offered a peerage. Do you think he would like it?"

"I really hardly know, your Grace—it comes as a great surprise."

"Well, you may hint it to him from me. Tell him I should be personally very pleased if it was offered and accepted. I have even suggested to the Duke

the title he might assume. What do you think of
Lord L—— of Muddipour?"

The announcement almost took my breath away.
Inwardly I knew Sir Edward well enough to be sure
he would welcome his new distinction. I assured the
Duchess I would do my best to favour her kind desire, and that since it was her wish that he should
accept the title, I would answer for him that it
would be so.

When I came to think of all the surrounding circumstances: of our wealth—amply sufficient to
grace such an advanced position—of our noble and
ancient family coming down in an almost unbroken
line from the Norman Conquest; of Sir Edward's
services, and of the oft-recurring difficulty of re-
warding him by promotion over the heads of older
officers, I came to the conclusion that he ought not
to hesitate on such a matter—nor, in fact, did he.

Muddipour is one of papa's best battles. It seems
it is somewhere up on the frontier of British India.
There is a big plain and a river with crocodiles in it.
It is a very rainy place at certain seasons. When the
battle was fought the whole plain on each side of
the river was a mud swamp with rice fields in it. It
was a Rajah who had revolted and collected a great
following to attack the British. However, we scram-
bled together some native regiments and a few
British troops. The Rajah attempted to cross the
plain with all his forces to the attack. His army
was nearly all cavalry and they wore great heavy
boots. They got as far as the middle of the swamp,
having forded the river. There they stuck. Neither
horses nor men could advance, or get back. There
was a great deal of firing of guns and cannons and

things. Then papa sent in his little Goorkhas—hundreds and thousands of them. They had naked legs and rather liked the mud. They caught all the enemy's cavalry and killed them, and their horses too, with their horrid knives. There was of course also a heavy loss on our side. A regiment which had been sent round to outflank the enemy lost its way in a defile. The natives did not understand a white flag and would not let the men surrender. They killed nearly all the detachment. It was a complete victory, however, for the Rajah was killed and the remains of his army dispersed. There was therefore an end of that war. Papa won immense praise from the government. The Radical papers said it was a butchery. The Irish members rose *en masse* and attacked the Ministry and poor papa. It all came to nothing, however. Papa got promotion and a medal. That was just before he came home.

"My dear, I want you to know Lord Endover. He is very anxious to make your acquaintance. Here he is. Allow me to introduce Lord Endover. Lord Endover, this is my young friend, Miss L——."

He was a rather old-looking young man, I thought. A line of wear and tear, the result, report said, of hard living, had already marred a fairly handsome face. He had been spoiled in society, but still remained a bachelor. He was popular among the men. His familiars called him "Endy." He was a noted sportsman and a keen follower to hounds. We danced a waltz together, then supper was announced by sound of a trumpet. Lord Endover took me down to a magnificent repast served in the cloisters below the great hall.

The Endovers are not a particularly old family.
A generation back they called themselves Endover-
Tipp. The grandfather of the present Earl managed to dissipate most of the family property and
died up to his neck in debt, every available acre
mortgaged to the hilt. His son married Miss Doro-
thea Tipp, the daughter of an enormously wealthy
Chicago provision man. Gaddernenus B. Tipp was,
as the French would put it: *"un pigs."* That is, he
possessed a factory in that city. It was an immense
affair, full of machinery. I have been told they
drove the swine in at one end, and the hams and
sausages and things came tumbling out at the other.
However that may have been, the Earl married the
rich American girl. She brought a large fortune to
him, paid off all his father's debts and besides purchased a beautiful seat in Cumberland which she
called "Chitterlings." The only thing old Tipp insisted on was that his noble son-in-law should add
the name of Tipp to his own. The present Earl,
however, had got over that difficulty. By the aid
of a couple of hundred pounds and the Herald's
College he had struck the Tipp off again and re-
verted to the original family name. Both his parents
were dead now and the Earl was very well off. Although he was reported to have spent a somewhat
dissolute youth, he had always the sense to keep
within his means. The estates had vastly improved
under his management. His ancestral seat, Normanstoke Towers, was undoubtedly the finest property in the county after the Duke's castle. Lord
Endover had the singularly good taste to prevent
his very evident admiration of myself from becoming too fulsome. He conversed sensibly on such

everyday subjects as interested him and appeared especially pleased when he found I was a good horsewoman and knew something about horses and stables.

It was already two o'clock. I had danced nearly every number on the programme. I found myself once more reclining under the shadow of the sub-tropical plants between the marble columns. The music at the moment was low and sweet. I was absorbed in following the cadence. A low voice sounded close to my ear from behind:

"Your future lies at your feet tonight. Will you stoop and pick it up?"

I started. I turned suddenly. The foliage securely concealed the speaker. I fancied the voice was familiar. I could not identify it.

"May I have the pleasure of this waltz with you, Miss L——?"

The request came from Lord Endover. I rose. I took his arm and we danced.

As I passed on Sir Edward's arm through the entrance hall, on our way out the same low, soft voice whispered in my ear: "Remember!" I turned my head sharply. A thickset, good-looking man with heavy whiskers and in plain clothes stood among the other servants. In a flash I recognised the voice. It was that of the ever watchful Dragon.

It was nearly four o'clock before I sat with my papa in the carriage on the way home. I was excited with the dancing, the gaiety, and the champagne. Sir Edward passed his arm round my satin waist. He pressed his lips to mine. He whispered burning words of love and passionate desire. He drew my softly-gloved hand within his own, his excitement equalling mine.

"Dear papa, we must not part tonight like this. We are both too much excited. You must enjoy your little girl as you wish; Eveline will not be content until she has had it. We shall be quite alone. I will see that Fanny goes off to bed and then—"

"And then I will be in the little boudoir where no one can hear our kisses."

"There no one can hear our sighs, our movements, or our transports of pleasure. Will it not be delicious, dear papa? Shall your Eveline come to you in her *peignoir*?"

"By no means, my darling, I want to have you as you are, in your ball dress. The white satin excites me horribly. Your pretty hands drive me wild. Feel here!"

He put my hand on his thigh. His limb was already at its full tension. I squeezed it and kept my hand there until the carriage stopped at our door.

"Fanny, you can undo my dress, lay my *peignoir* ready and then go to bed." It was very late—or rather very early. "Good night!"

"Good night, miss. Shall I call you in the morning?"

"No, Fanny. I want to sleep as long as I can. Now go to bed."

I watched her go upstairs. I heard her close and lock her door. The house was absolutely quiet. Everyone slept but us two. I descended to the boudoir. Papa was there in his scarlet dressing-gown. He seized on me. My dress being loosened, he pulled my pouting breasts over the top. He glued

his lips to them. I had retained my white kid gloves
to please him. I held his stiff member in my grasp.
I shook it gently up and down.

"Your little Eveline would like to suck it, papa."

I suited the action to the words. I sucked it for a
few minutes. I did not wish to finish him off just yet.
He threw me back upon the sofa. He turned up my
beautiful satin ball dress. He exposed my legs. He
devoured my fine pink silk stockings with a frenzy
impossible to describe. He began to whisper indecencies. I replied with suggestions even more lewd.
A demoniacal lust possessed us both. Our faces
glared with the hot passion we felt consuming us.

I stood again before him, in my stays, my long
silk stockings, my gloves, which I retained to please
him: long evening white kid gloves which fitted perfectly, of finest perfumed kid, extending up almost
to my elbow. I still retained my bracelets. My garters of rose velvet and old gold set off my glistening hose. To his view I must have appeared a perfect *houri*, with only my light *chemise* of finest
batiste to veil my satin skin, over which the delicate
flush of health and good nourishment cast a roseate
tint suggestive of joy and love's delight.

"Let us have our revenge now, dear papa. Let us
outrage this false society all we can. Let us invert
its hypocritical precepts. Let us be as indecent as we
can. Look at me, darling! I am your girl! I love
you! I love to give you pleasure. I enjoy only when
you enjoy."

I clasped his erected member in my delicately
gloved hand. I rubbed it again until it became purple with excitement. My jewelled bracelets tinkled
prettily as I played the harlot with him. He passed

his hand over my body—over my cool buttocks, rosy with health. My soft thighs, pink and plump, attracted his haggard eye—his wandering fingers. He felt me all over. I was in a rare bath of love's excitement, ready for any man or devil. I toyed with his nakedness. I commenced again to excite him further by my lewd whisperings, my murmured indecencies.

"Oh, my girl, my darling! I can wait no longer. I must—I must discharge! I must satiate this terrible longing with you, my Eveline. Do not keep me waiting. My member is bursting to bury itself in my little girl. I never knew what lust really was till I realised it with you, my child! Quick, slip off your things, your stays! Let me begin! I can wait no longer. We will wallow in lust—in pleasure. Yes, yes—I know—you little devil—you beauty—in *incest*—delicious, unbridled incest!"

"Take me—enjoy me! Do what you will with me! Be quick! I want you! I want to feel you in me!"

I unhooked the rest of my bodice. I threw it off. I stepped out of the skirts. I retained only my short *chemise*. He rushed upon me snorting with lust. We fell together, not on the sofa, but on the thick hearthrug. His stiff limb entered my body to the hilt. We lay in a bath of pleasure. He panted and pushed. I called on him to spend. He discharged. The sperm spouted into me. He wanted to recommence. I dissuaded him. We embraced and bid each other a good night. In less than half an hour I was fast asleep in my own soft and luxurious bed. Papa went off to his room tired out, but he said next day he had slept "like a top."

Chapter IV

"Good morning, Mrs. Sanderson, the little room upstairs will be at liberty this afternoon, I hope?"

"Yes, I will keep it specially, and you can drop in at any hour you may arrange."

"That is very kind of you. I will not forget your attention. You will please also take care that no one is about, either to see us go in or out."

"Trust to me, please. You had better come in by the front door of the shop and order something at the counter. Your friend had best come down the little passage, and in by the side entrance. I will look out for him, if you come first."

"That plan will be excellent. I will be here as near three o'clock as possible."

"Leave all to me. You will be satisfied."

The good woman laughed. She saw the double sense of her words.

"At least—I *hope so*! Good bye till then. I will see that everything is all right."

"Who is upstairs, Mr. Ferguson? There is a carriage at the door. This is hardly the time for visitors—only a quarter to twelve yet."

"Lord Endover has come by appointment to see Sir Edward, Miss Eveline. He is with him now in the study."

The fat butler had assumed his most pompous manner. It did one good to see the obsequious bow with which he announced this fact. John had often tried in vain to imitate his style. The butler was sublime, while John was only ridiculous. The obvious understudy made me laugh sometimes. Presently the Earl came down. I shut myself in the dining room while Ferguson bowed him out. A pair of splendid greys was harnessed to a neat brougham. A very unassuming device occupied the centre of the door panel. The men were in plain livery. Everything was in good taste. Lord Endover rose in my estimation. I no longer ridiculed him for dropping the "Tipp," though I wondered what he could want with Sir Edward at that hour. Suddenly I remembered he was holding office in the Ministry, though not in the Cabinet, and no doubt the Government wanted some information of a military character—or stop!—was it about the peerage? I had told papa all the Duchess had communicated. He was evidently gratified with the prospect I unfolded to him.

"Sir Edward would like to see you in the study, miss."

"Very well, Mr. Ferguson, I'll go there immediately. Please order my horse with the large saddle, at half past two, and tell Johnson he is to ride the mare."

"Yes, miss. I will go round myself about it."

I found papa in a glorious mood. He strove, however, with his usual prudence to hide his exultation.

"It never rains but it pours, Eveline. Here is news from Percy by the second delivery. He is on his way home from Montreal."

"Oh, papa, I am so glad! I shall be so pleased to see him again."

"But that is not all. Lord Endover brought the formal offer of the peerage. Are you pleased again?"

"I am always pleased when my darling papa is happy. I am simply delighted."

"But even that is not all. I have not got to the end of my list of news yet. I do not know, my child, if you will be pleased or not at the tag."

His voice wavered. He seemed anxious and uncertain as to his next words.

"Can you guess what else Lord Endover came about, Eveline?"

"I think I can. I would rather you tell me what he said."

"The Earl makes a formal request to be allowed to pay his court to you—nothing more."

"His lordship does me a great honour. I am too young for him. He will soon change his mind. Men are fickle. I have no desire to figure in the society papers as the *fiancée* of Lord Endover."

I had really no reason to feel piqued. I suppose it was only the waywardness of my sex which possessed me. I was really pleased. The man had done the proper thing. He was, at any rate, a gentleman. His way of putting the proposal showed a real regard for my own feelings. I watched Sir Edward's expression. It was dubious. A shadow rested on it which I thought had a foundation in a feeling of jealousy.

"What does my dear papa think of it?"

I sat on his footstool. I laid my hand on his. I waited for the reply which would give me my cue.

"I think, my darling, that sooner or later, you will have to follow the ordinary destiny of rich young ladies who are desirable matches for our aristocracy. You will marry, my dear Eveline. Under these circumstances, it is better to think of it while you have youth and beauty. You cannot remain always with me. Any day some unlucky *contretemps* might bring trouble. I sometimes dread to think of the horrible risks we run. It makes me often quite nervous. You must have observed it, my darling."

Indeed I had. I saw with great regret that the mental strain, quite apart from the exhaustion of the system at his time of life when the fresh vigour of youth has passed, already wore him down.

I threw my arms around him. For a moment a whirlwind of remorse encompassed me. It passed on. It left me calm again.

"Do with me as you will, dear papa. Your little Eveline will never cease to love you. It is as you say. I know it—I feel it."

"I shall write to the Earl that we shall hope to see him at dinner on Thursday next."

"Johnson, look to that girth before I mount—
loosen the curb a little. That's better!"

"Goorkha's very fresh, Miss Eveline, you should
be careful. I had him yesterday in the park for an
hour—that's all."

"I'm not afraid of him, Johnson. Now, put me
up."

The horse knew me and trusted me. I never made
him nervous. He had never played tricks with me as
he did with the groom. He looked round with a
snort of delight when he saw me come out. I am
convinced that horse in his equine heart admired
me as much as the men did. If it be true, as I think
it certainly is, that the affection towards the human
race of the so-called lower animals is founded on
gratitude and natural affection, I am equally sure
that a large share of deceit and duplicity unknown
to "lower animals," may be ascribed to my own
sex. How many women dupe and then ridicule men!
These women have no heart, and are generally
kleptomaniacs like the woman Osborn, who was
convicted of robbing her cousin of her jewels, and
tried to throw the infamy upon the husband of her
victim.

We were near the Powder Magazine in Hyde
Park—possibly that accounted for my present ex-
plosive frame of mind. I reined my horse up.

"Johnson! I want to speak to you—but not here.
I shall ride to Oxford Street and dismount. Please
call me a four-wheel cab there, put up the horses
and follow me to this address. Do not let it blow
away. And be sharp—do you understand? Bring
the bit of paper back to me at the address on it."

Johnson was Jim. I wore only a short riding

habit. I alighted. I entered the cab. Jim touched his hat. The driver whipped up his horse. I had already given him the address of the afternoon tea shop.

"You are early, but all is ready, and as it is still cold, I have had a fire in the room upstairs."

"Thanks. You will know my friend. He is dressed like a groom with belt and buckskins. He will be here presently."

I waited about a quarter of an hour. I heard a knock at the door on the little landing at the head of the spiral staircase. I gave the usual permission. Jim appeared. He had a rather puzzled look on his young and handsome face. He was splendid in his livery—white breeches and top boots.

"Come in, Johnson, and close the door. I want to speak to you."

"Yes, miss. I have put the two horses up as you told me."

"Now, Johnson, I desire to ask you if you are not sorry for what you did to me in the stable the other day?"

I had put on my most serious air. I pursed up my mouth and frowned viciously. My manner was a stage copy of Sir Langham Beamer.

Jim fidgeted with his hat in his hand. He looked very uncomfortable.

"Are you aware of the enormity of the offence you committed? You took advantage of my youth and innocence. You forced me down upon the straw. You violated me. Do you know the penalty for such a dreadful thing?"

"I thought miss—I felt sure, miss—I—"

"Wait a moment. What do you suppose would

happen if I were to have informed Sir Edward of
the shocking thing you did to me? He would surely
prosecute you. I am under age, and you are probably aware that under the recent Act—ahem!—
under the new Statute, you would certainly be committed for trial for a dreadful rape upon a young
lady. Then you would be tried by a jury of your
countrymen and you would be sentenced to at least
twenty years penal servitude, if not for the term of
your natural life. All this because you cannot keep
that nasty great thing between your legs in order.
What have you to say to all this?"

"I'm sure, miss—I don't know. I'm very sorry. I
thought you liked it. I thought you wanted it—and
gave your consent!"

"Well, Johnson, I may have been led away just a
little when you pulled out that instrument of tor-
ture, but you must not think that that fact would
weigh for a moment with a jury of twelve of your
countrymen—especially if I were to break down in
giving my evidence and begin crying in the witness
box."

"I'm very sorry, miss. I hope you won't let it go
any further."

"I don't think it could well go further, Johnson
—but if I could trust to you to keep the secret, then
perhaps I might be able to forgive you."

"Indeed you may trust to me, miss—indeed you
may! I have a good place. I don't want to lose it. I
would do anything to please you, miss; but if you
split on me I should be ruined. No doubt all you
say is true. I should be utterly ruined. I hope you'll
look over it, miss."

"Look over it! Well, I cannot easily forget it, Johnson—Jim, I mean. When I think of that monstrous thing you showed me, how can I look over it? Will you solemnly promise to be prudent and secret?"

"Oh, miss, only try me! I swear, I would not say a word to hurt a hair of your beautiful head. I could not help it! I was so awfully randy—and you came in—and then—and then you began to excite me until I did not know where I was."

"I only know, Jim, that you violated me on the straw."

"Yes, miss, but then you tickled my tool and led me on, and I thought I was free to stroke you there and then if I could."

"Well, Jim, just out of curiosity, I may have liked to feel it and tickle your—your tool just a little, but that could hardly give you the right to push that great thing right up my—my inside as you did, you know."

"Oh, but I was mad to go on! I could not stop. You were such a treat to a plain, working man like me, miss, with your beautiful face and beautiful clothes, and your soft and elegant limbs."

"Even so, Jim, you might have stopped in time, instead of letting out that thick white stuff and nearly killing me with your violence. However, since you have promised me to be faithful and secret I should like to forgive you."

I was actually wriggling about on my seat all this time. My lust was almost beyond my control. A look of pleasure came into Jim's eyes as I made the last remark.

"Indeed you may trust me, miss—I should be very ungrateful if I ever forgot your pardon for what I did. I couldn't help it."

I smiled as I looked on the strong, good-looking young fellow before me. The certainty that he was absolutely at my disposal to enjoy—to strip—to finger—to satisfy my voluptuous inclination, was delicious. I could wait no longer.

"Would you like to violate me again, Jim? Would you like to stroke me again? Would it be nicey nicey? Am I doing right to trust you?"

I suppose my expression reassured the young fellow. He put his hat on the table and grinned with the restless, uneasy grin of a man whose will is under restraint and who is afraid to let his inclination run riot.

"Come here, Jim! Help me to take off my habit. Undo those hooks. So—that's a good fellow! Do you like to feel my breasts, Jim? You shall stroke me as much as you like. Let me look at your tool once more, Jim. Undo your breeches—pull it out! I should like to see it again."

His restraint vanished. His trembling hands aided me to get rid of my habit. I was almost undressed. At my lewd invitation he opened his flap and exposed the monstrous limb already stiffly erect at the idea of enjoying me. I put my hand upon it. We stood closely together.

"Oh, Jim! Oh, what a big one it is!"

We both breathed hard and fast as we pressed our bodies together. His huge limb was in my grasp. His hand was up my legs. His fingers arrived at the centre. I was fearfully excited. I goaded him on.

"Oh, Jim, you shall stroke me now! You shall

violate me again. Won't it be nicey nicey? Do you like feeling there, Jim? You shall push this tool of yours in there, dear Jim. We will have such pleasure. I will roger with you, Jim."

I put my hot lips up to his. I sucked humid kisses from his mouth. He was wild with passion. His limb was immense and very hard. I quite dreaded it. I like large-made men. I forced him to take off his coat and breeches. I stood in my *chemise*. I seized his member again in my grasp. The big nut delighted me. We were both impatient to commence the lewd act of enjoyment. I leant against the soft bed in the corner. I raised my *chemise* with both hands.

"Look there, Jim—do you like that?"

I showed him my body naked to the waist. Half mad with the intensity of his passion, he rushed upon me. I mounted upon the bed. He placed himself kneeling between my legs. His monstrous limb stood erect and menacing. I anointed the knob with cold cream and also applied a little to my slit. He came down on me. I put the thing in between the nether lips. He pushed. I threw up my legs. I arched up my loins. It entered my belly. It passed slowly up my vagina.

"Oh, my goodness! Jim—you're into me!"

"My God! How lovely it feels—oh! Oh! Ugh!"

"Push, push! I can take it all! Do it slowly, Jim! Is it nicey nicey?"

Jim grunted and thrust as if his life depended on it. I was gorged with the monstrous thing. I had it up to the balls. Oh, how he worked me! How he slipped his huge member up and down! How the bed shook as he thrust in his pleasure!

"Oh, Jim! Stroke me slowly—so—slowly! Oh! Oh! It's lovely—it's heavenly now! Oh, Jim! Dear Jim! Stroke—stroke me! Oh!"

"My God! Oh, Miss Eveline, it feels as if I was up to your waist! I never had such pleasure! Ugh! Ugh!"

"Finish me, Jim! You're too big—but it's lovely all the same! Oh, my! I can feel it throbbing!"

Neither could articulate now. I clutched the bed-clothes. I rolled my head from side to side. My limbs quivered under the furious shocks of my ravisher. He sank upon me. His thrusts became harder and shorter. He discharged. Thick jets of semen inundated my womb. He was a long time finishing. I received the whole flood of his sperm.

It is at such moments as this that the transformation of woman takes place. She is helpless—irresponsible—*hors de contrôle*. The breath comes and goes in quick, short gasps. Inarticulate sobs come from her parted lips. Her face flushes. Her limbs quiver. Spasmodically she fights the air. She clutches at anything within reach. Her whole being is convulsed. Her body heaves and sinks like the waves of the sea. She is a woman possessed—possessed by a strong male. Nature has bestowed upon her this extreme condition of ecstasy in merciful compensation for her troubles—her pains—her cares of maternity.

"Oh, Jim! Dear Jim, let me get up now you have done! Why do you not let me rise? Oh, Jim! Not again! Take it out, dear Jim! It's getting so stiff again! Oh, my! Oh, my! Jim! It's as hard as ever—oh! oh! It's—oh! You're spending again, Jim! Jim —Jim! You know you are!"

At last he let me slip from the narrow bed. He had stroked me twice without withdrawing. What happened during the next three quarters of an hour I do not know. He seemed like one possessed by a demon of carnal lust. He kept me in a constant whirl of copulation. He must have discharged five or six times in all. I was almost unconscious when he at length desisted. I returned to the park. I remounted. I could hardly sit my horse. I fancied Goorkha looked at me reproachfully. I reached home. I threw myself upon my sofa—my ride had much fatigued me.

The evening was Thursday. I dressed for dinner. I had my cue. Lord Endover had accepted our invitation. Lady L—— condescended to preside. It was an infinite relief to me. No doubt she had her reasons. I made myself agreeable. I knew very well how to conduct myself on such occasions. I played my part. Papa said I was perfection. Lady L—— drank only toast and water. She had also a part to play. She revenged herself afterwards. After the guests had departed, I met the treacherous Sippett carrying up a basket. That night Lady L—— had a warning. Papa and I were roused to go to her at three o'clock.

Chapter V

"I do not conceal from you, Sir Edward, that it is serious—very serious. These cases are always difficult and complicated. We must have change and strict attention. Take her to the seaside. Eastbourne is the place of all others for Lady L——. I can promise nothing—very serious—very! You have all my sympathy—but—there we are! All we can do is to ward off another attack. Eastbourne—as soon as possible—very serious—Eastbourne—yes! Decidedly—Eastbourne. Good day—good day, Sir Edward—Eastbourne."

"Poor papa! I do pity you so much! You who love London; but it appears necessary. We ought to follow Dr. Proctor's advice."

"Yes, my darling Eveline, your mother will have to go away at once. It is very necessary—very desirable on many accounts. And Percy will arrive in two or three days. You will go with your mother. I will send Ferguson down to engage rooms. I will follow."

"A German gentleman to see you, miss. I can't read the name, but he's evidently a nobleman by the coronet on the card."

"I see. It is Count Blünderstein. Show him into my study—and please open the piano, Mr. Ferguson."

Count Blünderstein was my music-master. He was a celebrity in London society and in great request at concerts and musical receptions. It was considered quite a favour if he consented to give a young lady a few lessons at as many guineas. He had made no difficulty in my case, however. He seemed to my mind rather to jump at the chance. Possibly he caught a roguish glance in my eye when I asked him.

The Count—as he loved to be called—was short and fat. It was marvellous to see his hands fly over the keys. No doubt he was a talented musician. I was much mistaken if he was not a very sensual personage also. He was good-looking, but his small expressive eyes—his large nose—his thick red lips, all told tales. I have found that most musicians are sensualists.

This was his second visit. John had admitted him on the first occasion. I took care John should be out of the way now.

At first the German had taken me for possessing a very ordinary schoolgirl knowledge of music. I gradually undeceived him. Before he left he had expressed his great pleasure—his satisfaction to find I was so well advanced. I am a good pianist. I let him see it. He was delighted.

"It is so goot for teach de yong ladies dat are proficious. *Der* odders dat are behind zey gif to me much pain. I will now blay to you a piece of my own dat you may see *der* fingerin'."

"That is very fine, Count. Is it your own composition?"

"Ja, mein liebe Fräulein, I did make him in Germany."

"Where I suppose they made you, Count?"

He laughed until his eyes ran over and the tears stood on his plump cheeks. Then he subsided into little chuckles of delight at the conceit.

"Did you observe *mein* fingerin', *Fräulein?"*

"Yes, I like your fingerin' very much. Do you think you could make me clever with my fingers also?"

He laughed again—this time more softly.

Why should he have laughed? It was a very simple question—perhaps he noted a certain wicked look of encouragement in my glance as I turned my head.

"I tink so indeed. Blay dis *morceau* to me for *der* see."

He put his warm hand on mine as I played. He mechanically worked my fingers upon the keys. I thought he applied more pressure than was necessary. He stopped the playing. He still held my hand. Why did he also squeeze it?

"You can finger beautiful—I am sure."

It was now my turn to laugh. I blushed also. He looked radiant with pleasure.

"I will now blay you someting of Chopin."

We changed places. He sat himself on the music stool. I sat close beside him "for *der* fingerin'." My right hand was on the edge of my chair close—very close—to the Count's stool. His fat figure quite covered the round seat. He commenced a delicious piece of Chopin's.

"I will now see if you can mark *der* discords."

He continued to play. Suddenly I put my hand on his leg with a gentle tap.

"That was *one*!"

I never knew so many imperfect chords in Chopin's music. I marked each in the same way. Then he stopped. My hand stopped also. It lay on his thigh. He picked it up in his. He conveyed it to his thick lips.

"Such a beautiful hand must neffer be spoil *mit* blaying on *der* piano."

"I must take up some other instrument then, I suppose, Count?"

He replaced my hand upon his thigh without replying. He recommenced playing. The tips of my fingers marked the time.

"Please to go on—you know well to mark *der* time."

"That is a delicious *morceau*. What instrument would you suggest for me to play on, Count?"

My hand made a bold movement round his left thigh. His execution became more and more faulty. My hand advanced again. He appeared to favour the movement by pressing towards me. I felt something like a German sausage which throbbed. It extended some way down his leg. The Count made several rapid cadences, which were overloaded with accidentals and flourishes. I pressed my hand down.

I rubbed it along the thing in his trousers. I was right. He possessed what I expected. I am seldom wrong.

"Vateffer instrument you choose, *mein liebe Fräulein,* to blay on, take care it will not blay on you!"

The Count chuckled at his own joke. He had no modest scruples. Once assured of my intention, he expanded. He withdrew his left hand from the keyboard. He took charge of mine, moving it about over his trousers. He continued a wonderful performance with the treble. I contrived to insert one finger between the buttons. I dragged at it. It gave way. I worked my finger further in. I could feel his warm shirt. He made no difficulties, but with the greatest *sang-froid* he unbuttoned the impediment to my investigation and pushed my willing hand inside. I pulled aside the shirt with equal effrontery and laid hold of the thing I sought. It was stiff and hot. I clasped it firmly while the German continued his performance.

"*Ach! Mein Gott!* Dat *ist der* instrument to blay *mit*!"

He put down his hand again without ceasing to produce rapid passages with the other. He let fly the rest of the buttons. He swung the stool rather more round towards me. He half rose. He released a stout limb which I grasped anew at his suggestion. He sat down again.

I took a good look at it. It was as white and delicate as a lady's arm. Such a size—broad and rather flat! The head, completely covered with the foreskin, was entirely hidden. It was beautifully soft and warm. I felt the loose skin moving over the muscular portion beneath.

"You blay on him like dis!"

He held my hand on his own. He pressed it back
upon the member and uncovered the red nut. Then
he drew my hand up again. My cheeks burnt—my
lips parted—I became dreadfully excited. Seizing
the Count's idea I worked my little fist up and
down.

"*Ach! Mein Gott!* I haf lost *mein* chord!"

He stopped playing. He regarded his limb as I
continued the lewd exercise. He held back his shirt
and trousers with one hand, that I might get a better hold on it. No sense of modesty or shame
seemed to daunt him. My audacity equalled his. I
turned it about in every direction to examine it.
I pulled out his testicles. They were large. He was
evidently proud of them. I pulled down the loose
skin again. I made the nut pop out all shining and
purple.

"What a sweet thing it is, Count! Does that give
you pleasure?"

"*Himmel!* But *ja, Fräulein*—it is *sehr gut! Mein*
balls are full up. You make me feel bad to finish
der business. I make much mess if I come. What you
do now? *Ach! Mein Gott!*"

I stopped the fingering at once. The Count recommenced to play the piano with his right hand.
His left joined occasionally for the effect of a terrible thunder from the bass. Meanwhile, his limb
showed no signs of abating its rigidity—or of re-
signing itself to disappointment. From time to time,
his left hand would quit the keyboard to thrust
back his envious nether garments—to pull up his
fine linen shirt and expose his capacious belly, as
white and hairless as that of a young girl.

I was furiously excited. I felt it impossible to make any suggestions. He was too much master of himself to be led as I led others. At length he pulled out his pocket handkerchief. He enveloped his stiff member therein. Poor fellow! It was evidently not the first time he had been thus indulged by a lady pupil. I determined to afford him a more poignant pleasure.

"You had better keep the piano sounding, Count. Do not try to kiss me now. I promise you a sweet kiss before you go. We must be cautious. The *portière* is drawn, you see. We have time to arrange all, if only you are prudent. Play some gentle chords. I will give you all the pleasure I can."

"But I burn! I burn! *Mein Gott!* I am wanting to let off—vat you call it, eh, *Fräulein?* I am full— *mein* balls—*ach!*"

The last exclamation was caused by my removal of the handkerchief. I applied my lips to the tip of his member in a moist kiss. I never embraced a more delicious limb. I opened my lips a little more. I tickled the red nut with my tongue.

"You gif me dis pleasure? You beautiful *Fräulein! Ach, mein Gott!* Vat you do now? You die me *mit der* pleasure!"

I parted my lips. I pressed down on the big limb of the excited German. He was trembling with delight. His left hand still ran wildly over the keys. I placed my left hand under his enormous testicles. With the other, I rubbed his member up and down. I sucked—I tickled. He drew in his breath and exuded it in heavy gasps of pleasure. His fat white belly moved responsively. He bared his parts to facilitate my design.

"*Mein Gott in Himmel!* I go off! I come on!
Ach! Ach! Ach!"

His hand dropped upon the keyboard with a horrible discord. His fat face fell forward over the
piano. I took the head and shoulders of his stiff
affair all into my mouth. It was immediately filled
with exuding semen. He discharged abundantly. He
nearly choked me. His seed was lovely. It seemed
an age before the hot jets ceased to flow.

We hastened to adjust ourselves. The dear
Count had his kisses on my dripping lips. He
seemed to relish enormously the taste of his own
thick sperm. He rolled his tongue into my mouth
till I was obliged to caution him to stop.

Count Blünderstein departed. I heard the hall
door closed. Then I rang the bell.

"Has John returned?"

"He has just come in, miss. Shall I send him up?"

"If you please. He can help me to put away all
this music. He can bring up a glass of water at the
same time."

I arranged the *portière*. I pulled down the blind.

"Come in, John! Quick! Against the *portière* and
the door. I feel so naughty, dear John. Music always upsets me."

I placed my back against the door. John whipped
out his weapon. Robin was beginning to stiffen already. I pulled up all my clothes. I showed him my
white thighs—my belly. He stood up close to me.
Our bellies touched. My parts were sopping with
unsatisfied lust. He pushed his big limb into me at
the first thrust. He commenced having me in delicious earnest. In a very short time he seized me
by the hips. He strained his body forward. He dis-

charged copiously. Our spasms were shared. He quickly withdrew. He wiped the carpet with his handkerchief. He returned the dripping Robin to his cage. He opened the door, tray in hand. I passed out first. John held the door open. As I turned to go to my bedroom on the same landing, I saw papa coming up the lower flight.

"I heard your music-master go, my child, and knew therefore that your lesson was over. What does Count what's-his-name think of your playing?"

"He approves of it very much, papa dear. He was, I think, quite satisfied with my performance. Our last piece was a delicious duet."

"I want you in my study, Eveline. Come with me —I have no time to lose. I must go out."

We entered papa's study. He shut the door. He bade me sit on his knee. All John's spendings were running down my legs.

"Do you really wish to marry the Earl of En-dover, Eveline?"

"Yes, papa, if you think it would conduce to our importance and it suits your views."

"Needless to ask you, my child, if you love him?"

"I love only you, my darling papa. I have no one else to love but you."

"But do you think he would make you happy?"

"My happiness might not altogether depend upon him. I should be free. I should try to do my best to make him happy and to do my duty to him, but—"

"All marriages are not love matches, dear child. This affair is serious. You have a grand position within your grasp."

"I could never love anyone but you, my darling papa. Never—never—never!"

"My own! My sweet girl! My beautiful little Eveline!"

He kissed me passionately on the lips. His and mine united. We exchanged the doves' embrace. Our lips were glued together. He attacked me with his hand. I resisted. My defence annoyed him.

"Not today, darling papa—there are reasons. Let me feel your sweet thing. Is that nice? You are stiff already. Let your little Eveline play with it. Let me kiss it—so. Do I tickle it nicely? Is that nice? And that? Oh, how stiff it is now! Shall I go on? Do I give you pleasure?"

"It is exquisite, dear child. Go on as you are now doing."

"See, dear, how red it is getting. It wants to come."

I applied my lips. I opened my mouth. I sucked the stiff weapon of love. Sir Edward could not withstand my insidious caresses. Suddenly he pressed forward. He discharged in my mouth. I received a torrent of his seed—imbibed it all.

"Do you think you will like Eastbourne, Eveline? We are off in a day or two. Mind you take some beautiful gloves and some very pretty new boots."

"Indeed I will! Eveline knows how to please her darling papa."

He described the pattern and colours of the boots he wished me to wear. He selected exquisite gloves for my use. He was evidently preoccupied with his fanciful and lecherous ideas as to my personal appearance. I sat on tenterhooks. I was all swimming in John's sperm. I longed to beat a retreat. At last he let me go to my room.

Lord Endover called two days after the little dinner. I was at home. His lordship did me the honour to make me a formal proposal for my hand. I asked for time. He was most correct and polite. It was plain to see he was hopelessly in love..He pressed me for an immediate acceptance of his offer. I pleaded my youth—my inexperience. He used every argument he could think of, but I was determined not to decide without knowing more of him. I satisfied him at last. I promised him I would informally consider myself engaged to him, but without any distinct promise to marry him. I told Sir Edward the result of the interview. He expressed his approval. I pass over all his lordship's lovemaking. I thought it very insipid. His visits threatened to become frequent. Fortunately we had arranged to go to Eastbourne. Lord Endover had engagements which prevented him leaving town. The House was sitting. He was compelled to attend. The next day we left for Eastbourne.

Chapter VI

"My brother Percy has arrived at Liverpool. He will be in London tomorrow. He comes down to Eastbourne the next day. Papa returns to town to meet him. Lady L—— is no worse for the journey. Mrs. Lockett and John are left in town. Johnson has been sent down with Goorkha and another. We have secured excellent stables. Our apartments at the hotel are sumptuous and most convenient."

The above is the substance of the letter I sent to Lady Lessleton.

Sir Edward and I breakfasted together. The morning was lovely in its spring freshness. The sea was as smooth as glass.

The announcement of Sir Edward's elevation to the Peerage was gazetted in the morning paper. I was the first to kiss my congratulations. After the meal, the manager of the hotel waited on him also with the usual obsequious good wishes. It was intended kindly nevertheless. The afternoon post brought the following paragraph in *Society Peeps*:

"We announce with peculiar pleasure that a marriage has been arranged and will shortly be solemnized between the Right Honourable the Earl of En-

dover and the Honourable Eveline L——, only
daughter of the newly created Baron L—— of Muddipour, still better known as Sir Edward L——,
Bart. We rejoice that the noble Earl, who has so long
withstood the blandishments of very many eligible
ladies, has at length secured as his prize the beautiful and accomplished *belle* of this—her first season. Everybody will remember how, by her ideal
beauty, no less than by her charming style, and her
modest and frank deportment, Miss L—— took the
town by surprise and our hearts by storm. Many
will recall with pleasure Miss L——'s exquisite
piano performances when she so kindly assisted at
the concerts lately given in aid of the funds of the
Lying-In Hospital; the Hospital for the Special
Treatment of Corns and Bunions; and the Asylum
for the Victims of Misplaced Confidence. The Earl's
seats are the splendid pile so well known as Normanstoke Towers, in Sussex; and "Chitterlings," a
beautiful property in Cumberland, which has hitherto formed part of the jointure of the Countesses
of Endover."

When I had recovered from the perusal of this, I
said to myself:

"The Dragon has had a finger in that pie. I wish
at this moment—he had another—but no matter!"

The main fact was correct, however. Lord Endover had wrung a consent from me before we left
town. He was overjoyed and very kind. I only felt
ill at ease and uncomfortable. Sir Edward tried his
best to console me.

"You will have your freedom—a first-class and
leading position in both counties. 'Chitterlings' will
be settled on you as part of your jointure. It is a
lovely spot. I remember it well. The views of the

lake are magnificent. It has been admirab'y kept up. Eveline, my darling, you ought to be a happy woman."

"Let us forget it now, dear papa. Here at least we are out of the hurly-burly."

We agreed in our arrangements for the day. I was to ride with him in the morning. We would walk up the downs in the afternoon. Sippett was in attendance on Lady L—— as usual. He went to town next day to meet Percy and on business. I was left alone. Lady L—— made no scruple of her dislike to me. After breakfast I wandered along the Parade. I watched the sea and the boats. One old boatman interested me.

"Go for a row, miss? Beautiful mornin', miss. Sea like ile. Launch her down in half a jiffy, miss. Pull alongshore and see the bathin'."

The loveliness of the day tempted me.

"Which is your boat, my friend?"

"That's she, miss. Yon white one, with the red streak."

"She looks a safe craft. Does she rock about much?"

"Lor' bless your sweet soul! No, miss! Why look at her grand flat bottom, and her fine run aft! She can travel too. She's got legs on her! You should have seen her at the regatta. Better have an hour's row, miss."

I got into the boat. *The Locket, David Jones of Eastbourne,* was painted on the board against which I leaned. It was a nice big boat with good cushions in clean white covers. The old man pushed off and jumped in.

"You'll go past the machines, miss, o' coorse?"

"Anywhere you like, Mr. David Jones. I have confidence in you. It is quite warm on the water."

"Yes, miss. These are the ladies' machines. The gents' is further hup. We shall have to pass the ladies fust, but it won't take long."

"Where are you going then, Mr. Jones?"

"Why, o' coorse—past the gents. All the ladies goes past in my boat. 'Tis what they likes best—as is nat'ral. That's what they takes the row for."

The old fellow grinned. He screwed up his face into a comical expression. He actually winked.

The boat did travel well, as the poor old fellow said. It only took ten minutes to pass the line of gaudily arrayed, tall, angular female figures, of squalling children and shouting girls bobbing about knee-deep with their "flat bottoms and fine runs aft" presented seawards.

"What a number of people on the beach, Mr. Jones!"

"Yes, miss. They allus comes there to look at the ladies."

"I don't see very much to admire, but then perhaps it's because I'm a woman."

"Jus' so, miss. You wait a bit. It's all right, I knows what the ladies like."

Presently we passed the first of the men's bathing machines. Old Jones had pulled in closer.

"There we are, miss! Fine 'uns too among 'em today!"

I laughed—the idea was so crudely expressed. The fact was so evident that this was only an ordinary exercise on the part of the girls that I shook off the awkward feeling of restraint which troubled me. I looked boldly enough now. The men stood upon the machines with the doors open. They seemed to be employed principally in sawing their backs in a painful manner with bath towels. They were absolutely naked; their figures entirely and unblushingly exposed. Indeed when they saw me pass along with the old fellow they took special pains to exhibit themselves, their privates wagging proudly about in front.

"That's a fine 'un; ain't he, miss?"

I gazed in the direction in which the old man nodded his head as the boat glided by. I thought he even seemed to row slower as we passed. It was a tall man—white, handsome, well-developed—a patch of dark hair on his belly—a huge instrument of pleasure dangling between his thighs.

I held my breath. I noted the man well. I also observed the number of the machine—it was 33.

"Ah, he's a fine man, he is, miss, but he ain't half as fine a made man as what my son is. He's a sailor, miss, aboard of a big four-masted ship, he is, and comin' home tomorrow. He's been round the Horn to Valparaiso and he's been took very bad along of the Horn and the weather. He's been paid off today, and he's comin' down here to see his old dad again. I 'spects him by the first train. He's been ten months away, but he's bound straight here, for he's a good lad and nothing wouldn't stop him in Lunnon."

"Dear me, Mr. Jones, you quite interest me. And you think he would not stay to spend any of his money among the pleasures of London? He must be quite a model young man. I'm sure you must be proud of him."

"I am that, miss. Not that he's much of a muddle either—he's fond of his old father, but he's fond of a pretty gal too. He'll be here tomorrow, then you can tell me if I'm right or not. Lor', miss, you should just see him pull these oars about. He used to make *The Locket* fly, he did! I fear I won't keep him here long. Not that he wouldn't go to sea again, but he'll get rid of his money among the gals here. They'll all be after him like they was afore."

"What a sad thing, Mr. Jones. Don't you give him good advice?"

"So I used to do, miss. But Lor' luv yer, what's the good; lions wouldn't hold him, miss, he's that hot when he gets ashore. I got the missionary to reason with him, but it wasn't no good. He went about just the same again. No, miss, wild hele-phants couldn't hold him."

"I think, perhaps, if you removed him from such temptations; if you kept him to your boat-letting business now, under your own eye, you know, Mr. Jones, don't you think that might tame him down a bit?"

"P'raps it might, miss, if he'd anyone to read and talk serious to him, but I don't know no one; and he's that quick and impatient—"

"You make me feel very much for your poor son, Mr. Jones. I shall come round in the morning, and if he's there then I should be pleased to talk to him on his duty to his parents."

"I've been a widderer these twenty year come Michaelmas, so there's only me to look after the lad. He's more fit to look after me now. There's one thing I likes about him. He don't drink."

I had one of my headaches next morning. I have not always the remedy for them at hand. On this occasion I had left it in London. I thought the air along the sea front might do me good. After breakfast I strolled along the Parade to the far corner where Mr. Jones—who, by the by, was not a Welshman but a native of Sussex—had his boat.

"Good morning, Mr. Jones. I see you are an advocate of cleanliness. Your *Locket* looks splendid, after the scrubbing you are giving her."

A fine, tall, young fellow, fair and freckled, with his short curly hair shading his broad forehead, wielded a mop which belaboured the bottom and sides of the upturned skiff. His legs were bare to the knees. He stood like an old Northern Viking, a splendid specimen of the Anglo-Saxon race. The heavy bucket might have contained only waste paper from the manner in which he shifted it about, charged to the brim with sea water. He almost dropped it, however, as he turned and saw me. His mouth opened. He stood stupidly staring at me from behind his old father. I recognised the youth at once.

"Good mornin', miss. I don't know nothin' about no advocates, miss, but my son Bill is just a givin' her a rub round as we was a thinkin', the mornin' being so fine, I might see a young lady down for a row."

He had a twinkle in his eye which conveyed a silent hope that the liberal fee he had received the previous day might be repeated.

"So this is your son, is it, Mr. Jones? He must be of great service to you now you have got him."

"Oh, yes, miss—he's a main stronger nor me. You should see him capsize that there butt all alone by hisself. Why a rhinersorous couldn't do it!"

The old boatman was brimming over with pride
—satisfaction at recovering his long-absent son betrayed itself in every feature.

"You must be very glad to see your father
again."

"Yes, so I am, miss, and to find him so well and
hearty. You see, miss, he's getting on now. It ain't
as I'm so awful strong—it's that my old dad is a
gettin' a bit shaky in his timbers, miss."

There was something charming in the kindly
smile, and the rough, yet tender, manner of the
blunt young sailor towards the old man which made
me look him over more attentively. He was certainly a superbly built young fellow. His bare arms
and legs were furnished with a muscular development which is rare in these days of effeminacy. A
vigorous, healthy life upon the ocean had served to
enhance all his natural advantages. He was a man
to my mind. My headache increased—I wanted him
badly to cure it.

Between them, they turned the boat over again.
It was a good substantial skiff. I had been used to
boating with Percy as a child. I knew something
about rowing. I used to astonish the girls at the
pensionnat near Paris when we all went in a formal
party down the Seine from Suresnes. It suited me
now to pretend ignorance.

"I hope you will stop with your dad, and—and
be a good boy. He tells me you are too fond of—of
pleasure."

My manner was demure. I flashed him one of my
glances. He seemed struck. There is—they say—a
Freemasonry in love. I say there is *more*. There is
a magnetism in love which is conveyed from mind

to mind—from brain to brain—from heart to heart, if you will—but there is a power, subtle and irresistible, which speaks more powerfully than words. "I love you, I want you." Such was the influence which flashed between us now.

"We sailors don't get too much pleasuring, miss —but I've been ten months at sea, shut up in an old box of a ship all the time, four hours out and four hours in—and that's about the size of it. My dad ain't the man to deny me a fair run ashore now I'm home again. I know how to take care of the rhino all the same, but I mean to stay some time with him now and I shan't trouble about shipping again yet awhile."

There was a half serious, half comical air about the young fellow which showed he only partly believed in me. His keen blue eye followed me. He was noting me well from head to foot. He was distinctly struck with my appearance. Admiration was plainly, visibly written in his look. I read him like a book. I was a revelation to the young sailor. No doubt his appetite was sharp after ten long months at sea. I inwardly rejoiced. Meanwhile the boat was ready, the cushions in their places.

"If you've a mind for a row, miss, my son Bill will go with you and pull you about in the butt anywhere you likes."

I got into the boat. They launched her down. Bill swung himself in over the bow. He backed her out from the smooth beach. Then he sat himself down facing me and began to row steadily away from the shore.

"I really don't know if I ought to trust myself all alone with such a gay young man as your dad describes you, Mr. William, but after all he does not give you a bad character, though he does say you are somewhat—somewhat—what shall I say?"

"Oh, I know, he's a larky old customer, is my dad, and he thinks I'm not much steadier than he was when he was a young 'un. Which course shall we steer, miss—go along the Pevensey shore, or keep on out of the Bay a bit?"

"Let us get into deep water and right away from the sound of the noisy people ashore. How fast you row!"

He was pulling as if for a wager. We were already half a mile away, heading straight out to sea. He slacked a little as I spoke. All this time his gaze never left my person or my face. He was trying to sum me up. Speculating, probably, as to what sort of bedfellow I should make. He was very good-looking certainly. As he bent forward to his paddles, his loose shirt disclosed his broad chest covered with a fine sandy down. I felt impatient as I sat on the broad seat with a back to it. I faced him all the time. I sat cross-legged, my right knee over the left. As Bill pulled away at the paddles, my leg was jerked backwards and forwards. I took care he should have a good view of my feet and my stockings as well. I soon fascinated him. The black silk seemed a new sensation. He commenced to row still more unevenly. My leg moved in cadence. He could see at times up to my knee as the light breeze assisted his design. He was evidently getting excited. A strong lascivious expression extended itself over his features.

"So you have been shut up ten months on board

ship, Bill? That must have been trying to a fine young man like you?"

I could not beat about the bush. I wanted him. I meant to indulge my inclination—to have him. It was no time to waste in mere sentiment—in childish trifling.

"I guess it was, miss. Never saw a petticoat for over four mouths. We were not allowed ashore at Valparaiso, only in the daytime. It's a queer hole for British seamen, miss; nothing but rows and robbery."

"Poor fellow! But of course you have a sweetheart here?"

"Not I, miss. I only came home last night, or rather early this morning. I couldn't stop in London with the poor old dad here and he so old and feeble-like, so I jumped into the first train I could."

"You are a good fellow, Bill. I like you very much. What a long way we are from the shore now! I can't see the pier any more."

"We're over two miles from Eastbourne now. See that light-ship there—that's the Royal Sovereign shoal."

"How lovely it seems—how calm the sea is! We need not go any further out. You might not be able to get back, Bill."

"I only wish I couldn't!"

"Why so, Bill?"

"Because I haven't had the chance to see a face like yours in all my life, miss! There—now it's out!"

"Oh, Bill! You don't mean that? Come and sit here and tell me all about it."

I made room for him beside me on the broad seat with the backboard. The words "David Jones" were quite obliterated by our figures. Bill took up a rope and began undoing the end into four separate cords. Then he got the other end of the same rope, and served it the same. I watched him. Then he put two ends together, the four cords of each end interlacing.

"Why Bill! What do you call that?"

"That's what we sailors call making a splice, miss—when it's done."

"Do you ever think of being spliced yourself, Bill?"

"Sometimes, but sailors ought never to be properly spliced up, miss. There ought to be a slippery hitch somewhere. They're awfully true when spliced, but the gals ain't. They can't stand the long absences."

"Can you make a slippery hitch, Bill?"

He laughed. We both laughed. I looked into his eyes. He returned my gaze. I put my hand on his thigh. He slipped his left arm round my waist. He had dropped the rope now. We sat quiet a moment. The only sound we could hear was the low gurgling of the placid sea under the boat's bows and sides, as she lay idly rolling on the gentle swell.

"We are quite alone here, Bill—not a boat anywhere."

He had white canvas trousers on, turned up to his knees. My hand stole along until it was suddenly arrested by something hard and solid between his legs which lay along the inside of his left thigh. I lifted my face up close to his. Instantly he kissed me on the mouth.

"Oh, Bill! Oh, you bad boy!"

He seized me tightly in his arms. He covered me with kisses. He pressed my bosom with his great sailor hand. I closed my eyes and suffered all.

"Make me a slippery hitch, Bill dear!"

He pressed me again tighter than ever. My fingers pressed his limb. It seemed tremendously thick and stiff.

"Ten months! Only think, Bill, how bad you must feel!"

His hand was already on my leg. As I spoke it moved further up. I opened my legs and let it pass. Meanwhile I deliberately unbuttoned his canvas flap.

"I want to look at it, Bill!"

"So you shall, my dear. It's a whopper!"

A moment later, a huge naked limb stiffly erect and throbbing with eagerness for enjoyment was in my grasp. His hand had already taken possession of the centre of my desires. His fingers maddened me. Without more ado, I pulled the big member into the warm daylight. It was a beauty! White and red, with a large soft top and hard sides—very long and awfully stiff. We rolled about together in this position as the boat answered to the undulations of the sea. It could not last so, however, and so it came to pass that I slipped, cushion and all, off the seat. Bill and I found ourselves on the floor-boards of the skiff with the cushion under us. I still retained my hold of his limb. He reached out and secured another cushion which he placed under my loins. Then he tilted me back. He pulled up my clothes. I am afraid I helped him. He took one look at my exposed legs—at my white belly. I saw for a second his big truncheon menacing me within a few inches of my thighs. Then he threw himself upon me. I was quite as eager as he was. I helped him to his pleasure. The lewd business was about to begin —the curtain was up—the actor and the actress were on the stage.

"Oh! Oh! Bill—you hurt! Oh! Oh! You're right into me! You're too big! You're—Oh!—Oh!— Oh! My goodness, Bill!"

Nothing stopped him. The young fellow had had a long fast. I was getting the full benefit of his abstention. He pushed his great tool into me to his balls. He never spoke, but he set his teeth together. He worked up and down, thrusting at me like a battering ram. In less time than it takes to relate he sank on my chest. I felt a sudden gush of hot seed. I knew that his pleasure had reached the climax. He lay discharging, until a flood of thick sperm deluged my interior. My own pleasure was supreme. He gave me no rest. Instead of withdrawing, he recommenced. A few thrusts, aided by the natural elasticity of my vagina, restored him to all his virility. He commenced another course. Oh, the impatient fellow! How he worked me!

"Oh! Bill, dear Bill! Go slowly—do it gently, Bill! Oh, oh! You'll know the bottom of the boat out! Oh, my goodness! Oh!"

"Boat be damned!" was the polite rejoinder.

At last he got up. He adjusted his clothes. He wiped his smoking member. I raised myself on my cushions. I dipped my handkerchief into the cool sea-water and sopped up all I could of the tremendous overflow I had received. I made the best toilette possible under the circumstances.

"We can sail back easy. The wind is almost dead fair. Then we can sit together. Do you feel jolly now, my dear love?"

There was something that touched me beyond simple lust in this young fellow. There was an innate tenderness towards "his gal," to which they say sailors are particularly prone, just as one makes a pet of a dog.

I have heard of sailors at Portsmouth newly discharged from their ships and envious of married men who had found a ready-made progeny on their return, seeking to emulate them by hiring babies to carry up and down the Yard. I can quite believe it.

Bill set to work. In two minutes the mast was stepped; in two more the sail was hoisted and set, and the sheet, as he called it, hauled aft. The skiff sailed along merrily—too quickly I thought, as I sat on the cushioned floor of the boat with my head on the thigh of the young sailor who held the tiller. My restless fingers would not remain quiet. They sought their playfellow. Bill opened his flap. I pulled out his stiffening limb.

"Oh, Bill! What a big one! Do you feel any better now?"

"Why, yes, my lovely dear one, of course I do, and I'm damned grateful to you for the chance, miss. But I wish—that I do—we were not going to part so soon. I should like to have you all night."

"Oh, Bill! A pretty thing you'd make of me by morning!"

His limb rose again under the skillful touches of my nimble fingers. As I sat, my face was just on a level with his erect weapon. He held the tiller in one hand; with the other he caressed my neck and bosom. I bent forward. I examined minutely his splendid limb from end to end. I put my hand under and felt his testicles. I tickled him lusciously. I put the tip of the broad nut to my lips. I kissed it. I opened them—it entered. I sucked it. I rolled my hot tongue round the red head.

"Oh! Oh! Little lass! You are driving me mad, don't ye know! Stop a moment. Here, come stern on. I'll arrange all in the twinkling of a handspike. Now sit down between my legs. So! Oh, my God!"

He pulled me backwards. He had already raised my clothes. My buttocks were exposed to his salacious view. I settled myself down upon his thighs. I felt his thing pressing in between my pliant globes. The big knob was jammed between them. I put down my right hand. I placed his weapon between the moist lips of my little slit. I pressed down.

"Oh! Damn my eyes and limbs! My bowsprit's run you aboard, missy! It's right into you up to the gammoning! Oh, isn't it lovely?"

He seized me round the hips. He pushed home. With my left hand, I tickled his testicles. His big limb stretched me tremendously. I enjoyed it all the same. I shared his transports. I was mad with lust. I jogged up and down. My spasms came all too soon. I ceased moving. I could only moan now. Bill took up the movements. He pushed with fury.

"Oh, Bill! You'll upset the boat!"

"Upset the soup, you mean? There it goes! Enough for all hands!"

Truly the vigour of this active young sailor was tremendous. He had been ten months, remember, without copulation. His excitement, doubtless his enjoyment, was proportionate to the length of his abstinence. I was really glad when the boat's keel touched land.

"The Honourable Mr. Percy is in the drawing-room, miss."

"Arrived already, Ferguson? I had no idea the time had gone so fast. Oh, I am so glad! Say I'm coming immediately."

I found him so changed. The big boy of fifteen had expanded into a fine young man. He was handsome too. A speaking likeness of his father. My thoughts went back to the old days. Was he changed in character also? Hardly so, I thought. Did his mind revert to the time when we were last together? If so—what did he think of it all now?

"How you are altered, Eveline! I should have known you anywhere—but how you have grown! How you have developed! You are the most beautiful of girls! By Heaven, you take me by surprise! What a figure! I never saw so perfect a face in my life."

We stood together in the light of the window. He was indeed altered. No doubt he found me also very different from the little girl he had parted from so long ago. I seemed to astonish and attract him. He had lots to tell me of his foreign service—his friends and his comrades. We passed a quiet evening together. Papa had returned with Percy from London.

Chapter VII

If Lady L—— had no affection for her only daughter, she made up for it in the person of her second son. He was all in all to her. She had always spoilt him. His departure had ended what might have been a fatal obstacle to the formation of his character as a decent member of society and a soldier. My father saw the mischief in time. He interfered and separated them. Lady L—— never forgave him. Percy had left his mother a stout, strong woman. He returned to find a wreck. More than that, he could not feel other than shame at the state to which he saw her reduced by her own excesses.

"I have much work to do this morning, Eveline, my dear. I shall leave Percy to amuse you. He wants to drive you over to Lewes. The old town is well worth a visit."

"I shall be delighted to go, papa. We will take the phaeton. Percy, I hope you are a good whip and will not spill me?"

We started at eleven. We took the footman behind. He occupied the seat under the hood which was only partly thrown back. The morning was chilly for the time of year. The wind came over the Downs with a violence which made the fur rug very agreeable. Percy was in high spirits. He told me of Lord L———'s intention to get him transferred to the Household Cavalry on the first available vacancy. I told him all about my engagement to Lord Endover. He had already been informed of it by papa.

"You will be a horrid little Countess. I don't like the idea at all. I wanted to be a long time at home with you. I hoped to be such chums."

"Why, Percy, so we can be. I am not to be a 'horrid little Countess' for some time yet, you bad boy!"

"But it seems it is all settled. You are to be married and done for."

"Whatever do you mean? I am sure papa is pleased. You know, Percy, dear old boy, girls have to be married, or else become old maids."

Percy actually laughed.

"You'll never be an old maid, Eve dear. I don't like the idea of your going away from us—just when I've come back and am likely to stop in England. I had pictured up such jolly times. You don't know, Eve, how I've thought of you all the long years since we parted. Although I could not write my thoughts to you, yet nevertheless you were in them. I loved you better than any of the girls I met. None of them were a bit like you. When papa sent me your photo after you left school, I was told all round it was too beautiful to be true to life. They all said the photographer had touched it up—especially the women. Now I know that no photographer could produce so exquisite a picture as would give a just idea of the original. You have grown a splendid girl, Eve. Do you remember I used to call you 'Eve'?"

"Yes, and I used to call you Adam. But we must forget those times now, Percy, we are no longer children."

"Why should I forget? Because you are ten thousand times more winsome and lovely now you are grown up? Because I am a man with a man's strong passions? Eve, dear Eve, I am not likely to forget our childish frolics. I mean to renew them with you, I mean to repeat—"

"Oh, Percy—you must not talk like that! You must not refer to our old associations."

I laughed—I could not help it. In that laugh he saw the hollowness of my reserve. He became more confident—more passionate. He began in earnest to make love to me. He nestled close, put his arm round my waist and held the reins with the other hand.

"Percy! Percy! The horses will play tricks! For goodness' sake let go, and drive properly."

"Well, kiss me then, Eve—then I will."

I put my face up to his. I kissed him on the lips. He held me close.

"I was only a boy then, Eve, I am a man now. I only half had you in those days. I mean to have you in earnest now."

"Oh! Percy—if anybody were to hear you!"

"The hood is up sufficiently to keep all to ourselves. He can neither hear nor see over it, and the noise prevents all chance."

"Percy, you frighten me. We cannot be too careful."

"Trust to me for that. I am caution itself. We will play at Adam and Eve once more. I cannot let you marry and go without having tasted a real man, little Eve. Do you agree, my beautiful one?"

"Oh, Percy, you are too bad; you are exciting me shockingly!"

"Do you hear, my sweet? We began early. We are going to complete the thing now. Oh, Eve! My blood boils—I long to begin!"

"Hush, Percy! Pray be careful!"

"If you knew how I long for you! How I pant to snatch off that pretty bodice and let loose those well-blown breasts. I want to kiss them, Eve. I want to riot in kisses all over your beautiful body. How red your cheeks are, my charming Eve. You know you are as bad as I am. You want to play again with Adam. I know you do."

I cannot repeat all the bold and lecherous things he whispered to me on the way. We arrived at Lewes all too soon for my part. Percy drove to the best hotel. We descended and entered. He ordered lunch in a private room. It all passed pleasantly. He had the good sense to calm himself, but I made no scruple in allowing him to see that my inclination was as strong as his own.

We drove home to Eastbourne by Polegate. The air came fresher than ever over the South Downs. I nestled under the furs. Percy drove carefully. We had the hood quite up now. He was warm with the lunch and the wine. I shared his exaltation. A very little coaxing on his part induced me to keep my hand under the warm wraps upon his left thigh as he held the reins. I think a tailor must be an artist by birth. He always seems intuitively to understand that a gentleman's "unspeakables" must be cut much more commodiously on the left thigh than on the right. No doubt they take their measures, but as their absurd tape can hardly be supposed to produce the same effect as the delicate fingers of Eveline, I am at a loss to know how, unless they are as I suggest, artists by intuition, they can allow such gigantic inflammation as took place in that region on the present occasion. In fact, this tailor had not done his work at all as he would no doubt have done, had he only had the foresight to have employed his young daughter to take the gentleman's measure "up to the crotch." In any case, I was obliged to make more room for the increasing growth under my hand. I opened a couple of buttons; another flew off all by itself—my fingers closed on his stiff limb.

"Oh, Percy! What a dreadful thing! Why it's more than twice the size it used to be!"

"I believe it is, Eve; your little hand is making me furiously lustful!"

I could not keep up even a semblance of propriety with my brother. With him I subsided into the position of the little sister of old. With others it was different. I had a reserve to maintain, a presence to be insisted upon—a certain imperative necessity for prudence and forethought. With Percy I felt myself free from all restraint. I took up the position as of old. It saved my modesty, or what answered for it: my awkwardness and nervous apprehension of inspiring any other sentiment than desire.

I nestled close down to him. The sweet odour of

his manhood pervaded my nostrils—stole over my senses with irresistible impulse. I even furtively sucked my fingers when I could find a decent excuse for relaxing my grasp. He had certainly realised my hopes and expectations. The volume of his limb was undoubtedly doubled since the time when, as children, we made our pleasant investigations into the mysteries of the sexes.

"No, Eveline, you will never die an old maid. You are too wise, and you know too much for that. At the same time, my little Eve, you cannot make me believe you have not found, in all this time, a serpent to tempt you, though I really do think it might require a *pair of apples* to do that. Tell me— was it before you left school? Who was the lucky reptile? A music-master? A youth of subtle insinuations? A man—or a snake?"

"How can you talk such nonsense, Percy? You are really too bad!"

"But I am right, little Eve. A girl of your temperament could not resist if she tried. I am not in the least jealous, you may be sure, dear girl, nor do I blame you for following a purely animal instinct. We men all do it, then why not the girls? Confess then, little Eve?"

"It was not a serpent, and it was not an apple; nor even *two apples,* Percy, and I don't see why I should satisfy your inordinate and most improper curiosity even if I had anything to confess."

"Well, at any rate, the devil that tempted you had the best catch he ever made in the whole course of his administration. You must be a treat for the gods, and much too good for imps of the other persuasion."

"For shame, Percy! But tell me if you are serious? This wicked thing feels anxious to try its luck."

"Serious? Of course I am serious! I mean to have you, Eve dear. It will be no joke now. I am a man and a strong man too. We will take all necessary precautions—but have you I must, and before we are many hours older."

"Well, Percy, what must be, *must*. But I hope you will be very prudent—very quiet and very cautious. You take matters too easily. You do not seem to see the risk we may run."

"Do I not though, my Eve? Indeed I do! Remember the more risk we run to obtain what we want, the sweeter is its possession. There is only one consideration which can make it sweeter."

"What is that, Percy?"

"The fact that it is dreadfully 'improper.' Therefore it is dreadfully nice. It is the extreme limit of the principle 'naughty but nice'—the very essence of it carried to its fullest excess. It is *incest*, my little sister! Therefore it will be divinely nice!"

"Oh, Percy! You make me horribly agitated. I already wish it was night."

"Why night, my sweet Eve?"

"Because I want you, Percy. Because I have a plan. Your room adjoins mine. I thought of that when we set out the apartments in the hotel. There is a door of communication from your chamber to mine. I have had *portières* put up on both sides. Also across my door into the corridor. I hate these hotel doors of communication, you know, Percy. Do you not see I have only to turn my key and you are in my room. I will oil the lock, the key and the hinges."

"What a cultivated Eve! By Jove, you have well thought of all. Did you also provide a garland of fig leaves?"

"No, Adam, we haven't fallen yet. You might prefer me in my pristine innocence. I am worth a study."

"Good day, Mr. David Jones. Your boat does not look as if it had been launched today."

"No, miss—no more she ain't. I ain't got the strength of the young 'uns. My son's been telegraphed for to go back to Lunnon."

"What! Left you already! How is that?"

"Why, miss, yer see the owners of his ship—the one as he come 'ome aboard of—offered him a berth as third mate. He's gone up to Lunnon to school in the Minories and get book larnin' to pass the Board o' Trade. He'll do it, miss, no fear. He's a sure hand to push 'isself in anywhere, and he's strong and steady too."

"Yes, Mr. Jones, I am sure *he's all that*. What is the name of his ship?"

"They calls her the *Priapus,* or maybe it's the *Priam,* or the *Pegasus,* but I think it's the *Priapus,* miss. A fine four-masted, full-rigged ship she is too, and over five thousand ton o' cargo they stows away in her. I didn't know you, miss, up there, aboard o' that rampin' great 'orse."

"Oh, I'm very fond of horse exercise! The bumping up and down does me good. I'm off for a gallop on the South Downs before dinner."

"Well, miss, all I 'opes is you won't tumble overboard. Good day, miss, and thankee very much for this 'ere yellow boy."

"Good bye, Mr. Jones. I wish your son luck. Now, Johnson, I'm off! Follow me up close."

I gave Goorkha the rein. He got clear of the town and the houses. He flew up the chalky road to the Downs. My weight was as nothing to him. He seemed rather to like it. He was full of mettle. He appeared, however, as if he knew the fragile nature of his burden. Poor fellow, why had they robbed him of his horsehood? Why was he not a stallion? I really think I should have loved him even carnally had he only been one. As it was, he was in my estimation first cousin to the Centaur. We were soon on the open downs, heading away for Beachy Head. On the right was a large chalk pit with a road for carts into it. One could see all round for miles.

"Is there anyone in view, Johnson?"

"No one, miss, that I can see for over a mile round."

"Get down then and see to this girth."

We had pulled up a little out of the road and up the narrow cart track which led into the pit. Johnson got down and came to my side.

"Isn't it too slack, Jim? Don't touch my leg, you wicked man! Don't put your hand there. Do you hear, Jim? Oh, Jim! Let me alone. Take your hand away, I say!"

"No one can see us now. We are quite alone. Do let me lift you down, miss. We can go into the pit there quite easy."

"No, Jim. It won't do. How are you going to leave the horses? You know very well we cannot leave them. Besides——"

"Besides what, Miss Eveline? Don't be angry with me, I feel so awful randy. I can't help it."

I looked down at him. His buckskin breeches bulged out in front.

"I have reasons why I cannot allow you to repeat your outrageous violence, Jim. All the same, I should like to get off and stretch my legs a little."

Jim handed me down. We stood between the horses.

"Pull it out, Jim. I want to see it again."

The groom needed no coaxing. He unbuttoned and instantly let loose his monstrous limb, throbbing with desire and obstinately erect. I took it in my gloved hand. There was something ineffably indecent in the idea of this man's huge member clasped in the delicate white kid gauntlet glove of a little hand like mine. I skinned it back. I gazed on the big nut.

"What can we do, Jim! I dare not move away from here."

"Toss it off, miss. Oh do, miss! It's so awfully stiff, I shouldn't take a minute. We are quite alone. No one within miles of us now."

He held both horses by the bridles. I moved my hand up and down his big thing. It grew red and stiffer—harder than ever. My hand flew up and down the long shaft. Jim groaned and staggered. I abated my movement a moment.

"Is it so very nice, Jim?"

"Oh! Oh! Miss, it's lovely. Only I wish it was up

your belly—like—like—last time. Oh, what a game we had—didn't we, miss?"

I pulled the loose skin of his tool down with a gentle jerk at each stroke, so that the delicate nut presented itself all shiny and bent forward to my eager gaze. I thought it could not last more than a few seconds more. Already a drop of pearly dew issued from the little opening. My gloves were evidently doomed. I should be smothered in another minute. Only one thing occurred to me as a natural resource. I stooped. I kissed the dewy tip. I opened my moistened lips. I rolled my tongue round the big nut.

"Oh! Oh! I can't stand it! I'm coming! I'm coming! Oh!"

The next moment he discharged. The first outflow came in a great gush. It went straight down my throat. Then, responsive to my jerking tender movements, jet upon jet of thick sperm spouted from him. I continued as long as the spasms lasted. I only desisted when the source ran dry and the big limb fell away from my grasp.

Jim made haste to set himself to rights. The two horses had stood as quiet as the wooden ones at the coachmaker's in Long Acre.

Jim asked me to kindly hold the reins a moment. The young fellow was awkwardly situated. But nature is nature everywhere and after all we have to be subservient to her dictates. Jim therefore wandered round the corner of the chalk pit at the entrance of which we stood. As he turned the angle of the cutting I noticed he stopped. A wild expression of astonishment spread suddenly over his face. He raised his hand and beckoned to me. I advanced with the horses a few paces. I could now see round the corner. I must have assumed the same look of blank amazement as he did.

Not twenty yards further and within the chalk pit, upon a little plateau of debris which had slipped down from the rim of the great cutting and still retained its verdant carpet of the fine grass of the Downs, were a man and a woman. They were lying upon this dainty spot. The woman on her back, the man on her body. They were evidently in the act of copulation. It was equally evident they had been too well occupied to have suspected our proximity. The woman had seized the shirt tails of her companion and had pulled them up to his waist in her excitement. The man was engaged in stabbing at the person of his friend beneath him and his posteriors were naked as the day, while his broad buttocks worked up and down with a velocity which promised to bring their pleasant pastime to a speedy issue.

"Oh, Lord, miss! Only look at that! Ain't he a ramming of it in? Ain't she a-getting of it? Oh, my!"

The pair were too much occupied to heed anything or anybody. Jim was simply struck silly. He stared open-mouthed. He was immoveably rooted to the spot. It remained for me to act.

"Oh, dear! How shocking! Johnson, come back! How dreadfully indecent! Do you hear, Johnson? Come here! Help me to mount. I feel ill—take me away!"

We withdrew quietly. I rode home slowly. I felt a little indigestion. I think it must have been the *œufs sur le plat* I had at lunch. However, I didn't "tumble overboard" as Mr. David Jones had feared I might. I appeared in perfect health at dinner.

"Hush, Percy! Are you sure you have locked your door?"

It was midnight. The church clock had just struck. I had prepared everything. I had only a *peignoir* of blue, my favourite colour, and my fine soft *chemise*. I retained my black silk stockings and my little bronze shoes. I had thrown a dressing gown over all.

For full a minute we stood listening. We looked at each other. My brother's gaze was penetrating in its fierce intensity of desire—in its audacious incentive to animal concupiscence. There was no attempt at disguise on either side. No other sentiment for the moment than acute desire. I longed for him. I had waited so long. I had thought of him —dreamt of him. Now I was to have him! He was to possess me—to revel in my embraces. To yield his manhood and his virility at my shrine. I was to know all the ecstatic emotion of his incestuous contact. To aid him to his enjoyment. To watch his contortions of voluptuous excitement. To participate in all.

"Where have you been, Eve, all the afternoon? I looked for you at tea time. You had flown."

"I galloped over the Downs on Goorkha. I wanted air. I thought it best to leave you to yourself. I wanted you to think. You were very silent at dinner, Percy."

"I was thinking of what was in store."

"Are you determined to go on? Don't you think it would be best to go back to your own room, Percy?"

He caught me in his strong arms. He covered my face with his kisses. His trembling hands invaded my bust. His lips settled upon mine in a lascivious kiss. I quivered with excitement. He did not utter a word, but he bore me gradually back towards the bed. I knew he was preparing himself for the fullness of his pleasure. He had only his dressing-gown over a *foulard* night-shirt. He slipped the cord. I beheld him almost naked within the wrapper.

"Oh! Percy—dear boy! Pray be cautious! I am so frightened!"

"There is no cause for fear, Eve, we are absolutely isolated at this end of the corridor. My room is the last. All the lights are out. All the servants have gone to bed. Only a night watchman down below. Let me see your beautiful legs, dear—let me feel your satin thighs. Oh, my God! How lovely! How plump! How luscious! What beautiful bosoms! How firm! I must kiss those strawberry titties. Dear little darlings! Let down your hair, Eve! What luxuriant locks—how glossy! What perfume! How sweet you smell! Your skin is like ivory with a touch of carmine in it. You are a beauty all over—and now—my Eve—my darling Eve!"

He put me gently on the side of the bed. He parted my willing thighs. Instantly he glued his eager lips to the centre of my desires. His hot tongue worked around my clitoris. It rose to meet his salacious caresses. My hands toyed with his hair—my head fell back in the sensuous enjoyment he was giving me. He groaned in his delight.

I rose panting from his luxurious embrace. His face, flushed with longing and excitement, looked more radiant than ever.

"Now I must look at you, Percy! How you have altered!"

I twisted myself from his grasp. I turned swiftly and dropped my *peignoir*. I slipped into bed. He followed me. His strong arms encircled my light form. His kisses covered my face—my bosom—my shoulders. His body lay on mine. His warmth thrilled me through all my being. His touches conveyed a magnetic sympathy I was unable to resist. I suffered all. He mounted upon my body.

"Oh! Percy! We were children then—now—Oh! Oh! Pray not now! Oh! Percy! Oh! Oh!"

It was already too late—our bodies were in closest conjunction. I felt the penetration of his limb. It slipped impatiently up my vagina. The throbs of the solid shaft of muscular manhood secretly delighted me. We writhed—we struggled in our agony of sensuous enjoyment. His thrusts were violent. I felt them at my very womb. He was in my body to his utmost extent, yet he set his teeth and pushed. He groaned and slobbered in his pleasure. It was my paradise to witness his transports. My parts were swimming. My own spasms were almost continuous.

"Oh! My darling Eve! I never knew pleasure till now. You make me thrill all over! You drive me mad! Take that, you little devil! I love you! I have you! Oh! How I wish I could finish so! I dare not! My sister—my beautiful—darling sister!"

"Why not? My dearest boy—why not? Finish me—finish your Eve. She loves you—she has no fear. All will be safe—give me all! I want it—all! Oh! Oh!"

The response came all too soon to my supplication; involuntarily I arched up my loins. I spread my limbs, my thighs clung to his hips—my whole being was at his disposal in expectancy. It came. He sunk upon me with a groan of blissful rapture. A torrent shot from his bursting member. It invaded my vagina—my womb. It came from him with a force I could feel in my vitals. We clung together with convulsive shudders until he had expended all his pent-up manhood.

During the half hour which followed we lay locked in each other's arms, forgetful of all the world beyond ourselves. Percy exploited me from head to foot. He praised all he found in extravagant terms. We had no reserve now. We were boy and girl again together. We exercised the greatest caution—we spoke in whispers; these again so subdued that they were inaudible half across the bedroom. Our faces were close together. We conversed of all we would be to one another.

"You will have to carry out your engagement, Eve. I see that of course. You will marry Endover. They say he has led a tolerably fast life. His name is associated with more than one of the actresses. Well, what of that? Whose is not, nowadays? But he looks older than he is, they say. I have never met him; some of our mess know him though. He's good across country, they say. He has looked well after the family possessions. No doubt he is well off."

I held my peace.

"You will have more liberty when you are married, Eve. You will have your house in town—your carriages. You will have Normanstoke Towers for a country residence, and above all, to my mind, 'Chitterlings,' which I hear is lovely."

"Will you come and see me there, Percy?"

"Won't I, little Eve! But turn over, get on your back. I want it again—feel that! Stiff! So—I want to put it in all by myself. You beauty, how lovely and soft you are! Oh! Oh! Ugh! There it goes. It's in!"

"Ah, Percy, not so hard! The bed creaks. Take care! You are too strong! Oh, my goodness! How big it is! Oh! Oh, my dear boy! It's—it's lovely! Ah! Quick, I'm coming!"

He thrust his limb into me to the fullest extent. He discharged a volume of his sperm. We swum in voluptuous delight. At the first appearance of daylight Percy returned to his own room. I closed the intervening door. I slept soundly far into the morning.

END OF BOOK TWO

Book Three

Chapter I

"A temperament like yours, my darling child, requires constant attention. You are no ordinary girl. You have need of change, of variety, of sufficient venereal food to keep you in health. You have developed within you so much vitality, so much necessity for sensual gratification—if I may use the term—that you have urgent need to feed the fire. Like the ancient flame which burnt—and still burns—on the altars of followers of Zoroaster, you must keep it going; replenishing it as may be necessary, never letting it languish. If it does so, you will not be well. Eveline will not be herself."

"I feel the force of what you say, dear papa. I love you devotedly—but—"

"Yes, my child—I see it—I know it. At my age, with all my various occupations and engagements, I am not likely to be all to you that your nature demands. When you are married—"

"Do not speak of that, dear. It will be time enough hereafter. I do not anticipate any pleasure from my married state—not in the sense my darling papa can bestow it. I look forward to it with disgust rather than with satisfaction. I feel very dejected on the subject."

"Listen to me, Eveline. Your nature requires sexual excitement. You know it as well as I do. It is medicine to you. You must take your medicine; or rather, being healthy, the *beau idéal* of a perfect and beautiful girl, your nature, having once tasted, requires constant nourishment. Take it then, only be careful that you imbibe naught but what is good and wholesome. I would be your physician, if you would follow my advice."

"I am always ready to be guided by your counsel, dear papa."

"Well then, Eveline, having sufficiently explained my views, which I am sure you understand, I will obtain you the necessary medicine."

"And I will take it, for whatever you provide for little Eveline is sure to be nice."

"It shall be something extra nice. Something that will set your pretty mouth watering—your eyes sparkling—your whole being alert with anticipation of enjoyment. Something that will wring sobs of delight from your darling heart—sighs of the most intense rapture from your parted lips—something which shall possess your body and your senses with ecstasy—something irresistible in its noble manhood—solid, stiff, and strong!"

"Oh, papa! You excite me too much. I already long for this delicious medicine. When may I commence my course of it? Or is it only in small doses, to be taken sparingly? I am ready for all. Let it be large and solid—stiff and strong!"

"Your capacity for enjoyment is wonderful, my child. You require a male well furnished with sexual organs, in full vigour; perfect health; robust and extraordinarily well developed. I will provide you such. I will enable you to take your fill of pleasure without risk—without danger."

"I think you are right, papa. In the meantime, I want this thing which is already so stiff in my little hand. See how its head shines? It enters! Oh! Goodness, dear! How you excite your little girl! Push now! Now! Oh! Oh! It comes! It is squirting into me! Oh! Give me all your delicious seed! Dear love! You kill me with pleasure!"

"I have in store for you, my darling child, a delicious treat of the senses. To see you enjoy it will be to me a supreme excitement. We will roll in ecstasy. Our senses shall float in a world of pleasure. Give me only a few days to arrange all. Your medicine will take a novel form. The medium is deaf and dumb!"

"Oh, papa! How dreadful!"

"By no means, Eveline. We only desire the means —the instrument. So long as that has no surroundings which are positively objectionable or repulsive, it matters little—we shall possess all we require. I promise you that in the present case it is neither, but, on the other hand, attractive in every sense. You will be charmed and even sympathetic when you know more."

"You excite my curiosity, papa. When may I take my first dose?"

"As soon as we are back in town together. They say the implement of love is immense, and that its owner is singularly gifted in sexual gratifications."

"Oh, papa! You are too good to your naughty little Eveline. You offer her a banquet—it will not be medicine. It will be a draught of pleasure. My mouth waters already. I long to taste it."

Percy had been at Eastbourne three days. We had not altogether lost our time. I determined to run up to town. I went by an early train alone. I entered the station some fifteen minutes before the train started. On the platform was a gentlemanly looking man in a tweed suit. I thought I had seen his face before. I could not recall where. We passed each other. He looked pointedly at me. Certainly I knew his features. I never forget, if I take an interest in a man's appearance. I liked the look of this tall, well-built fellow in tweeds. He appeared to be about thirty-five to forty years of age——hale and hearty. I gave him one of my glances as he passed me.

"This way, miss. First class——no corridors by this train. You will be all right here. You're all alone at present."

"Thank you, guard. Does the train go up without stopping?"

"Stops at Lewes, miss. That's all——then right up."

I saw my tall friend pass the carriage. Another glance. He stopped——hesitated——then opened the door and got in. He took a seat opposite me. The newspaper appeared to engross his attention until the whistle sounded. We were off.

"Would you object to my lowering the window? These carriages are stuffy. The morning is so warm."

I made no objection, but smilingly gave consent.

"How calm and beautiful the sea looks! It seems a pity to leave it."

"Indeed I think so—especially for London."

"You are going up to London? How odd! So am I!"

I could not be mistaken. I had seen him somewhere before.

"I shall miss the sea very much. We have no sea baths in Manchester. I love my morning dip."

It struck me like a flash. I remembered him now.

"You must have enjoyed it very much, coming from an inland city."

"Well, yes, you see I had a good time. They looked well after me. Always had my machine ready."

"I have no doubt of that."

"No. 33. A new one—capital people—very fine machine."

I suppose I smiled a little. He laughed in reply as if he read my thought. Then he folded up his paper. I arranged my small reticule. It unfortunately dropped from my hand. He picked it up and presented it to me. His foot touched mine. We conversed. He told me he lived near Manchester. He had been to Eastbourne for rest. His business had been too much for him, but he was all right now. His gaze was constantly upon me. I kept thinking of his appearance all naked on the platform of the bathing machine as old David Jones rowed me past. We stopped at Lewes. My companion put his head out of the window. He prevented the entry of an old lady by abusing the newspaper boy for his want of activity. The train started again.

"I think Eastbourne is one of the best bathing places on the coast. You know where the gentlemen's machines are?"

"I think I know where they keep them."

"Well, I was going to say—but—well—what a funny girl you are! Why are you laughing?"

"Because a funny idea struck me. I was thinking of a friend."

His foot was pushed a little closer—very perceptible was the touch. He never ceased gloating on my person. My gloves evidently had an especial attraction for him. Meanwhile, I looked him well over. He was certainly a fine man. He roused my emotions. I permitted his foot to remain in contact with my boot. I even moved it past his, so that my ankle touched his. His face worked nervously. Poor man, no wonder! He gave me a searching look. Our glances met. He pressed my leg between his own. His fingers were trembling with that undefined longing for contact with the object of desire I so well understood. I smiled.

"You seem very fond of the ladies."

I said it boldly, with a familiar meaning he could not fail to understand. I glanced at his leather bag in the rack above.

"I cannot deny the soft impeachment. I am. Especially when they are young and beautiful."

"Oh, you men! You are dreadfully wicked. What would Mrs. Turner say to that?"

I laughed. He stared with evident alarm. It was a bold stroke. I risked it. Either way I lost nothing.

"How do you know I am married?"

My shaft had gone home. He had actually missed the first evident fact. He picked it up, however, quickly, before I could reply.

"It appears you know me? You know my name?"

"Well, yes. You see I am not blind."

I pointed to the label on the bag above his head. It was his turn to laugh.

"Ah! You have me there! What a terribly observant young lady you must be!"

He seized my hand before I could regain my attitude. He pressed it in both his own.

"You will not like me any the less—will you? I thought we were going to be so friendly."

"On the contrary—they say married men are the best."

Up to this point, my effrontery had led him on. He must have felt he was on safe ground. My last remark was hardly even equivocal. He evidently took it as it was intended. I was equally excited. The man and the opportunity tempted me on. I wanted him. I was delighted with his embarrassment—with his fast increasing assurance. I made no attempt to withdraw my hand. He crossed over. He occupied the seat beside me. My gloved hand remained in his.

"I am so glad you think so. You do not know how charming I think you. Married men ought to be good judges, you know."

"I suppose so. I rather prefer them."

I looked in his face and laughed as I uttered the words. He brought his very close. He passed his left arm round my waist. I made no resistance. The carriage gave a sympathetic jerk as it rushed along. Our faces touched. His lips were in contact with mine. It was quite accidental, of course, the line is so badly laid. We kissed.

"Oh, you *are* nice! How pretty you are!"

He pressed his hot lips again to mine. I thought

of the sight I had seen on the bathing machine. My blood boiled. I half closed my eyes. I let him keep his mouth upon mine. He pressed me to him. He drew my light form to his stout and well-built frame as in a vice.

I put my right foot up on the opposite seat. He glared at the pretty tight little kid boot. He was evidently much agitated.

"Ah! What a lovely foot!"

He touched it with his hand. His fingers ran over the soft pale cream-coloured leather. I wore a pair of papa's prime favourites. He did not stop there. The trembling hand passed on to my stocking, advancing by stealthy degrees. It was then he tried to push forward the tip of his tongue.

"How beautiful you are and how gentle and kind!"

His arm enfolded me still closer, my bosom pressed his shoulder. His hand pressed further and further up my stocking. I closed my knees resolutely. I gave a hurried glance around.

"Are we quite safe here, do you think?"

"Quite safe, and, as you see, quite alone."

Our lips met again. This time I kissed him boldly. The tip of his active tongue inserted itself between my moist lips.

"Ah! How lovely you are! How gloriously pretty!"

"Hush! They might hear us in the next carriage. I am frightened."

"You are deliciously sweet. I long for you dreadfully."

Mr. Turner's hand continued its efforts towards my knees. I relaxed my pressure a little. He reached

my garters above them. In doing so he uncovered
my ankles. He feasted his eyes on my calves daintily
set off in openwork stockings of a delicate shade of
pale brown.

"Oh, you are too bad, really! I ought not to let
you do that—no, really! Pray do not do so—oh!"

It was a delicious game of seduction. I enjoyed
his lecherous touches. He was constantly becoming
more confident of his sudden and uncontrollable
passion. He strained me to him. His breath came
quick and sweet upon my face. I lusted for this
man's embrace beyond all power of language to
convey. His warm hand reached my plump thigh. I
made pretence to prevent his advance.

"Pray—oh, pray do not do that! Oh!"

A sudden jerk as we apparently sped over some
points. I relaxed my resistance a trifle. He took instant advantage of the movement. His finger was
on the most sensitive part of my private parts. It
pressed upon my clitoris. I felt the little thing stiffen, swell and throb under the touch of a man's
hand. His excitement increased. He drew me even
closer. He pressed my warm body to his. His kisses,
hot and voluptuous, covered my face and neck.

"How divinely sweet you are! The perfume of
your lovely breath is so rapturously nice. Do let me
—do—do! I love you so!"

He held me tight with his left arm. He had withdrawn his right. I was conscious he was undoing his
trousers. He had left my skirts in disorder. I saw
him pull aside his protruding shirt. I secretly
watched his movements out of a corner of my eye
while he kept my face close to his. Then appeared
all that I had seen on the bathing machine, but

standing fiercely erect, red-headed and formidable
—a huge limb. He thrust it into full view.

"My darling! My beauty! See this! See! See
to what a state you have driven me. You will let
me—won't you?"

"Oh, for shame! Let me go—pray do not do that
—you must not. Your finger hurts. Don't—pray
don't! Oh, dear! Oh! Oh!"

The jolting of the carriage favoured his operations. His hand was again between my thighs. His
second finger pressed my throbbing button. My
parts were bedewed with the fluid begotten by
desire. He was inspecting the premises before
taking possession. I only hoped he would not find
the accommodation insufficient for so large a
tenant.

"Oh, pray don't! Oh, goodness! What a man you
are!"

With a sudden movement, he slipped round upon
his knees, passing one of my legs over his left arm
and thus thrust me back on the soft spring seat of
the carriage. He threw up my clothes. He was between my thighs. My belly and private parts were
exposed to his lascivious operations. I looked over
my dress as I attempted to right myself. I saw him
kneeling before me in the most indelicate position.
His trousers were open. His huge privates stood
menacingly before my eyes. He had so far loosened
his clothing that his testicles were out. His belly
was covered with crisp black hair. I saw all in that
quick feverish glance. I saw the dull red head of his
big limb drawn downward by the little string as it
faced me, and the slit-like opening through which
the men spurt their white venom.

He audaciously took my hand, gloved as it was, and placed it upon his member. It was hard and rigid as wood.

"Feel that—dear girl! Do not be frightened. I will not hurt you. Feel—feel my prick!"

He drew me forward. I felt him as requested. I had ceased all resistance. My willing little hand clasped the immense instrument he called his "prick."

"Now put it there yourself, little girl. It is longing to be into you."

"Oh—my good heavens! It will never go in! You will kill me!"

Nevertheless I assisted him to his enjoyment. I put the nut between the nether lips. He pushed while firmly holding me by both hips. My parts relaxed—my vagina adapted itself as I had been told it could without injury to the most formidable of male organs. The huge thing entered me. He thrust in fierce earnest. He got it fairly in.

"Oh! My God! I'm into you now! Oh! Oh! How delicious! Hold tight! Let me pull you down to me—so—oh! My God! How nice! How soft! How exquisite!"

I passed my left arm through the strap. My right clutched him round the neck. He put down his hand. He parted the strained lips round his huge intruding weapon. Then he seized me by the buttocks. He strained me towards him as he pushed. My head fell back—my lips parted. I felt his testicles rubbing close up between my legs. He was into me to the quick!

"Oh, dear! Dear! You are too rough! You hurt —you push too hard! My goodness me! How you are tearing me. Oh! Oh! Ah! It is too much! You darling man! Push! Push! Oh!"

It was too much pleasure. I threw my head back again. I grasped the cushions on either side. I could not speak. I could only gasp and whine now. I moved my head from side to side as he lay down on my belly and enjoyed me. His thing—stiff as a staff—worked up and down my vagina. I could feel the big plum-like gland pushed forcibly against my womb. I spent over and over again. I was in heaven.

He ground his teeth. He hissed. He lolled his head. He kissed me on the lips. He breathed hard and fast. His pleasure was delicious to witness.

"Oh! Oh! Hold tight, love. I am in an agony of pleasure. I—I—can't tell you! I—never—tasted—such delicious poking! Oh! Ugh!"

"Oh, dear! Oh, dear! You are so large! So strong!"

"Don't move! Don't pinch my prick more than you can help, darling girl. Let us go on as long as possible. You are coming again. I can feel you squeezing me! Oh! Wait a moment—so—hold still!"

"Oh! I can feel it at my womb—you are up to my waist! Oh, dear! Oh! Oh! You are so stiff!"

"I cannot hold much longer. I must spend soon!"

Bang! Bang!! Bang!!!

The train was passing over the points at Reigate. The alarm was sufficient to retard our climax. It acted as a check to his wild excitement—to the coming climax.

"Hold quite still, you sweet little beauty. We do not stop. The speed is quickening again. Now push! Push! Push! Is that nice? Do you like my big prick?

Does it stir you up? You are right, my sweet. I can feel your little womb with the tip."

He assisted me to throw my legs up over his shoulders. He seemed to enter me further than ever.

"Oh! You're so large! Oh! Good Lord! Go on slowly—don't finish me yet! It's so—so—so nice! You're making me come again. Oh my!"

"No, dear, I won't finish you before I can help it. You are so nice to poke slowly! Do you like being finished? Do you—oh, my God! There, push! Push! Do you like to feel a man come?"

"Oh! Not so hard! There! Oh, my! Must—must I tell you—I—I love to feel—to feel a man spend —all the sweet sperm!"

"You'll feel mine very—very soon, you beautiful little angel. Oh! I shall swim you in it! There! My prick is in now up to the balls—oh! Oh! How you nip it—oh!"

He gave some exquisite short stabs with his loins. His thing, as hard as wood, was up my belly as far as its great length could reach. He sank his head on my shoulder.

"Hold still—I'm spending! Oh, my God! How luscious!"

I felt a great gush come from him. It flowed from him in quick hot jets. He groaned in his ecstasy. I opened my legs. I raised up my loins to receive it. I clutched right and left at anything and everything—I spent furiously. He gave me a quantity. I was swimming in it. At length he desisted and released me.

A few minutes sufficed in which to rearrange ourselves decently. Mr. Turner asked me many questions. I fenced some——I answered others. I let him believe I was professionally employed in a provincial company. I told him I had been unwell and had been resting a short time at Eastbourne. He was delicate enough not to press for particulars, but he asked for an address. I gave him a country post office. In a few minutes more we stopped on the river bridge to deliver up tickets.

The train rolled into the station. My new friend made his *adieux*. He dexterously slipped two sovereigns into my glove as he squeezed my hand. I was glad. It proved the complete success of my precautions.

I hailed a hansom and drove direct to Swan and Edgar's. Outside the station, my cab stopped in the crowd. A poor woman thrust a skinny arm and hand towards me with an offer of a box of matches. I took them and substituted one of the sovereigns. As I alighted in Piccadilly, a ragged little urchin made a dash to turn back the door of my cab. He looked half starved.

"Have you a mother? How many brothers and sisters?"

"Six of us, lydy; muvver's out o' work."

"Take that home as quick as you can."

"Blimy! A thick 'un! There ain't no ruddy copper lookin' to pinch it off me! Muvver'll plant it away, so as 'ow favver won't have no cause to bash her for it."

He had never been taught to say "thank you." He took one hasty glance in either direction and darted away in the throng.

I discharged the cab. I made quite sure I was not followed.

Meanwhile my late companion was no doubt speeding on towards Manchester where he said he must dine that evening with Mrs. Turner. I hope the good lady was reasonable with her spouse.

I drove home. I found Mrs. Lockett ready to receive me. It was yet morning. I lunched alone. John was radiant with happiness.

"No more chicken, thank you, John. How is Robin? There are some ginger nuts for him in a bag on the hall table. You see I did not forget him."

"Thank you very much, miss. It's been very dull since you went away. Mrs. Lockett ain't very lively company. As for Robin, miss, he's been as sulky as possible; the poor thing is left quite alone. In the mornings he comes up the bedclothes and he stares me in the face, miss, as much as to ask where you've gone to. I'm ashamed to look at him."

"Poor dear! Why, John, how shocking! It's quite stiff now!"

I had only just tapped it with my finger tips through the red plush breeches. The unruly monster was already stretching itself down his plump thigh as its owner leant forward to pour me out a glass of wine. The door was shut. I let fly a button. My hand passed inside.

"Oh, John! It's shameful! It's bigger than ever!"

I gave a twist of the wrist. His fat member sprang out into view. I squeezed it as I examined the rubicund top.

What a beauty it was! The true perfection of

what such things ought to be. I pulled down the skin. I delighted to see the effect of my touches.

"He likes that, John, doesn't he? He seems to enjoy being stroked just like a tame cat."

"Yes, miss—puts up his back for it. You can almost hear him purr."

"You must not let him get too much excited. We will keep all that for tonight, John. I think we must let him out then, but you cannot be too cautious. Mrs. Lockett sleeps in the wing, doesn't she?"

"Yes, miss. She always turns the key of the door on the landing. A fine scraping it makes too when she locks it at night. The maid sleeps on the top floor. There is no one on your floor now, miss."

I made my arrangements. I finished my lunch. I dressed myself very plainly to go out. John called a cab. I drove straight to my bootmaker in Great Castle Street. Monsieur Dalmaine was not an ordinary bootmaker. He was an artist in boots. He only made for ladies, and his terms would be considered extravagant by the ordinary customer. His shop was small and unpretentious. Personally he was stout, short, and fair for a Frenchman. He might have been some eight and thirty. His wife kept the accounts and assisted him to collect them. His boots and shoes were not ordinary either. They were the perfection of his art. He took a real pride in them. The assiduity of the poor man to turn out boots to my satisfaction—and what appeared to be even of more importance, to his own—was sufficiently apparent. He was in the shop when I entered. Madame Dalmaine was out collecting accounts as usual of a Monday.

"Good morning, Monsieur Dalmaine. Are my

boots, *couleur crème*, ready? Have you completed the slight alterations to the *bleu pâle* lace boots?"

"Both are at your service now, miss. I will try them on if you will step into the showroom."

There was a small well-arranged room behind the shop with several glass cases. In these were deposited boots which had been made for celebrities. They were by no means old or worn, but this extraordinary man had obtained them from the ladies in question after they had only served on a single occasion. Monsieur Dalmaine persisted that they did not please him. He thereupon supplied a second pair. He retained the first for his *musée*—as he called it.

I sat myself in the easy chair in which he fitted all his lady customers. It was a great event if he made a pair of boots in a fortnight. He had, however, prepared mine considerably within that period. He brought out both pairs. He held them up. He turned them about. His keen little grey eyes sparkled with evident delight.

"*Les voilà, mademoiselle!* But they are superb! It is not often that I make for so beautiful a foot. *Mon Dieu!* One would say the foot of *mademoiselle* had been sculptured by Canova himself. It is a study."

He knelt before me. He placed my foot in its openwork silk stocking upon his knee. He gave one affectionate look at this object. He cast another at his work. He then proceeded to fit the artistic little boot in its place. Several times he inserted my foot. As often he withdrew the boot for some trifling adjustment. I tired of his minuteness. I amused myself in worrying the good man by avoiding his grasp. Sometimes I slipped my glossy, silk-covered little foot on one side—sometimes on the other. At last it slid from the approaching boot and was jerked between his thighs. There it alighted on the muscular development of Monsieur Dalmaine's most private personal effects. I distinctly felt a something pulsate beneath my toes. The artist in ladies' boots flushed. He was arranging the lace of the new *chaussure*.

"Please give it to me, Monsieur Dalmaine. I have not yet examined it myself. Is not the toe a little more pointed than usual? You know I do not wear those hideously impossible toes to my boots."

He handed it up, holding my ankle as he did so. I rubbed my wicked foot a little very gently against his person as I took it from his hand. At the same time, the man must have seen the half comical, half lecherous glance with which I met his eye. A sudden inspiration almost overwhelmed me. This artist *cordonnier* was a victim to his own creations!

He had fallen in love with his own work, like Pygmalion with his statue. The discovery set me on fire at once. What joy to play on this man's weakness! I allowed him to fit on the boot. He smoothed down the yielding kid as it glistened with its soft sheen on my foot, the perfection of *chaussage*—the delicate leg which attracted so many followers. His eyes followed his nervous fingers. His lips moved as though he longed, yet dared not extend his too evident fascination into an actual embrace. I pushed my toe again towards his person. The quick blood of the nervous Frenchman was evidently stirred. There was an unmistakable enlargement in the region of his trouble. My warm foot did not let it subside. I was conscious of a certain throbbing against the sole of my foot.

"How long have you been in business? Monsieur Dalmaine, you have evidently a passion for your art. You are not like the ordinary shoemaker."

"No, *mademoiselle*, I am not so. I am a man different. I am one man by myself. No other man understands me. Sometimes a lady she comes to me. I make the boots for her. I fit them to her. She like my work—she come again. More work—more boots. But—oh, no! She comprehends not. She know not my heart!"

Monsieur Dalmaine pressed his hand upon the article in question—or as near to it as he could get. He bowed his head with its light curly hair over my legs as he knelt in the pursuits of his calling. His air was patient—if not pathetic. It seemed to say, "I suffer—I am content to suffer."

"What is the matter with your heart then? Is it so very susceptible? Or is it really a matter for a physician?"

"Ah, *mademoiselle*, can you ask? Can you doubt?"

My active toes were tickling gently all the time between his legs, where something very like a cucumber had gradually developed itself within the folds of his clothing.

"I am afraid your art is too much for you. You are too much engrossed with fitting the ladies. Why not work for the men?"

"The men? Me! Dalmaine make boots for the beasts? I am not a *maréchal-ferrant*! What you call him? Farrier? I do not make shoes for the horses!

Mon Dieu! When I no longer make the *chaussures des dames* I die! I go dead! I inspire—direct!"

In the agony of his desolation, good Monsieur Dalmaine had seized my foot and ankle in his nervous grasp. He even emphasised his anguish by raising my leg so that a portion of my calf was visible. I laughed so heartily that his confusion became even greater. Raising my other foot, I almost pushed him backwards in my assumed merriment. Thus he had a chance of a private view certainly not calculated to calm his excitement. His features proclaimed his delight. A sudden look of sensual longing spread over them as he saw my brown-stockinged legs. I let him enjoy the exhibition as long as he liked. My foot was all the time in contact with the cucumber. At last he could stand it no longer. He put down his hand. He himself pressed my little foot upon the sensitive spot.

"Ah! *Mon Dieu!* You are the most beautiful young lady I make for! You do not know what you make me suffer. When I see—when I feel these lovely little boots, I am mad—I am mad! When I make them I have pleasure! When I see them on your beautiful feet, I go crack!"

I did not reply in words. I only raised my foot to his face as he knelt. He seized it again. He covered it with kisses. His white apron had slipped on one side. The violent erection of his limb was plainly visible in his loose blue cotton trousers. From the position he occupied I am sure he could see above my garters. I made no scruple in encouraging his passion.

"Poor Monsieur Dalmaine! Are you so very bad?"

"Oh, you most beautiful! I must fook with you—
or burst. Oh, dear! Oh, dear!"

"I should be sorry to make you suffer. Will it do
you good, do you think?"

"I must fook you—I must fook! You are the
angel of my dreams, I must—*il faut que je m'assou-
visse avant de mourir!*"

His whole being quivered with excitement as he
knelt, his hands convulsively clasping my ankles as I
reclined in his *fauteuil*.

"Are we quite sure not to be disturbed? Poor
Monsieur Dalmaine, you shall not be disappointed.
Only be prudent. Pray do not hold my legs so high!
How dreadfully indecent! Oh, really!"

"But first I must taste of your sweet *parfum*—
of your essence divine. I must enjoy! Oh, yes! Oh,
yes! My beautiful young lady! I have wanted you
for a long time! Now! Now!"

In another instant he had separated my legs.
Plunging forward, he inserted his head between.
He forcibly opened a passage. Before I could op-
pose any resistance to his attack—even had I been
so inclined—his face was upon my naked thighs.
He pressed forward. In pretending to protect myself, I assisted his design. With a stifled cry of
bestial delight, he covered my parts with his lips.
He drove in his long hot tongue. I felt him sucking
my clitoris with all the fury of a satyr. The taste—
the perfume appeared to drive him to a perfect
frenzy. Finding no further resistance, he clasped me
round the loins. He continued his salacious gratification, steeping his mouth in the amorous secretion
with which I liberally dosed him. I was almost beside myself with the pleasure he was giving me. I

spent continually. Presently his right hand released me. I guessed his object. He raised himself from his recumbent position but without quitting his vantage ground. His face was red and inflamed with lust. Raging desire had taken possession of the man. I had led him on. It was not in my power to stay it now. I had not long to wait. He tore open the front of his trousers. I saw his limb fiercely erect—red-capped and ready to do its work. The lewd sight destroyed what little remained of prudence. He threw himself upon my willing body. I raised myself to favor his assault. We neither spoke, but with a great gasp of acute delight I felt the stiff insertion of the Frenchman's long member into my parts.

Monsieur Dalmaine went to work at once. He was so fiercely charged with unappeased desire that he made haste to quench his passion upon me. In the midst of his desperate thrusts he took care to seize one of my feet in either hand. He thus had me at his mercy. I felt his desperate movements within my belly where his limb was pushed as far as its great length could carry it. It was perfectly strong and rigid. I enjoyed the act as much as he did. All too soon I knew he was about to discharge. He spent in a burst of semen which overflowed my parts. He sank groaning upon my bosom.

"Oh! Monsieur Dalmaine, is this what you call 'going crack'?"

Chapter II

Our reduced establishment closed early. By eleven
o'clock all the inmates had retired for the night.
Mrs. Lockett was heard to shut and turn the key. I
thoroughly believe John had purposely rusted that
lock. Sometimes a drop of salt water is as useful as
oil—but in a contrary sense. At midnight the mansion was wrapped in slumber—all save John and I.
At a quarter past twelve I admitted the footman.
I lay with him that night. He entered noiselessly.
He had on felt slippers. I had thought of all. We
were absolutely safe and alone. It was delicious to
feel free to gratify all one's voluptuous inclinations
and indulge without restraint all one's libidinous
ideas and conceptions. One great advantage was
that, under the circumstances, my stallion—for so I
considered him—could mount me—neigh and whin-
ny without fear and to his heart's content. My
greedy nerves vibrated as I closed the door of my
chamber after the impatient fellow. I motioned him
to a seat. He submitted with the prompt obedience
of a well-trained menial. We neither of us spoke.

He watched me as I undressed. I intentionally afforded him a delicious prospect. I saw his hands clench—his lips quiver—his nostrils dilate as he took in all the points I wantonly exposed for his intoxication. I let fall my skirts. I stood in my *chemise*, my stockings, and my corset. His greedy eyes followed every movement. I knew I was working the man into a state of almost unendurable longing. It was delightful to me. I grew excited beyond measure. I watched the keen, fierce, lecherous spirit overpowering all reserve—all prudence. I threw myself upon the large soft couch.

"John, you may undress. I want to see you naked."

It had pleased me to act the school miss in my intercourse with this man. It seemed to come natural to me. It served as a silly excuse for my precocious wantonness. It assuaged my *amour propre*. It gave me unbounded confidence in my character of an innocent led astray by the blandishments of a good-looking, full-grown man. John's natural vanity did the rest. To him I was the condescending young lady of the house seduced by his modest behaviour, his rich livery. Above all by his manly proportions and his capacity for affording her sensuous delight.

I therefore looked on while John cast off his coat and divested himself of his striped waistcoat, depositing both within the room adjoining. Then came the turn of his scarlet breeches. I smiled at the semi-modest, stupid air with which he let them fall. My mouth watered and my lips parted at the sight of his erected limb, his hairy belly, as his shirt flew up.

"Come here, John. I want to feel your Robin."

In another second, my stallion was beside me. My eager hand closed around his huge member. I shook it. I caressed it. I lowered my head. I sucked it. It was delicious to my overwrought nerves. I took his big testicles in my grasp. I played with them.

"How shall we do it, John?"

"You'll let me do the job for you this time—won't you, miss? Right into you, I mean, miss. I'll do it beautiful! You'll feel as if you were in heaven when Robin is pushing himself up and down your beautiful little belly. It's all very well against the door, standing up, but lying down with your sweet legs open, he goes at it so free. He seems to get up almost to your waist, miss."

As if to give point to his argument, the rampant fellow opened my thighs. His face went between; his eager tongue inserted itself in my moist slit. I was in no humour to refuse him anything. I bore down on his thick, sensual lips. The scenes of the past day came back to me. They passed as in a panorama before my closed eyes. John luxuriated in his prurient employment. I seemed to be exhaling for his delight the concentrated essence of previous luxury. The thought added poignancy to the sensations he forced upon me. I shivered with ecstasy.

"Oh, John—dear John—you are making me come!"

The delighted footman revelled in the solution of bygone pleasures with which I now liberally bedewed him. I rose to my feet. I beheld his strong member, red-headed, stiff as a bar of metal, menacing an onslaught upon my delicate person. I saw him gloating over my naked slit.

"Hush, John! Whisper only. How shall we do it, dear John?"

He clasped me to him. He pressed his big hairy chest to my tender form. He carried me towards the bed. He sat me on it.

"Oh, miss, do let me do it so. Let me put it into you. See how stiff I am. It's bursting, nearly. It's so full of the white stuff you are so fond of."

"So, John—on the side of the bed. Now push it into me—oh! Oh! How big you are, John! Oh! Oh! Go slowly—it hurts! Oh!"

Huge as it was, the thing went in—up me, till I felt the two big testicles pressed against my bottom. My stallion was at work upon me. The lewd fellow lolled back his head. He rolled his eyes in his luxury. His hands clutched nervously at my haunches as he pulled me toward him. Then he thrust slowly in and out—up and down in my little belly where he had said he longed to be.

I love to look on a man in this condition, filled with a bestial sense of desire unappeased, struggling in his libidinous embrace, his eyes turned up and vacuous, or burning with fierce lust at the contemplation of the object of his passion extended and at his mercy beneath him. The picture is a delicately delicious one to my luxurious temperament—it enhances enormously my own enjoyment. It is the sacrifice of modesty upon the altar of lust—it is the reversal of all that is reserved, becoming, and dignified. It is its enormity which is its charm. It is its utter abnegation of personal respect, the prostitution of virtue to vulgar passion which is its fascination.

The enjoyment of my poor John, alas, came to

its end as all things must. It grew too poignant to last and it burst. I was the recipient of his exhaustive efforts. He left me bathed in his erotic efforts to my intense enjoyment, and to his loss.

⁂

"A telegram for you, Miss Eveline. I would not disturb you sooner. Fanny told me you had given orders not to be awakened."

"Oh, thank you, Mrs. Lockett; but I have been awake already a couple of hours. I have even had my tub, as you see."

I tore open the telegram. It was from Eastbourne—from Percy.

"Mother has suffered a fresh attack, is extremely unwell. Lord L—— desires you to remain. Await further news."

The "further news" arrived an hour later. I had anticipated. It was from the local medical practitioner.

"Lord L—— desires me to inform you that Lady L—— succumbed at three o'clock this morning. He is much distressed but is writing particulars. He begs you to be calm."

I pass over those particulars. They have no place here. Enough that Lady L—— had paid the inevitable penalty of her folly and that poor papa was free. Sippett lost a profitable employment. I was told that her luggage was heavy and voluminous when she went away.

"A gentleman to see you, miss. He says he has

come on business. I told him you could see no one but he insisted—here is his card."

"Mr. William Dragon, Bow Street. Quite right, John. I will see this gentleman. Show him into Lord L——'s study. I will come up directly."

The blinds were down. The house had already assumed the usual hypocritical, dolorous, and lack-adaisical appearance of society grief. At such times one receives odd visitors—always on business, of course. It was not yet ten o'clock. The situation was already quite conventional. Everyone went about their duties as usual, only they spoke lower and whispered, and looked solemn instead of simpering.

"I should not have called, but that I thought I could do so without fear under present circumstances. I was already in the street and on my errand when the boy left the first telegram. We had the news at six this morning direct to Bow Street."

"I am sure you are very good and you would not have come unless for some useful object. I feel bewildered."

"I know—I know. Do not trouble to explain. I only want to caution you. Of course, I know your position is a little—just a little—difficult. Take my advice—will you? That's right. I knew you would —for it is honest. Do not delay your marriage. Listen to me: I told you—little Beauty—once, not long ago, your fortune lay at your feet. You had only to stoop and win it. It lies so still. But you must act."

"How do you mean? What must I do?"

Dragon looked cautiously round. He even closed the slide over the keyhole. He waited a moment and listened acutely.

"I know much more than you think. Your groom is not to be trusted. Young men are vain and they boast. He is steady, but he is no better than his fellows. You have elected to pick up what lay at your feet. Another trouble may arise. Women are plotting. They are devils when they are jealous. Do not delay on account of what has happened. Try to shorten the time. Lord Endover is surrounded by interested toadies. Women are there in his councils also. You are safe yet. Strike the iron while it is hot; you know what I mean. Do not give him time to let them get at him. They will ruin you if they can."

He looked at me appealingly. His manner was most respectful.

"I really hardly see—and yet—I know you are good and honest in what you say. Frankly, I will take your advice. You frighten me. I thought I was so safe—so guarded."

"So you are *as yet*. That is why I have come to reassure you and to caution you. I know all that passes about Endover. Take my advice. And now good bye. Look all the facts in the face and— *marry him quick!*"

Dragon rose. He bowed with an almost mock solemnity which had its significance. In another moment he was gone.

The day passed wearily enough. In the afternoon, Lord Endover called. He was all sympathy and condolence. His passion was obviously at its zenith. He regarded me evidently as the object of his most cherished desires. The position was difficult. I told him I had not yet seen my papa. I would consult him. My *fiancé* was evidently alarmed lest a long delay should be added to his probation. I did my best to reassure him. He quitted me in better spirits. He had my permission to return the day following. I told him he was welcome. I said I desired his companionship and his advice. He left me much pleased and flattered.

I passed the evening with Mrs. Lockett. She brought her needlework to my sitting room. At an early hour I retired to rest. She supplied the place of my maid. I had never known the tender offices of a mother. I was grateful for her sympathy. I cried myself to sleep.

When I rose next morning, I had resolved all my difficulties. I had made my plans. I prepared to put them into execution.

For malignity there is no expression to equal the intensity of the simple pronoun "she," hissed through the lips in an undertone when a woman speaks of another member of her sex behind her back. It seems to convey not only the absence of all respect, but the full measure of contempt which the utterer can bring to bear on an absent, and possibly an innocent acquaintance.

I felt I was being discussed, and probably in quarters where I desired to appear at my best. I felt quite equal to the emergency, but there was no time to be lost. I resolved to act at once. Thanks to Dragon, I was warned and therefore armed.

"Ah! What a pleasure, I never expected to see you, my lovely one, this morning—and so early too! Why, business has been so dull lately that I have closed quite early. The season is a lot too good for us doctors; no colds, no bronchitis! What is London coming to? But you look anxious and not quite so well as usual."

"Well, I am very glad to see you, all the same. I am not quite so well perhaps as usual. I have had bad news. No, do not ask me about it. You remember our compact. It is because I rely on your word of honour that I am here. I want your advice. I have lost a relative, but that is not the immediate cause of my visit. It has raised complications. I am uncertain what to do for the best."

My tall, fair, young disciple of Aesculapius consigned the care of the establishment to his lad. He ushered me into his back parlour with a look of radiant delight on his handsome face.

"Now, my beautiful! Tell me how I can be of use. I am entirely at your service. I hope the matter is not very grave. You look weary."

"You remember the conclusions you arrived at with regard to the difficulty in the way of—of— well, I need not be reserved with you, my friend— I mean in the way of my conception?"

"Certainly I do, and I am still of that opinion. I am absolutely certain that every physician who took the same pains in the examination and who was proficient in his practice would confirm them."

"Then you are still sure that I could not bear a child to my husband if I married?"

"Quite sure—nor, for the matter of that, to anyone else."

"But that if I submitted myself to an operation —a slight operation—in that case, I should have the same chance as other healthy young women?"

"Exactly so. I believe more than an even chance, because you are so beautifully—so perfectly formed. Without going into professional particulars, let me tell you: You should sit for a friend of mine who is an artist, as our mother Eve, for your figure is the perfection of all that is desirable for the procreation of the race."

"Oh, you wicked serpent! But seriously, is that your solemn declaration? Much may depend upon your reply."

"It is, my Eve, my most serious opinion, which you may have confirmed any day you please."

He had placed me in his easy chair. He now came and sat beside me. His face wore an anxious and dejected look.

"So you are going to be married. I might have guessed so beautiful a young girl with so much self-possession, forgive me for saying so, with so much force of character, would not be long without a choice of husbands."

"You may be right, but what then? We are already very good friends."

"There, my darling, we are good friends, and if I could think—well, let me explain. If you would not give me up altogether, but if you would come to me sometimes, I—well, I should not be jealous."

I felt piqued. I hardly knew why. He seemed almost to catch at the idea of my marrying as something to be desired, and yet he was not at his ease. He waited a moment. He evidently saw my perplexity. Then he continued:

"To be plain with you, my sweet little friend, you are the most delicious girl I ever had in all my life. I have always had a fancy for married women.

If only you were really married you would drive me
mad with lust to enjoy you. Your enchantment
would simply be doubled."

"Is that so? If that is your whim, I will not fail
to gratify it. You shall have me all to yourself as
soon after I am married as I can contrive it. Are
you satisfied?"

He took me in his arms. He became furiously indecent. His face, his voice, his movements all united
to betray the desire which raged within him.

"Oh, my darling, my love! You have given me
such pleasure. You promise me? You will? You
will let me have you first after your marriage?"

"I promise!"

We were standing face to face. He pushed me towards the wall. He pressed himself lewdly upon
me. He covered my face with hot kisses and took
me in his arms. In a second his trousers were open
and my hand closed on his limb.

"Oh, how stiff you are! What a size! Do you really like married women? Are they so nice? Is it a
part of your enjoyment to know you are committing a real adultery?"

"It is horribly—awfully delicious to enjoy a married woman. Your promise maddens me. I consider
you are one already. Come, let me have you! I
must! I want you so bad! What lovely legs! Don't
try to stop my hand! Oh, yes, skin back my thing.
That is so nice, your fingers are so warm and soft.
Kiss—kiss me! Give me your tongue. You would
like to suck it? So then—take it between your
pretty lips. What a stupid fool your husband must
be! I am going to spend into his wife's belly."

He seized me in his arms. He lifted me panting,

my lips exhaling the ambrosia of his huge tool. He laid me on the sofa. He was evidently madly excited with his strange, lecherous idea. I determined to encourage it.

"But what would he say? I am his property now. I cannot really let you abuse me. Oh, stop! Fie, take your hand away! Oh! You are so strong—so cruel to me."

He forced me down. He pressed his long and powerful form upon me. My thighs were easily parted. His stiff limb wagged between them. I felt him divide the moist lips. The next moment he was into me.

"Oh, Christ! What a lovely girl you are! How tight it is! There! There! Now take it quite in! Does that please you? Is that better than your husband's? What a fool! What an idiot! I'm going to spend into his wife!"

"Oh, shameful! Let me go—you must not finish! Take it out! What would he say! Don't you know you are committing adultery?"

"Yes, that's it! Adultery! Oh, how tight you are, my little married friend! No—I shall not take it out! I shall spend into you—do you hear? Right up into your delicious little womb."

"Oh, my poor husband! You are killing me with your great thing! What will he say? Oh! Oh! You are going to spend! You are coming! Oh—oh—so —so—am I! Oh! The syringe! Oh! What a stream! Oh! Oh!"

A few hours later, my wedding was fixed to take place within three months. Lord Endover left me in a transport of pleasure. He declared his intention to come very frequently if I would allow him to do so. I was most amiable. He received every assurance of my affectionate consideration.

I think I have already demonstrated that I am a hypocrite. Society obliges everyone to be a hypocrite. The difference is only in degree; the necessity is universal. I never care to do things by halves. I am therefore a very great hypocrite. The higher your position in society, the more consummate must be your hypocrisy. The attribute begins with the highest. Is not every evasion of the truth a smooth —a plausible hypocrisy? Nobody believes it all the same; that is the strangest part of it. It is offered and accepted. Everybody excuses it, weighs it at its own fictitious value, and passes it on. "Tell the truth and shame the devil"—that somewhat shabby proverb goes a certain way. I almost think, after a careful study of the subject, that society would be more ashamed, in spite of its usual disregard of that sentiment, *if it had to tell the truth*. Weighing one opinion with the other, I fancy His Satanic Majesty is decidedly in the background. He could set to work to render his own society so much more select if he only would—there being so much material to choose from. A just sense of the value of hypocrisy, of its judicious use, its employment, is absolutely necessary if you would shine in the flickering light of society. Yet I am not afraid of criticism. I defy criticism to do me any harm. It could certainly not do me any good. No more than Marie Corelli herself. But I have no necessity to rack my brains to produce demons and divinities. I find, in my exalted position, enough of both in society itself. I meet in every *salon*, in every boudoir, the saintly canon who cannot keep his fingers off his choristers; the elderly lordling who apes the vices of a Domitian or a Nero; the minister of religion who ministers to the lambs of his flock in more senses than one; and the blatant, pretentious man about town who divides his attention between his exaggerated shirt collar and his simpering partner. He would delight to be "the very devil himself," if he only knew how! There, too, are the lonely, loving hearts, who in that never resting vortex watch long and sadly for the coming of the one they dreamed of in days now gone, or who mourn unceasingly the one who will never return—whose hope never flags, whose faith is intact beneath the false mask they must wear—who will be as content as I shall be to give up all—to submit to the inevitable when it comes.

Chapter III

"At last I have my darling girl again with me! It has been a terrible time, my dear Eveline. You were quite right to remain in town as I directed."

"My dear papa had only to express his wishes. Eveline is always ready to gratify them."

"I hope you got on well here in this lonely house, dear child."

"Yes, papa. Mrs. Lockett was very sympathetic. John got on too very nicely. I managed to keep things together. We felt it acutely."

Over a week had passed since the news had been telegraphed to me. All was now over. The house had resumed its wonted appearance. Lord L—— had returned. Percy was at the Depôt. Only our sombre costumes which conventional habits enjoin betrayed to outsiders the changes which had taken place so recently.

"You have brought Johnson back with you, papa, of course? How is Goorkha? Does he look after him? Do you know, papa, I am not overly pleased with Jim, as you call him."

"Why so, Eveline? I thought he was rather a favourite with you."

"Yes—well, so he was—but to tell the truth, I mistrust that young man Johnson. I believe he is inquisitive. I had occasion more than once to be careful when you and I were riding together, dear papa. He tries to overhear our conversation. I am sure of it."

"Is that so? Then Jim must go!"

"Did I not see your old friend, Sir Currie Fowles, was going out to take up his new appointment in Madras?"

"By Jove, yes! And he asked me to find him a groom to take out with him. He knows I am like him, averse to natives and prefer an Englishman in charge of my stables in India, so he came to me. Johnson would suit him exactly. I will see to this at once."

Ten days later Jim was tending horses on board a P. and O. mail steamer in the Red Sea, as head groom to the new Vice-President of Madras. He received a considerable advance in wages. I was well rid of him.

We sat close together. We spoke of the future. I explained the arrangement for my wedding and told Lord L—— the date I had fixed. He willingly assented to all. He said it had his entire approval, and that Lord Endover had already written to him on the subject. We could not help feeling that we were now more than ever thrown together. The sentiment of mutual confidence had become riveted between us. There was just a touch of sadness in his voice as he spoke of my forthcoming marriage. I thought I detected a certain feeling of jealousy in it which pained me.

"We shall always be the same to each other as

we are, dear papa, shall we not? Nothing shall ever change your little girl as regards her love for you, dear."

"My only anxiety is that no harm may befall you, my dearest child, no awkward *contretemps* take place before your future is assured."

"Have no fear on that account, darling papa. All is quite safe and will continue so."

"Where are you going, Eveline? That black silk bodice and the lace become you charmingly."

"I was going to my bootmaker, dear papa. I want some more black kid boots."

"Extravagant little puss! Why those you are wearing are lovely!"

"Do you like them? See—they do not fit badly—what do you think?"

I turned my foot about to show him. I raised my skirt sufficiently to exhibit my dainty calf in its glistening silk stocking as well.

"By heaven, my dear child, you tempt me frightfully!"

He caught me in his arms. He sat me on his knee. With trembling hand he fondled both boot and leg. Our lips met in a long, hot embrace.

"What is to stop you, dear papa? Certainly not your Eveline!"

His excitement increased. We were safe in his room. I was sure of him now. I wanted it so badly. He could read the flames of lust in my eyes. He drew me still closer. I put my hand on his trousers. His limb was quite stiff. It was so long since I had felt it—so long since it had had any enjoyment. His pent-up passion betrayed itself in every muscle of his face—in every movement of his nervous frame.

He put me off his knee and stood before me.

"Oh, Eveline, my child—I must have you at once. We have a good chance. Oh, my God! How I long for your enjoyment; how I pant for the pleasure we shall give each other!"

His passion rose as he spoke. He threw his arms about me. I unbuttoned his trousers. I caressed his handsome limb in my new black kid glove. Papa glared at the lewd spectacle as my little hand moved slowly up and down the standing object in my grasp.

"Is this dear thing so bad, dear papa? Eveline will comfort it. It shall have all the delight it wants. We are alone. Let us do all that will give us the most pleasure."

I put my lips to his ear. I whispered so indecent an invitation that with a low growl of lascivious frenzy he bore me towards the sofa and raised my clothes. I fell backwards. He fell upon me. I was all aswim with longing for the incestuous encounter. I guided the shiny knob of his thing to my eager parts. The strong and erected instrument slipped voluptuously into me. He positively foamed at the mouth in his agony of enjoyment. For a few seconds no sound was heard save his stentorian breathing and the rustle of my black silk dress. My spasms became delicious. My womb seemed to open to him invitingly. His limb hardened throughout its length. He discharged with a low groan of rapture. I received every drop of his thick seed—the seed of which I was mad. When he retired I kissed off the slippery exuberance of his spendings from the drooping head of his limb. I rearranged the disorder of my condition, baptised as I was in his rich sperm. I made my preparations to go out. I went alone. The cab set me down at the corner of Great Castle Street. I entered the shop of Monsieur Dalmaine. I had made an appointment with the *artiste*.

"Good morning, Monsieur Dalmaine. Are my new boots ready?"

"But certainly, *mademoiselle*! Am I not always of the most exact; besides how could I keep waiting my most beautiful client?"

"Let us try them then."

He led me into his back room, beyond which was his *atelier*. I seated myself in the large chair. Dalmaine produced the boots from a glass case. He held both pairs up for my inspection. His little eyes danced with pleasure as he scrutinised the glossy black *peau de chevreuil* and the exquisite work of his skilled assistants.

"They appear perfect. I trust they are not too tight. Not like *souliers de vingt-cinq*—you know, monsieur."

"They are the correct fit for your lovely foot, *mademoiselle*. I know not your *souliers de vingt-cinq*. What are they?"

"They are *neuf et treize et trois*, Monsieur Dalmaine; consequently they are *vingt-cinq*."

"Ah, *mon Dieu!* Now only do I discover you! It is too good! *Neuf et très étroit! Mais c'est splendide!*"

He sank down at my feet. He removed my boot. He inserted my toe into the new one. I pushed my other foot against his apron. The cucumber was already in evidence. I could feel its magnificent proportions. Meanwhile without noticing my proceed-

ing the Artist in Ladies' Boots became wholly absorbed in regarding the elegance and the delicate
fit of his darling study. He no sooner had my foot
in, than he commenced the lacing in the most exact
manner, his face beaming with smiles as he drew
the silk cords together. Not a sign escaped him to
show that I had ever permitted any undue familiarity. Nothing marked his conduct beyond the most
respectful attention to do credit to his employment.

"I think you had better put on the other boot
also, please, so as to make sure there is nothing
amiss."

He trembled with delight as he beheld the pair
invested duly into office. He moulded them. He fondled them alternately. I pushed my right foot towards the cucumber, now evidently getting beyond
control.

"Ah, *chère mademoiselle,* it is too much! You
make me so bad! It is not possible to resist. You are
so beautiful."

He pushed his hand up my leg. He lost suddenly
all his reserve. His other hand was engaged in re-
leasing his member. He turned up my dress as carefully as if he was my own maid. I saw him fix his
gaze upon my thighs. His fingers pressed on higher
yet. He met with no restraint. Suddenly he bent forward, his face pressed upon my naked legs. He
pushed on until his head was quite buried beneath
my clothes. He found his way to the central spot of
his desires. I felt him seize on the coveted spot with
an exclamation of rapture. I pressed his naked limb
between my feet. I parted my legs to give him room.
His large tongue was now rolling upon and around
my clitoris, already excited and swollen with the

previous exercise papa had given it. He gave me delicious pleasure. I pressed down upon him, continually responding to his amorous caresses with renewed effusions. At length I drew back. He raised his streaming lips. He pulled aside his white apron. I saw his huge member, red-capped and shining, stiff as a bar of ivory, distended in front of him.

I gloated on the luscious morsel before me. It resembled John's. It was just as handsome. I seized on it—I fingered it all about.

"Stand up—it is my turn now."

The excited *artiste* obeyed only too willingly. The stiff limb was within a few inches of my face. I examined it thoroughly. I pressed back the thick white covering skin which lay around the glistening head.

"So this is what you go 'crack' with, Monsieur Dalmaine?"

He was apparently too engrossed to reply. He glanced toward the shop door. He saw that the bolt was shot. All was quiet. He smiled.

I imprinted a moist kiss just on the little opening in the head.

"*Oh, mon Dieu, mademoiselle!* You will drive me to the mad!"

I repeated those moist kisses; my pointed tongue even took part in the salacious game. The cucumber acknowledged my condescension by stretching its warm length eagerly for my caresses.

I delighted to watch the voluptuous effects upon my companion. I continued my kisses—my tickling touches—I worked my little hands in unison.

With the unerring instinct of his countrymen, the Frenchman divined my intention. He still further loosened his clothing and drew back his shirt and trousers. He exposed his belly—his thick bush of hair—his large testicles. closely drawn up beneath his standing member. I noted all. I determined to gratify him to the utmost. My whole being vibrated with prurient exultation at the delicious prospect. He pushed his loins forward. My lips opened—they engulfed the head of his limb.

"*Ah, quel plaisir!* You are giving me the pleasure celestial!"

The contact, the pressure, the suction of my lips seemed to madden him to frenzy. To say that he enjoyed conveys but a faint idea of his condition. His eyes were half closed or fixed alternately on my face. His breath came in gasping sobs. He was acutely sensible of the delicious friction I was providing for him. I continued my voluptuous task. He replied by gentle pushes which served to thrust his stiff limb backwards and forwards on my palate. The hollow beneath the ruby nut rested upon my tongue. My fingers worked continuously along the white shaft. I stopped suddenly. I drew back. It was the pleasure of anticipation on both sides. I looked on the throbbing limb close to my lips.

"Do you like that? Is it nice? Shall I recommence?"

"Ah, *mademoiselle*, you are so kind! You give me such pleasure."

"Would you like to finish like that?"

"Ah! But yes, sweet *mademoiselle*. Make me to finish in your lovely mouth."

"Oh! You shockingly naughty man! What! You want to make that thing finish in a young lady's mouth?"

"Yes, oh, yes! I will give you great pleasure also!"

"You have already afforded me pleasure. If this pleases you let us recommence. I am ready to gratify you."

"Ah, mon Dieu! I shall be quick! I shall have the pleasure of the Gods immortal—oh!"

Even as he spoke he pushed the broad head of his thing between my lips. I sucked it voraciously while my gloved hands caressed and stroked the shaft.

Dalmaine bent forward. He placed his hands on the back of the easy chair. I took in all I could manage of his big member. The game was too good to last long. He gave a little cry. He pushed forward. The next instant my mouth and throat were filled with a flood of sperm. I was greedy. The hot spurts followed each other in quick succession until all was over. I rejected nothing. We had mutually gratified each other's perverted instinct.

It rained for the best part of two days. London was out of season. Only the necessity of making preparations for my approaching nuptials kept Lord L—— and myself in town. I began to feel that insupportable *ennui* and lassitude which cause one to fly to almost any distraction to escape from it. Papa remarked my dejection. He attributed it to the right cause. He was always shrewd and careful of me. Divining a means of relief he hastened to make his proposition.

"You remember, my darling Eveline, our conversation at Eastbourne, when I proposed a pleasure of unusual sensuous delight?"

"Oh, yes, dear papa, certainly I do. Only our preoccupation has prevented my curiosity from becoming importunate. When is it to be? When am I to make this new experience?"

"We have nothing to do in particular this evening, dear child. I propose we spend it in the indulgence of this pleasure."

"Oh, papa! That would be lovely! To tell the truth I am dreadfully dull and ready for anything. Besides you told me it was physic for me!"

"So be it then! We will dine half an hour earlier and sally out together. All can be in readiness. I will complete the necessary arrangements at once."

"Dear, kind papa! You are always thinking for your little, loving Eveline. You are dull too, and not looking so well as usual."

"We will have a dose of sensuality that will rouse us both."

"Indeed it will! I already feel better. I will go and put on my most enticing things to please my dear papa."

I had time to make my toilet before the afternoon tea was served. John brought it in. Lord L—— had gone out. I well knew his errand. The footman shut the shutters, drew down the blinds, and placed a chair at the table for my convenience. The door was shut. We were all alone.

"It is three whole days since you noticed poor Robin, Miss Eveline."

"So it is, John. Bring him here—pull him out."

In another second John had his limb out. It showed white and red against the black hair on his

belly. It was half erect already. The perfume of the
male organ began to excite my senses. I laid hold of
it. I kissed it—I sucked it for a moment. It rose superb and rampant at the contact of my warm lips.
Then I stopped.

"Not now, dear John. Perhaps tonight or tomorrow night upstairs I will give you a chance. I am
not in the humour now."

The man looked disappointed. I thought him
even surly. It occurred to me whether I was wise to
continue this *liaison*. Was it not time to break it off?
Mischief might come of it.

John put away his unhappy Robin. He buttoned
his plush breeches. I thought I caught the muttered
words, "a reason for that, perhaps," as he left the
room.

Lord L—— returned in excellent time for dinner. I could see by his cheerful manner that he had
reasons to be content with himself and his mission.

"All is arranged and will be ready. We will be as
secret as the stones of Troy."

"Where are we going, dear papa?"

"You will see all in good time! How ravishing
you look, Eveline!"

I wore a black satin bodice and skirt trimmed
with black lace, somewhat open in front and ex-
posing the upper roundness of my bosom. My hair
was simply caught up and twisted behind. It was
well secured with pins. Black silk openwork stockings of very fine material, black glossy kid shoes
very thin, soft, and with high Louis Quinze heels
set off my little feet and ankles. The rest was duly
arranged as I knew he loved to have it.

We drove to a second-rate theatre. Lord L——

sent the brougham home. We slipped out again. Papa took me on his arm. We threaded more than one small street. We made sure we were unobserved. Then suddenly we started on again. A door opened—we entered a house. I thought I knew the place. I had been there with Dragon. We went upstairs; a little woman in black pushed open a door. I found myself in a narrow corridor. About six feet in front was a second door. A third was on the left. The right-hand side was apparently a blank wall. Lord L—— himself pushed open the door immediately in front. It gave access to an elegantly furnished chamber. A soft light came from the screened electric lamp which hung suspended from the centre. There were pictures on the walls. Two rather handsome carved wood brackets occupied places on either side of the doorway. On them were two heavy Chinese vases.

"Here is a delicious little temple of pleasure, Eveline. This place so secret and retired has never yet been disturbed by vestries or police."

I kept my own ideas to myself. I waited for more.

"It is here I have arranged for your dose. The substantial medicine, my dear girl, you require I have ordered. To drop all metaphor, you will meet here a very fine young fellow whose very condition and surroundings preclude all risk. His actions are circumscribed. He is as I told you, both deaf and dumb. He was so born."

"Poor fellow! I do not think I shall be afraid of him. Is he—is he so very nice, dear papa? So very strong—you know what I mean?"

"My informant is a medical man—a member of my club. In the course of conversation he related

the case to me. He tells me he is possessed of a surprising degree of copulative power. I was told how
I might see him nude and I went to a public swimming bath. I soon picked him out. He was a study
for a sculptor—and, oh, my darling girl, as the
costermongers would say, such a *lovestick*!"

I have the acquired habit of blushing when I like.
I did it then. It is not difficult when you know how.
It is also useful.

"Here is a luxurious bed, Eveline. I wish you all
the pleasure you are capable of in this delightful retreat. I shall come and fetch you when all is over.
Meanwhile I shall not be far off. You are quite safe
here. You can make yourself quite at your ease.
You have everything to enjoy, my darling, and
nothing to fear. Ta ta! I will send him up. His
name is Theodore."

He left the room. I heard him close both doors.
Almost immediately Theodore made his appearance. I was at once struck by the young fellow's really distinguished appearance. His apparent awkwardness of manner was evidently only due to so
unusual an introduction, but his bearing, his personality were conspicuous. They were more: they
were most uncommon.

He was rather fair than dark. His height could
not have been less than six feet two inches. His
hair, of a rich auburn, was naturally curly and
glossy. His complexion was clear and bright; his
eyes remarkably fine and expressive. Poor fellow!
It was sad to think he could neither hear a human
voice nor express his ideas in speech. His individuality, however, compensated in some measure for
these defects.

He came straight up to me with a rather weak smile on his face, as if he was shy. So, in truth, I found him. I motioned him to sit down by me. I made room for him on the sofa. I noticed how he watched furtively all my movements and seemed to be impressed by my personal appearance.

"You are a very handsome young man."

There was no answer. He produced an elaborately mounted slate to which was attached a crayon and a sponge.

I remembered my mistake. I wrote my remark on the slate. He broke into an intelligent smile at once. His whole being seemed to wake in response to my sentence. He was evidently vain, poor fellow. He commenced writing rapidly. I followed his pencil.

"Nature has not been wholly unkind to me. I am strong. I am young. I rejoice in life. I have the means to enjoy it."

I smiled and, putting my left hand on his shoulder, I wrote: "Can you make love?"

"It would not be difficult for anyone to love you. I could die for a girl like you. I have never seen a more beautiful woman!"

"Are you in earnest? Would you really like to make love to me?

In an instant his arms were round me; his lips pressed mine. His breath was sweet as an angel's; his eyes shone into mine with the awakening of uncontrollable passion. He wrote rapidly: "I love you already—you are so sweet! I want you! You will let me, will you not?"

I took up the crayon: "We are here to make love together!"

Again there was no use for the slate. He pressed

my form to his. He thrust his trembling hands towards my bosom. I denied him nothing. He panted; he breathed in heavy jerks. It was plain he was becoming more and more excited. He covered my face, my neck, my hands with burning kisses. Love and desire have no need of words. It is a language understood without sound, communicated without speech. He felt its influence. Its intensity brought with it an insupportable necessity for relief.

He wrote rapidly on his slate: "Do I make myself clear? I possess unusual advantages with which to please a beautiful and voluptuous girl like you."

I read. I believe I blushed. I playfully pulled his ear. He kissed me on the mouth in mock revenge. He became enterprising. He essayed familiarities which were hardly decent. I feigned sufficient resistance to fan his rising flame. Suddenly he released me again to write:

"I conclude there need not be too much modesty between us to interfere with our mutual pleasures?"

"No. I am here for your pleasure. You are here for mine. We should enjoy together. Let us make love in earnest."

His eyes shot flames of lust. He took the slate.

"You are no less sensual than beautiful. We will drown ourselves in pleasure. I love pleasure. With you it will be divine."

He threw off his coat. He assisted me to remove my bodice. Soon I stood in my corset of pale blue satin and a short skirt of the same colour and material. He rapidly divested himself of his outer things. He caught my hand. He carried it under his shirt.

"Oh, good heavens! What a monster!"

His instrument was as long as Jim's. It was even thicker. It was stiff as buckram. It throbbed under my wanton touches.

He pressed my hand upon it and laughed a strange silent laugh. Then he wrote on the slate:

"What do you call that?"

This was evidently intended as a challenge. Not bashful, I took it up.

"I call it an instrument—a weapon of offence—a limb."

"I call it a cock!"

"Well, he certainly has a very fine crest. He carries himself very proudly—his head is as red as a turkey-cock—he is a real beauty!"

The slate was thrown on one side. Theodore drew me on his knee. He tucked up my short, lace-trimmed *chemise*. I made only just sufficient remonstrance to whet his appetite. He lifted me in his strong arms like a little child. He bore me to the bed. He deposited me gently upon it. He was by my side in an instant minus all save shirt, which stuck up in front of him as if it was suspended on a peg—as indeed it was. Theodore laid his handsome head on my breast. He toyed with my most secret charms. My round and plump posteriors seemed specially to delight him. I grasped his enormous member in my hand. I ventured to examine also the heavy purse which depended below. His testicles were in proportion to his splendid limb. I separated them from each other. There seemed to be something I did not understand. I felt them over again. Surely—yes, I was correct—he had *three!* He led me eagerly to the soft couch. Once on the bed he recommenced his amorous caresses. I seized him

once more by his truncheon. It was so nice to feel
the warm length of flesh—the broad red nut—the
long white shaft, and the triangle of testicles which
were drawn up tight below it. It was so strange too
that this fine young fellow could neither hear nor
speak! The spirit of mischief took possession of
me. The demon of lust vied with him in stimulating
my passion. I slipped off the bed. Theodore followed
me. I raised my *chemise* up to my middle and laugh-
ingly challenged him to follow. The view of my
naked charms was evidently appetising. He tried to
seize me again. I avoided his grasp. He ran after
me round the table which stood at one end of the
room. His expression was all frolic and fun, but
with a strong tinge of sensuous desire in his humid
eyes and moist lips. I let him catch me. He held me
tight this time. I turned my back to him. I felt him
pressing the brown curls of his hairy parts upon my
plump buttocks. He pushed me before him towards
the bed. His huge member inserted itself between
my thighs. I saw its red-capped head appear in front
of me. I put my hand down to it. To my surprise,
he had placed an ivory napkin ring over it. It reduced the available length. It certainly left me less
to fear from its unusually large proportions. I had
already taken the precaution to anoint my parts
with cold cream. I adjusted the head as I leant forward, belly down, on the soft bed. The young fellow pushed. He entered. I thought he would split
me up. He held me by the hips. He thrust it into me.
It passed up. I groaned with a mingled feeling of
pain and pleasure. He was too excited to pause now.
He bore forward, setting himself solidly to work to
do the job. I passed my hand down to feel his cock.

as he called it, as it emerged from time to time from the pliable sheath. Although I knew he could not hear, yet it delighted me to utter my sensations—women must talk—they can't help it. I was every bit a woman at that moment! Besides, I could express my ideas in any language I liked, as crudely as I chose—there was no one to hear me—no one to offend—no one to chide. I jerked forward.

"Oh! Take it out! Don't spend yet! I want to change—it's so delicious! How sweetly you poke me—you dear fellow!"

The huge instrument extricated itself with a plop! Theodore divined my intention. He aided me to place myself upon the side of the bed. I took his cock again in my little hands. I examined it voraciously. It was lovely now—all shining and glistening, distended and rigid in its luxury.

"I want it all—all—all!"

He evidently understood. He slipped off the napkin ring. He presented it again to my eager slit. It went up me slowly.

"Oh, my God! It is too long now. Oh! Oh! Never mind—give it me all—all—oh! Ah! Oh! Go slowly! You brute—you are splitting me! Do you hear? Poke! Oh! Push—push now! I'm coming, do you hear? You cruel brute! Coming—oh, God! Oh!"

He perceived my condition; he bore up close to me as long as my emitting spasms lasted. My swollen clitoris was in closest contact with the back of his weapon which tickled ecstatically.

I clung to him with both thighs. I raised my belly to meet his stabbing thrusts. I seized the pillow. I covered my face. I bit the pillowcase through and through. When I had finished he stopped a little to let me breathe.

"You have not come yet, but you will soon. I know it. I can feel it by the strong throbbing of your cock. I want it—oh! I want it! I must hold your balls while you spend. I want your sperm!"

He became more and more urgent. He was having me with all his tremendous vigour. His strokes were shorter—quicker—my thighs worked in unison. His features writhed in his ecstasy of increasing enjoyment. He was nearing the end. I felt every throb of his huge instrument.

I draw the veil over the termination of the scene. I cannot even use ordinary terms to describe it. My whole nervous system vibrated with voluptuous excitement. My senses deserted me.

When I recovered consciousness, to my astonishment, my companion had disappeared. Papa was standing over my prostrate form. How he had been occupied I did not then know. His face was turgid with satisfied lust. His hands trembled. His dress was disordered. He held in his hands a towel with which he was bathing my aching parts.

He assisted me at my toilette. As I passed out with Lord L—— I noticed that the door on the left of the corridor was ajar. I peeped through. It gave access to a little cabinet, not larger than the inside of a double brougham. In the partition which separated it from the chamber where my adventure had taken place there was one bright point of light which shone from a round hole the size of a wine cork. A hasty glance explained all. The carved fretwork of the bracket on which stood the China vase was perforated just under the shelf, and quite invisible from that side. I understood all with that streak of light.

Lord L—— had witnessed everything that had taken place. I hastily followed papa who had already descended the stairs. He awaited me. I am not a fool. I kept my discovery to myself.

Chapter IV

Wedding bells! The usual bustle and fuss. The usual ceremony. The usual lies on both sides. The usual hypocritical admiration of everybody for everything, and behold the day had come—in fact, had half gone—when I was made Countess of Endover.

The marriage was necessarily quite a quiet one. The ceremony was made as short as possible. A few intimate friends appeared at the church. The dear old Duchess of M—— insisted on being there. She was one of the few whose compliments were not all flattery.

Lord Endover really looked almost handsome in his uniform as Lord Lieutenant of the county. Papa and Percy paid him the honour of acknowledging his military standing as Lieutenant Colonel of militia by also arraying themselves in their state panoply of war.

The three sisters of my husband were present of course: the Honourable Maud, a confirmed old maid; the next a widow, Lady Tintackle; the youngest, plain, spiteful, and nine-and-twenty, yet a spinster, with every chance of remaining so, Margaret by name. She had begun life with one or two notorious escapades, from the result of which nothing but her brother's influence and position had saved her. The wave of disdain with which society overwhelms offenders flagrantly transgressing its unwritten laws and detected never quite ceased to ruffle her future. The men were shy. All three sisters regarded me with little favour, jealous already of a new influence asserting itself between their brother and themselves. I foresaw a great need for caution in my intercourse with my noble connections.

We were all relieved to get home. Lord Endover and papa were closeted in the latter's study with the family solicitors. The ladies were whiling away the half hour before breakfast in the drawing room. I had found an excuse to escape to my room. I bolted the door. I sat down in my favourite armchair before the glass. I was engaged in admiring myself in my beautiful wedding dress. I was so glad to be alone. I wanted to think. I had many ideas to arrange.

We were to spend the honeymoon—how I hated that word!—at Endover Towers. The state rooms had been specially prepared. The place was said to be arranging a festive reception for the Earl and his young bride. The village was *en fête*. It was all to be very gorgeous and gay.

I was still before the glass. Five minutes had not yet gone since my entry. Already there was a tap at the door. I rose and opened it. My brother Percy pushed his way in. He immediately closed and locked the door again.

"Now I shall have at least a private view."

"What do you mean, your naughty boy?"

"Oh, it's no use riding the high horse with me, little countess! Your ladyship will please descend to the level of ordinary life."

He had seized me by the wrist; his other arm was round my waist in an instant.

"Oh, Percy! Please leave me alone! Someone may come."

"I'm going to give the new Countess of Endover her first lesson in—Why! You have no drawers on! Fancy a countess without drawers!"

"You really must not tumble my skirt! Percy! For shame!"

He had put me before the large armchair. Before I could prevent him I was made to kneel in it. He began raising my skirts from behind. All protestations were in vain. I was in horrible fear someone would want to come in. Still nothing was more natural than that my brother should come to offer me his private congratulations. He had only seen me before that day in the church. We had scarcely exchanged a word.

"Oh, Eve! Dear, Eve! I've sworn to have you first after your marriage. I will not be denied. You looked so divinely beautiful at the altar—like an innocent angel of light. I declare I could hardly keep the buttons on my trousers. Turn your head, dear Eve, and look!"

I did as I was bidden—all power of resistance seemed to pass away. What I saw fired my hot blood.

"Oh, Percy! You wicked boy! It is bigger and bigger! Make haste then! I shall have to go downstairs in a few minutes."

He pressed his belly to my bottom. My wedding
dress and underskirts were thrown over my back.
In another instant he was into me, up to the balls.
There was no time to lose. He knew it. He worked
fast to arrive at his climax. My own arrived. With
a low groan I sank my head on the cushioned back.
His weapon straightened—hardened, and with a
sigh of lustful frenzy Percy discharged.

Ten minutes later I entered the drawing room.
Breakfast was announced. Lord Endover was com-
plimented on all sides. He disposed my beautiful
bouquet on a side table. There was no fuss—there·
were no speeches—only our healths in champagne.
Then a retreat to the drawing room and conserva-
tory. That evening at five-thirty we entered the
village and drove straight to the Towers. The
local volunteers with their band bade us welcome
at the station. All was in readiness for our reception at Lord Endover's noble seat. It was a grand
old pile. The family had bought it some two hundred years before from the original noble family
who had held it since the time of the Conqueror.

I pass over that portion of my history which relates to my early married life. I am not a hypocrite
from choice, but from the necessities of my position. Lord Endover never relaxed his fondness for
me. I became disgusted with myself. Incapable of
reciprocating his passion, I sought a retreat in our
beautiful country seat in Cumberland. The autumn
session of Parliament had been summoned. There
were weighty political issues in the balance; my
husband had to be present.

It was then I heard sad tidings from my old
home in F—— Street, Mayfair. Lord L——

wrote often. In one of his letters he told me that
John, the footman, having been sent to St. John's
Wood on an important commission, had met with
an accident. He had been run over by a cab. He
was badly hurt. Conveyed to a hospital he never
quite recovered consciousness. All that could be
made out was a ceaseless cry for "ginger nuts."
Papa bought the poor fellow some pounds of them,
but all they got from him still was "ginger nuts!"
And so he died.

It was in the strong bracing air of the country
that I revelled, until the obligations of my position
necessitated my return to London. Lord Endover
had gone to Scotland where he had taken a moor
I had decided not to accompany him. The weather
had turned cold and wet. A week on a visit to my
old home would be enjoyable. Papa received me
with a transport of delight.

"My darling papa is always in the thoughts of
his little girl."

"My sweet Eveline! You are more beautiful
than ever. You have become rounded and fuller in
the figure. The country air has been most beneficial
to you. I have had no news from you lately of a
private nature. Tell me, my darling, has Lord
Endover any hopes that—"

"I know all you would say, dear papa. He has
none, nor do I desire he should have. It is never
likely to be as you suggest."

"I am not surprised, my dear Eveline; it is then
as I thought."

"I am determined, papa, never to perpetuate the race of the Endovers. It is bad blood. If ever I nad a child, a son—my offspring should have a father capable of procreating a new and healthy race which should endure—otherwise I am content to remain as I am."

He took me in his arms. We mingled our kisses in tender dalliance. We were alone. The opportunity was propitious. It was not lost. Our gasping sighs of ineffable enjoyment alone broke the silence.

"Oh! My Eveline! What pleasure you give me!"

"My sweet papa! You drown me in ecstasy! I am yours—yours only! What sweet adultery!"

"Oh, Eveline, my child—incest is sweeter still!"

In lascivious whispers we expanded the ideas which served to whet our ardent passion. Monstrous perceptions of enjoyment floated through our minds—they added poignancy to our lust—fuel to the fire of our already heated temperaments. We paused in our fierce and ravenous enjoyment. We lingered even as the epicure delays to complete his fill of a sumptuous repast that we might digest our luxurious piecemeal sensations. We worked ourselves almost to the point of consummation. Then we broke off only to recommence. I excited my darling papa with every lewd suggestion my prurient imagination could devise. He made such proposals under his bated breath that only demons could have prompted. We were both drunk with lust—overwhelmed with the intoxication of this renewal of our intimacy.

I made no secret of my discovery of his peephole. I went further—I asked him if he had enjoyed the exhibition; whether it had kindled his lust. Nay, whether he would like me to act the scene over again—or another, a more obscene and outrageous one in which there should be three actors. In this way we laid our schemes. Thus we invented plans of voluptuous gratification which we determined mutually to carry out. In the midst of our transports, while our imaginations ran riot in a red whirl of satanic excitement, we rushed together to the final spasmodic struggle. Hissing forth a volley of erotic expletives, papa drove in his swollen limb and flooded me with a volume of his seed. Exhaustion succeeded nature's overwrought efforts. A sweet, refreshing slumber in each other's arms restored the vigour we had so recently expended. Our fixed determination alone remained—we could indulge our voluptuous inclinations in the future as we had already proposed. We had invented a new pleasure—a lewd distraction of no ordinary kind.

Lord Endover had come up to town. It had no doubt strong inducements for him. I knew him too well to suppose he would be firm enough to free himself entirely from the meshes which the early allurements of fast life had woven about him. All I feared was some lasting taint, some loathsome encounter which might entail ruin upon myself as well as my husband.

He would return home very late, or rather very early in the morning—of course, from his club. Always the club! If not *this* club—then *that* club. It was so necessary he should show himself in the

Lords too. I grew quite accustomed to these excuses. I received them all with imperturbable good humour. I only ventured to remark that I thought he worked too hard for an ungrateful country— but I took care to provide myself with a separate room—one which suited me well in every respect and communicated with a beautiful boudoir beyond.

There is no more ill-treated an institution in London than a man's club. The poor thing has to stand all the responsibility and receive all the vituperation of that large section of society women who suffer from the husband who returns with the milk in the early morning. It is certainly remarkable how many of them believe—or pretend to believe —in the power of that select circle of men of good standing, to spread its blandishments in the shape of whist, cigars, and brandies and sodas around them to the extinction of all natural desire to seek the warm and genuine embraces of the loving and still fresh wife at home. I drop a ready veil over the picture. It is all unreal. The awakening comes suddenly, and with it, in too many cases, the natural impulsive revenge of an angry woman, surrounded by temptations, to carry her neglected charms to a more profitable, if not more congenial, market.

Lord L—— was naturally a frequent visitor. I drove him in the park. He took me to the Opera during the season. When there was none, we visited the theatres. My husband was rarely of the party. Percy was quartered in Scotland.

"Tonight, Eveline, in accordance with your wish, I have arranged our little *divertissement*. We start at nine precisely. You are still determined on the attempt? Not afraid, eh, little woman, of this double encounter?"

"I am ready, dear papa. Indeed I long for the fun. We will do all we talked of. You will be near. You will look on and enjoy it too, will you not? Oh, it will be delicious if I only know you enjoy through me, that our ideas are so mixed and interchanged."

We drove to our quiet street. I wore a veil. Lord L—— was also unrecognisable. He took me from the cab. We walked a short way. We were absolutely alone. He turned a corner. We stood at the door of the same house. He turned a handle. We passed in. A tall, fair, young woman received us in the hall as if by appointment.

"The young men are here. Will you walk up stairs, please?"

I heard all she whispered.

"They quite understand everything—the lady will be pleased with them. I know they will amuse her—they are only too glad of such a chance."

We followed the loquacious woman up the stairs. She ushered us into the same room. The two carved brackets were in their places. On them stood the somewhat meaningless Chinese vases as on my last visit. Papa made haste to disappear. Presently the door opened again. Two young men entered. Then the door closed. We were all three alone.

My first inclination was to laugh. We must all have looked a little awkward. They were fine handsome young fellows, stout and broad-shouldered, with what Lord L—— would have called "plenty of grit" in them. They were evidently of the well-to-do artisan class, with healthy features, well-cleaned persons and supple limbs. Just the sort of young men that Eveline loved to enjoy. Appearances certainly promised well. She was not likely to be denied her pleasure, nor, to judge by their look of pleased excitement, were they in any danger of a disappointment. A few words, and we were soon on a social footing. They never took their eyes off my person. I sat on the sofa. They came uninvited and sat by me—one on either side.

"You are not afraid of me, are you? You can be quite at your ease. You both know what a young woman is, don't you?"

"Yes, of course we do! Don't we, Tom? But we don't often see one like you! You're a perfect beauty!"

"She's a lovely bit, Bill! She's—oh, my, I can't say any more! I'm longing for it already!"

"How nice you both look! What are you longing for? Give me a kiss!"

They vied with each other in snatching kisses from my hands—my lips—my cheeks. I let them pull me this way and that as they listed. I shut my eyes. I let my imagination wander. My attention was quickly recalled. One young fellow had insinuated his impatient hand under my clothes. His friend was kissing me on the mouth. I laid a hand on each side of me. I encountered their thighs. I had no difficulty in discovering the condition of their privates. Both were already violently erect. They moved excitedly under my touches which I made pointedly indecent. My right-hand neighbour put his arm round me. He pulled me towards him. I kissed him on the lips. The other man put his left hand on my bosom. I turned and kissed him also.

"Let us be at our ease. Take off your coats—
take off everything that is in the way. I want to see
you as you are."

They rose quickly. In an incredibly short time
they stood before me stripped to their shirts—
their trousers flung into a chair.

My spirits rose. I was consumed with longing
for the game to begin.

I raised their shirts as they stood before me. I
grasped their stiff hairy members in my little hands.
I determined to be as plainly lewd as possible. I was
well aware I was overheard. I desired to make rich
amends to the listener for his sacrifice. I knew he
would appreciate every indecency—every salacious
incident of the performance.

"What sweet pricks you have!"

They were in reality both splendid specimens of
vigorous manhood; broad-headed, red-capped,
their members confronted me menacingly as I commenced to finger each in turn. I bent down my
head. I tickled, I kissed them. I played round the
soft warm things with my hot tongue. Both became
furiously excited. They assisted me to undress. I
slipped off my skirts—my bodice. I stood in my
corset, *chemise*, and stockings. I retained my pretty
kid boots. Then I threw off my corset and gave
them my warm body with which to play.

"What a lovely girl you are! I am longing to
get into you!"

"See, Tom, what a bottom she's got! Isn't she
awfully well made?"

They felt me all over. Tom went on his knees.
He divided my legs. He kissed my thighs all over.

Then he pressed his face forward. He tried hard to arrive at my orbit. I put down my hand and shielded it. Resistance only made him more eager.

"We must both have you, my dear. How would you like us to do it?"

"Say which of us you will have first? I'm sure you're a randy one when you've got a man up your sweet little belly."

I delighted in their rough indecencies. I knew someone who would also be enjoying them, but of whose proximity my companions were both ignorant.

"Will you lie on your back, my girl, on the sofa first, and let me put it into you so? I'll be very gentle."

I pretended to become a little frightened.

"I don't know, I'm sure. Your things are both so dreadfully large and stiff."

In another second I was on my back on the sofa. It was exactly opposite the Chinese vase to the left of the door. I gave a despairing look in that direction as the young fellow his friend called Tom bent over me. He inserted his knees between my thighs, while the other, with the greatest good humour, arranged a soft pillow for my head. Tom lay prone on my body, his hairy chest pressing my soft breasts. My parts were in no condition to resist him, potent as was this monstrous rammer. I was actually swimming in the moist exudation which kindly nature provides in such an emergency. Already I felt the broad head of his instrument thrusting itself within my slit. With steady pressure he continued to penetrate.

"Put your hand under her bottom, Bill. I'm half

in already. She's—she's—oh! She's awfully nice. It's heaven! That's it! So—raise her up!"

"Make haste and give it her! I want my curn!"

Tom began a gentle undulation, supporting himself principally on his knees and hands. He raised his head. He looked me in the face.

"Oh, my! You're into me! Oh! Ah! Pray go gently—you're so strong! You're too bad! Oh! Ah! But it's nice now!"

Bill's broad palm was still under my buttocks which he raised up in unison with his friend's movements.

"Is that nice now, eh? Is he stroking you nicely? Hasn't he got a fine tool?"

It was impossible to answer. I stretched out my right arm. My hand encountered Bill's stiff weapon only waiting the other's vacation of my parts to be itself inserted in its place. I gasped with pleasure. Meanwhile the act was proceeding with the utmost vigour. The young fellow was up to his balls. His rough belly, covered with curly black hair, rubbed upon my satin skin with an exquisite sensation of lustful friction. I felt his limb vibrating with delight whenever he stopped for a moment the determined thrusts with which he belaboured my poor body.

"I've got my finger on the line between his balls. I think he'll spend directly. You'll get a lot. He just can let it out!"

"Oh, Bill! He's up to my womb now! He's so long—so hard! It's awfully nice! Oh, my! Oh!"

Here were two men assisting in the single act! It was a new sensation. I found it delicious. My flexible parts were stretched round the stiff instrument like a glove. The other's finger seemed to act as a spur upon the man's genitals. He drove up and down furiously. He worked away with indescribable energy. I felt the short spasmodic thrusts which precede the discharge. I came. He lay on me pouring out his rapture. His sperm burst from him. It deluged my longing parts in rapid jets. When all was done he withdrew with reluctance, urged thereto by his friend. Before I could even rise, Bill sprang upon me. He got between my legs. He contemplated my naked body, red and bruised by the rough contact of his companion, as a hawk might gloat over its tender quarry. He lay down to his work, stretching my thighs open to receive his loins between. He pointed his strong limb to my already reeking slit. He drove it into me until I felt the crisp hairs on his belly chafe my mount. It was a new sensation for me. I found it exquisite. The heat, the slippery condition I was in, the knowledge that the young fellow would end by doubling the flood I had already received, wound up my imagination to fever heat.

"My God! Tom, she's heavenly nice! Put your finger down and tickle me between my balls. I'm up to her waist. Oh! My God—oh!"

The big member of my second ravisher seemed to swell to an enormous extent, caused probably by the fervent temperature of my own parts. He seemed very long in bringing the lewd business to a climax, though his limb hardened 'til it more resembled a truncheon of wood. He worked away with frenzy. At length, I felt him spend. He spouted a second emission into me. He was so long in doing it I thought he would never finish. At last

the final drops were expended. The human cascade
ran dry. My *chemise* was saturated with their
sperm. Even the holland cover of the sofa was
marked by a big round patch. I hastily rose. I made
my toilet behind the screen which covered the position of the necessary furniture. We all three then
reposed upon the sofa, pressed together like sar-
dines in a box. Each of my new friends vied with
the other in their indecencies and their libidinous
suggestions.

How I passed the entire hour during which these
two delicious young men kept me wantonly at their
service it is impossible to record. I only know I experienced a round of voluptuous sensations indulged in amid smothered cries of intense nervous
exaltation. At last, I believe, I slept. I recollect in-
distinctly a quaint triangular *adieu*—a long silence.
Then the voice of Lord L—— sounded in my ear
and I threw my arms about papa's neck. He had
been a witness of all that had passed. He explained
the secret of the little cabinet. He showed me the
interior. I looked through the opening. It could be
effectually closed with a wine cork. There were two
of these peepholes, arranged both for the eye and
also for the transmission of sound. Securely
screened among the carved foliage of the bracket
and immediately under the shelf on which stood the
large Chinese vase, no one could suspect their
presence which was rendered doubly unlikely by
the blackened corks when not in use. The partition
between the two rooms was only a thin panelling of
wood.

"I should like to be with you, dear papa, and
share your curious pleasure by witnessing some-

thing also. Could we not see on another occasion just as today you have seen us?"

"I have no doubt it could be managed. I will make inquiries. Money, my dear Eveline, will buy anything in London."

"No, papa dear. No money could buy off the love—the wicked, willful, ardent love that Eveline has for you."

"Well spoken, my darling! However, it will serve our purpose in this matter. Next week, if you have time and opportunity, we may bring off an exhibition of a peculiarly interesting character."

Chapter V

How sweet is this country air! How lovely the
blue water of the lake which sparkles in the sun
beneath the shadow of the trees! Yet winter is
upon us—winter in Cumberland. I have no taste to
remain to encounter the snow, the cold. Chitterlings is delicious in the summer. It is not altogether
such a residence as I should select for the winter
months. Endover is still away in the North—shooting. I feel also much inclined for a little sport,
though I fancy I should be on more congenial
ground were I to be shot at and become the target
of some gallant gun.

These subjects revolved themselves in my mind
as I reached the great iron gates which gave entrance to the avenue. Mrs. Hodge, the gatekeep-
er's wife, ran out all wreathed in smiles to open
them, a buxom, good-looking woman of some seven-
or eight-and-twenty years of age. After her came
toddling a chubby lad of some three summers. A
second held on by the lodge doorpost, just getting
firm on his legs. I looked on well pleased to pause

in my solitary walk, to regale my sight with a picture so rural, so natural, so unobtainable. No, money cannot purchase all. There are gifts for which nature refuses such dross, blessings which are sometimes unobtainable for all that wealth may have to offer.

"Good morning, Mrs. Hodge. Why bless me! What fine boys! Are those both your own?"

"Well, yes, my lady. They are mine—and my man's too. This is my eldest. Yonder one's my second. That's all, my lady—all at present, but there's another on the way."

"Ah, Mrs. Hodge, you are a lucky woman to have such splendid children. They are perfect little cupids."

"I don't know about cupids, my lady, this 'un's christened Christopher. The parson gave us the name, which it was a merchant captain which sailed over to America. Christopher Columbus his whole name was. That's Columbus standin' by the door. He's just a year old last week, my lady, and can walk and run till it's all I can do to catch him. But Lor' bless him! He's a good little lad, and happy as the day is long."

"I quite envy you. I fear such happiness is not for all the world. Have you a good husband, Mrs. Hodge?"

"Lor' bless you, my lady, that I have! My Jock is never so happy as when his work's done and we sit inside together of an evening. He reads a lot then aloud to me, for you see, my lady, he works hard in the woods, cuttin' timber all day on the estate out yonder, and he takes his supper hearty, he does, and then he sits, and smokes, and reads."

"How long have you been married, Mrs. Hodge?"

"Nigh on to four years now, my lady."

"You've not lost any time, I perceive." I laughed. The good woman joined in my merriment.

"Lor', ma'am—your ladyship, I mean—I beg pardon—if you only knew how rampageous my Jock gets! Why, I had all the trouble in life to keep him decently quiet when we were courtin', and since we're married there's no holdin' him. He's like a mad horse, he is!"

"And what age is your husband, Mrs. Hodge?"

"Jock's nigh on a year younger nor me, my lady."

"Younger is he? That is rather unusual in these parts, is it not?"

"I dunno, my lady, but savin' your presence, his parents were both dead and gone. He had no home. I had saved up a bit o' money here in the dairy, and so they gave me the chance of the lodge if we chose to marry and look after it together."

"You're a happy woman, Mrs. Hodge."

Something in my voice seemed to raise all the woman's tender sympathy. She looked at me inquiringly.

"I hope, my lady, you won't think me too bold, but we've all of us on the estate been hopin' as how my lord might have a hare."

I pretended not to understand.

"I always thought hares were unusually plentiful this season about Chitterlings."

Mrs. Hodge looked nonplussed.

"I don't mean hares wot run, but thems wot's bred and born."

"Oh, I see! Yes, now I see! It's very kind of you, I'm sure. At present, Mrs. Hodge, we must be content as we are."

The good woman drew closer. There was an air of mystery in her open honest face, a look almost of trouble. She shook her head as she slowly uttered her next remark.

"*I shouldn't*. No, there's something wrong somewhere. Savin' your presence, my lady—and your ladyship'll excuse me—but a lovely, beautiful, well-grown young lady like your ladyship has no call to be childless. Ye may send me off for my impertinence, or turn us out of the lodge, but after being brought up on the estate, and it's now nigh on twenty-nine year ago I was born on it, I do say as how your ladyship ought to *have a hare*. I shouldn't—no, I shouldn't."

There was something in Mrs. Hodge's kindly meant comments which touched me. There was even a dimness in her eye as her broad, good-humoured face looked almost affectionately into mine.

"No, I shouldn't be content. I know there's a main difference in the livin' and ways of great people and the likes of us poor folk, but if I were the lady of the manor without a hare I know that all the village would want to know the reason why. I can keep my mouth shut, my lady. I'm not a woman to go about gossiping about what don't concern me. I keeps to myself, but if your ladyship heard all they said you would find they knew it wasn't your fault."

The woman looked so kindly sympathetic that I suppressed a natural inclination of resentment. It

rose in my throat. What! I, the Countess of Endover, Lady of the Manor of Chitterlings in my
own right, to be thus spoken to and pitied by a
peasant on my estate! No, but it would not do. I
broke down. The position was too strained. The
tears rose to my eyes. Mrs. Hodge saw my distress. The kind, good-hearted woman's own sweet
natural disposition came up beaming in her sympathetic look as she took my hand and kissed it.

"I know, I know, my lady. My lord takes his
shootin'—takes his huntin'. He can do a long day
in the covers, perhaps, but he's—he's not to be
compared to us poor folk *under the sheets.*"

"What do you mean, Mrs. Hodge? My husband
—Lord Endover—is all that is kind; all that is—"

"Ah, no! My lady, you must excuse me—I mean
no wrong. I only talk as I feel for your ladyship.
It's not your fault. It's *his* !"

I withdrew my hand. An angry light must have
shone in my eyes. My red blood flew to my cheek.
I drew myself up. This woman's insolence should
not go unpunished. It was bad enough to have
been accosted thus, but to be an object of down-
right pity—no, this was too much! My husband
too! The Earl to be thus discussed at my own park
gate!

"You are angry, my lady—and no wonder! I am
only a poor ignorant woman. You are a great lady.
I hope you will forgive me. I cannot bear that you
should be angry with me. I meant all for the best. I
could tell you more—that which would show you
that I want to serve you truly."

I hesitated. There was an air of reality about
the young woman I could not mistake. Her earnest-

ness moved me strongly to listen further. She was quick enough to divine my thoughts.

"Come in here, my lady. I will explain all. I will tell you all I have to tell. The Lor' knows I have no cause to hide it. It's too well known already."

I entered the comfortable dwelling. Mrs. Hodge carefully dusted a chair with her apron. I sat down. She dropped on both knees in front of me, hiding her bonny face in her hands. Suddenly she looked up, her confidence seemed to return—her cheeks were wet with tears, red and mottled by contact with her hot hands.

"I want to tell you all about it. I always said to myself I would. It was not all my fault. I was so young then—only fifteen. He was old enough to have known better than to take advantage of a poor girl without experience. He was eddicated and rich, with ladies all round him ready for his asking. I was taken with his winnin' ways. I was foolishly proud of his noticin' me. He did what he liked with me. More's the pity. He said it was all a bit of fun and nonsense and that he would take care of me. So it was for *him*, but not for *me*. Father come to hear of it. Mother was dead then. The village all heard of it. They sneered at Father. It broke his heart. He beat me and turned me out o' doors. An old neighbour took me in out o' charity like. It killed Father. I was left alone. The Countess was kind to me—the last Dowager, I mean. She's dead now, and he—can you guess *who* he was? Yes, I know you do, my lady."

Down went her head again between the hands. I heard a low sobbing moan. Then she spoke again.

"Fortunately nothing come of my wrong doin'.

I lived down most of the talk. Then Jock come in
my way. He was always a good lad. A bit studious-
like. Clever at farm work, strong, and cheery. I
took to him. We married. The Dowager Lady
Endover had left directions that they were to take
care o' me. They gave us the lodge. Jock is keeper,
as your ladyship knows, and woodman too."

Mrs. Hodge looked all round. Seeing that we
were quite alone, but for the two children playing
on the floor, she went on:

"It was then I knew why nothing had come of
my wrong doin'. *He* was not like my Jock. He had
not the way of doing what men who take up with
young girls ought—I mean are expected—to do.
He was weak. Almost without any force at all
after the novelty passed off. It was different with
my Jock—my goodness, yes, my lady! I couldn't
hold him. He was like a cage full o' lions under
the blankets. There wasn't no stoppin' him. Under
ten months my baby was born. My second was
planted the first time as ever he touched me after
I gave up sucklin' the first, and my lady, I don't
mind telling you, my third is a-comin' the same.
He's a good lad, my Jock is, and a quiet steady one
as loves his home, and I'm a happy woman."

Mrs. Hodge rose to her feet. She was quite dra-
matic in her excitement. As she unfolded her narration, the truth had gradually come home to me.
It was the old story—only a penny novel. But
there was more than that in it. This view struck
me also. Every word was evidently true. She had
told me at least one fact I recognised only too well.
Very naturally she had fallen into an error in her
knowledge of only half the facts. Very possibly as

regarded my matrimonial affairs there existed a *double* disqualification. I felt angry at having been deceived. I had been married only a year. I felt I was looked upon all round as a failure—a disappointment. In a flash it occurred to me why the three sisters of the Earl had suddenly commenced a course of subservient patronage towards their cousin, the heir apparent to the title and the entail. It was even said the youngest was going to marry him. Many things hitherto hidden from my understanding became clear. If the cousin, a worthless, idle creature, obtained the title, Chitterlings would one day be his. My woman's instincts were aroused, my pride revolted.

"Go on, Mrs. Hodge. I am much interested. Alas! I think it is much as you say, but still I fear there is nothing to be done. I must be content to be as I am. You are blessed with two beautiful children, boys fit to be kings. You have a fine young fellow for a husband replete with health and strength, while I—"

The good woman dropped on her knees again. She came closer and gazed up into my face with a puzzled look I could not decipher.

"*I shouldn't!* No, my lady—not in your place— I shouldn't. It ain't in nature. What! Let all go to nobody knows where? A fine title! A fine estate! When all might be for you and yours but for the fault of a certain person who has passed his time in ruining his faculties. See, my lady; only see what might be yours! Look on my boys there—my Jock's the man that knows the trick! Oh, my dear lady, *try my Jock!*"

Mrs. Hodge clutched my hand, took it between

her own, and slobbered it with her kisses as she knelt humbly before me.

🌼 🌼 🌼

"What, Eveline, my darling child, you are in town again—so unexpected too! I thought you had intended remaining some time longer down at Chitterlings."

"So I did, dear papa, but I have changed my mind. Ladies are apt to be fickle you know, and they are privileged to change their minds."

"But you are not fickle. You stick to your old love, my sweet girl, or your darling little hand would not be where it now is."

"Do you like to feel your little Eveline's warm hand there, dear papa? Is it nice? Does it make you feel you love your own little girl? Do you like my kisses? Do they give you pleasure? Is my tongue warm and soft? Is it all that which makes this sweet thing so stiff and broad and long? Oh, dear papa, let me caress it—let me—"

"Oh, my God, Eveline, you kill me with pleasure. Your tongue and your lips are maddening me. Take care—I shall fill your mouth!"

"Well, papa, and what then? Do I not love your sweet sperm?"

"Oh, stay—you drive me mad—not again! Oh! Oh! It is in your mouth. You are rolling your hot tongue round the nut. Oh! Good Lord! If you will —you must—there! There! Take it—take all! I spend! I die! Oh! My God, what pleasure!"

"You and I will sleep together tonight, dear papa, shall we not? You will make the bed go crickety crack when you are on the top of your own girl, will you not, papa?"

"There is a ball at Lady A——'s in Eaton Square. You had an invitation, I know. It is for the day after tomorrow. Will you go, Eveline? A dance will do you good. If you will say yes, I will take you myself."

"Then I will go, dear papa. Endover is coming to London. I have sent for him to the North."

"What can be the matter, my darling? I hope nothing is wrong."

"Nothing is wrong in an ordinary sense, but I have come to a decision. I am not satisfied with the state of my health; not altogether sure that things might not be set right as regards my——my present condition, papa."

"Eveline, you alarm me. One would fear you are not well."

"I am quite well—and quite resolved. One thing is certain: I have been married over twelve months. Endover is becoming morose. He has given up domesticity. He goes here and there. He writes to inquire after every interval we pass together if I have any news for him. I understand what he means. I have none."

"My poor darling!"

"You remember our conversations, papa. Who knows what may be the cause of my sterility, for such it is. I have decided to consult a London physician. I have sent for my husband to hear his opinion after a proper examination. I should like you to be with him on that occasion, dear papa."

"I think you are very wise. The stake is an enormously important one. It is worth playing for. I will not disguise from you that the Earl has already lamented the loss of all his hopes in my hearing."

"We shall see. At any rate I will not leave this chance untried."

"Are you ready, Eveline? The carriage is at the door. Although you will not want for partners, I should not, in your place, be late. The supper is arranged, they tell me, for an unusually early hour. Lady A—— likes her guests to dance, as sailors say, with the champagne all aboard."

"How dreadful, dear papa. I want no such stimulant. I have not danced since my marriage. You must give me a square dance. I do not think I shall care to waltz, though you know how I love it."

"Never mind. As Percy would say, 'let's make a night of it!' I must leave you early. I have an important engagement to meet the new Viceroy at the club. He could only come down there late."

"Yes, I mean to make a night of it, papa. I may not have such a chance again. But come and take me home."

Papa laughed. I could see my humour made him nervous. He changed the subject.

"How superbly beautiful you look, my dear child! How lovely your dress, yet how simple! It does not look good enough for the Countess of Endover though; but it becomes you superbly. Oh! What gloves! Your long white kid gloves are absolutely ravishing. They look so infinitely delicate and soft. They fit like the skin they are, but then your darling little hand is perfect. Your bracelets too are selected with exquisite taste, so simple and yet so chaste. Your dress is curiously made—almost a divided skirt."

"Let us go then, dear papa. You kill me with your kindhearted flattery. Endover cares nothing now for all the points, as he would call them, that you enumerate."

The dancing had been in full swing for some time when we arrived. I found a chance to give papa his quadrille. Several young men were presented to me. I selected one—an old acquaintance. We waltzed together. He danced well. The music was good— the time perfect. I thoroughly enjoyed myself. The strains of the melody died away. The dancers stopped. Supper was announced. My partner thought himself the happiest of men to lead me downstairs to partake of it. I was thirsty. The champagne was grateful to my feverish palate. I left the table at the first opportunity. I wanted air. My head ached. I found myself in the entrance hall. The house door was open. An awning had been erected down to the kerb. A solitary footman stood in attendance just below the steps. The night breeze was so refreshing. I looked behind; I was alone. I advanced a step or two beyond the doorway. I drew the hood of my opera cloak over my head.

"Looking for your carriage, miss? Shall I find it for you? It's too early, I think. Ours is the only one here at present."

"Oh, no! Thank you very much. It is not here. I felt faint. I want to breathe the fresh air. It is so fine tonight. The heat inside is oppressive."

"Yes, miss—lovely night—all the stars out. Would you like a quiet turn round in our carriage? It would do you good."

I took a rapid survey of the man. He was of the ordinary type—tall, good-looking to a certain extent, and wearing a livery which I did not recognise. It was equally evident he did not know me.

I flashed such a glance at him as I flatter myself Eveline knows how to lance with effect. He caught it in all its intensity.

"It would perhaps be nice. I suffer so—but— Well, take me just round the half of the square at a walk. I think it would do my head good."

The footman whistled. A large closed landau and pair came up out of the darkness. He held open the door. I swiftly stepped in. As I half suspected he would, the man followed. He closed the door, giving a quiet direction as he did so to the coachman. The footman sat himself opposite on the edge of the seat with his back to the horses.

"I still feel faint—my head aches badly—the heat of the rooms was dreadful."

My self-imposed companion promptly whipped a fan out of the pocket behind him. He began agitating it gently before my face as I reclined on the comfortable cushions. The horses were going at a walk. The night was moonless. The gas lamps alone threw an uncertain streak of light into the carriage at intervals as we passed them. By their aid I furtively summed up my neighbour. He was evidently much agitated. His whole bearing betrayed an eagerness hardly compatible with his innocent employment. He had bent forward in order to fan me. The better to steady himself he had rested his left hand on my knee. He pushed one of his sturdy legs between my knees. I felt his calf against mine. I was conscious of the pervading perfume which exhaled from myself in the close atmosphere. He evidently respired it. It seemed to madden him.

"There! You're better now, miss. It'll soon pass off."

I could see that his eyes were intent on my face which had emerged from my hood. He stole fervent glances at my bosom, also particularly on the gloved and delicate hands with the left of which I held my cloak not too tightly closed. The right pressed my lace kerchief to my lips. An irrepressible feeling of the absurdity of the situation possessed me. I had difficulty to restrain my inclination to laugh. He advanced his left hand a little further. He even pressed closer with his fingers. He moved his leg at the same time more boldly between mine.

"Oh! You must not do that. You are shockingly indelicate."

There was only coquetry in my voice; only an invitation in my glance. The man noted both. He grew bolder still. I felt quite as wanton as himself. My position became exceedingly critical.

"I think you have fanned me enough, thank you. It rather makes me cold. Oh! Pray, pray do not put your hand there. How dreadfully wicked you are!"

He closed the fan. It fell between us. In stooping to pick it up, his hand touched my ankle. Instantly I felt it slip up my calf. Just then we crossed the lamplight. I saw his face all flushed, his lips apart, his eyes dilated with strong sensuous craving. There was no stopping him now. I could stand it no longer. I tittered through my kerchief.

"Oh! Don't—pray don't! You must not do that! Indeed you are too bad! You tickle me!"

His hot hand advanced. He touched my knee. His left was under my clothes still. I put down my own in a well-feigned effort to restrain him. He seized it with his. He caressed it softly. He fondled the well-gloved fingers. He stroked the perfumed kid on my wrist and arm. Suddenly he drew my hand towards him. He pressed it down upon his person. He was now fairly aflame with desire. My hand, retained in his strong grasp, detected his condition. Within his garment I felt his limb. It was evidently a fine long one—stiff as buckram and very thick. The contact excited him further. I was just as bad.

"How delicious you are! Don't take your lovely little hand away."

A gentle squeeze was all my response. He took care I should not leave off my digital inspection. It fired my blood. He slightly jerked his loins. I bent my body nearer to his own I repeated the squeeze even more suggestively. He pressed and rubbed my hand on his person.

"Do you feel so very naughty then? Let me look at it!"

He released his grasp. He quickly unbuttoned his trousers. He pulled up his shirt. A big red-topped member started out. Oh! How long it was, so dreadfully stiff! Curving slightly up, the swollen head already naked and staring me in the face. I put my gloved hand upon it. I took it in my palm. My right covered the protruding knob. I shook it. He could hardly retain his seat. He thrust his eager fingers into the front of my low dress.

"What shall I do with this? What a large one you have!"

I pressed back both my hands. He tried to raise my dress. I stopped him.

"Oh, no! It is impossible—you would rumple my skirt. You must be very gentle. Sit still—oh! Pray do!"

I love to finger a man's limb when it is of such splendid proportions. This man's was exquisitely moulded. It stood awaiting my inspection. There was no reserve between us now. Modesty had flown out of the window We understood each other perfectly.

"But what can we do? Pray do let me put it into you. I won't hurt you. I'll be as gentle as a lamb. I won't tumble your clothes. It won't take a minute. The coachman is 'fly'—no one will know. Let me pass my hand up. Let me feel all you've got."

"Ah! No—no! It won't do! I must go back. What do you think they would say to me if they saw me enter all tumbled and rumpled? Sit still— sit still! Oh, pray do! Is that nice?"

I moved both my hands gently up and down his huge limb. Each stroke covered and then exposed the red gland. He breathed heavily. He ceased his attack. He pushed his loins forward. His thing got harder still.

"Nice? Oh, yes! My God! It's delicious—it's heaven—but I can't stand it! You'll bring it on!"

"Bring it on? Do you mean that I should milk you? Is it so very nice? Like that? And so—like that? Do you like me to play with it?"

"Oh, yes! It's lovely—you'll make me come if

you go on! You'll milk me, miss! Oh! Ah! Ugh! Do please stop a little!"

The horses had stopped. The carriage appeared to have drawn up under the trees close to the square railings in a dark place on the near side. I bent my head lower. I examined the man's limb as well as I could by the uncertain light. It was a model of manly health and vigour. I stooped lower still. My wet and eager lips touched the purple tip. How soft it was! How delicious the masculine fragrance. I kissed it repeatedly. A second later it slipped into my mouth. The man seemed to resign himself. He sighed with delight. My tongue thrust itself below the velvet plum-like nut. He pushed the head and shoulders quite into my gullet. I sucked it all I could. My gloved hands tickled and pressed the long shaft. He commenced to wriggle on the edge of the seat. He straightened his legs wide apart. He threw back his head.

"Oh, my God! Stop—no—go on! Go—oh! I'm coming!"

I obeyed—he thrust forward. I received a mouthful. He spent furiously. I held on. I caught it all to the last drop. I was half mad with the erotic pleasure. He groaned aloud in his spasmodic discharge as I drew spendings from him. I wiped my lips with my lace handkerchief. He sat up and re-arranged his clothes. We listened; then my companion cautiously opened the carriage door and got out. I heard another voice. The door was closed but the window was on the last button.

"What have you got inside, Chris?"

"Oh! Don't ask—a reg'lar stunner! It's a young

lady from the ball at No.——. She's all right—she's
—oh my! I can't speak yet, I've just done it. I've
had such a time!"

"Well! Get out of the way! Keep a lookout for
the sergeant—he won't be back along here just
yet."

The door opened again—a strong light flashed
into my face.

"Hullo! What's up here? What's up?"

The carriage door opened wider. A policeman
thrust himself in and sat on the front seat.

"I don't know that I oughtn't to run you in, miss
(they all called me 'miss'). There's been fine go-
ings-on here! Well, I never! A handsome, beautiful
young party like you! Why it makes my blood bile
to look at yer! What have you two been adoin' of?
I think I know. He's a nice young chap is Chris, but
he's that clumsy, that's what he is. I should like a
go at it myself! Give us a kiss, my beauty. There,
don't be shy. It's only my way, you know!"

"Oh! Please, you mustn't put your hand there.
You hurt—you are so rough. You will tear my
dress. Let me alone, I say! Oh! Pray don't—don't
do that!"

"Sit quiet. I'm in with these chaps. Why, they
couldn't do nothing without me. It's on my beat,
you see, miss. Sit quiet, I won't hurt you, but I mean
to have you—like Chris did."

All this time he was pulling me about with his
right hand. He was engaged in unbuttoning his
clothes with the other. He had no shame. He pulled
out a long white member. He shook it impudently
at me in the uncertain light. He was a strong, tall
man.

"Now, miss, you just keep quiet, or I shall have to spring my rattle."

"Oh, my goodness, policeman, how dreadfully naughty you are! But—oh, dear, dear me, what shall I do? Tell me—are you a married man?"

"Yes, I am that. I've a missus at home and three kids, but she ain't a patch upon you. You're just to my liking—a real beauty! But what do you want to ask that for?"

"Well—I don't know—but if you are really married—and if you are very, very gentle, perhaps—"

"Oh, shut up! I can't wait—here turn up your skirt—I want to see your legs."

The wretch put down his hands—he begged me to help him. I did all I could to save my dress. He saw my stockings up to—above the knees. His truncheon was stiff enough in all conscience now. I saw it plainly sticking up in a wild erection. He pulled me forward to the edge of the seat. He slipped onto his knees. He had shoved one hand up my clothes. His other arm was round my loins pulling me toward him. His eager fingers were already in contact with my most private parts. Secretly I enjoyed his rough toying. My skirts were up now until he could see my white belly. He rudely pushed my thighs asunder.

"Oh, Christ! What a fine little bit you are! You make me awfully randy! Here! Take this in your hand. Come! No nonsense now. I can't wait, I tell you. I won't hurt you—put it in yourself."

He forced me to take his truncheon in my gloved hand. I squeezed it. It was level with the place he sought. He thrust forward. I let it slip in. He no sooner felt the hot contact than he pushed it up me, dragging me close to him. He thrust it in to the balls—he began to move.

"Now, I'll do the business for you, my lady! How do you like that?"

"Oh, policeman, how you do push! Oh! Oh! Ah! Not so hard—oh!"

The man worked violently up and down my vagina. He was too excited to be long over the job. He seized me as in a vice. Almost immediately I felt him spending. I went off also. I was in an agony of sensuous delight. His sperm was thick and hot. He waited a moment to recover his breath. He drew his limb out and got up. As he did so, I noticed a face against the window. It was the footman. He opened the door.

"Come out. I know you've had the young lady. I saw you through the glass. I'm awfully randy again. There's time yet. There ain't no one about. Look out a minute while I have a go."

He entered the carriage and closed the door. He let loose his huge member. It seemed stiffer and bigger than ever.

"Now, miss, I can't help it. I'm not going to be left out. He's had it, so shall I!"

"Oh, you beast! What are you doing? Let me alone—don't thrust my legs open—you'll kill me. What a size it is! Oh! Dear! It will never go in! Oh! Ah! Oh! Oh! You hurt—you're right into me!"

He had already penetrated. He forced the huge thing into me till he seemed to be right up my womb. He uttered no words. He only breathed hard and pushed me upwards in his strong excitement. Then his head fell on my shoulder. I knew he was spend-

ing. He emitted in short spasmodic jerks. Like his
friend, he made haste to escape.

Before he could reclose the door, I heard the
flick of a whip. A new and very gruff voice exclaimed:

" 'Ere, I say! What the 'ell are you fellers
about? I'm agoin' to get down. The old box is
a-shakin' about that hawful, I can't 'old the bloody
horses!"

Just then I heard a scramble. The policeman
rushed across the road. The footman got up beside
the coachman. The carriage was turned rapidly
round and then went slowly back towards No. —.
I adjusted myself as well as I could. I pulled my
large opera cloak over my head and was set down
once more. I passed hastily in and gained the ladies'
retiring room. I found myself alone. The wild
strains of a lovely waltz were filling the air. I re-
paired damages and changed my gloves.

"Oh, my dear Eveline, I have been looking for
you!"

"Poor papa! I had a headache, but it is better
now. Have you been making a night of it? I have
enjoyed myself thoroughly. Take me home now—I
have danced enough!"

Chapter VI

Dr. Brooksted-Hoare was a dapper little man. He came of a medical family. His father had commenced life as assistant to an apothecary and subsequently practised as such himself. The doctor's curly brown hair, already tinged with grey, was crisply arranged round his small and shapely head. His finely cut features presented nothing in their repose which betrayed his exalted opinion of his own powers or person. When he spoke, however, his animation increased imperceptibly. His mode of expression was adapted to the circumstances of the case. He was obsequiousness itself to the wealthy and the noble—short and terribly decisive to the meek and lowly. He emphasised his opinion with a sort of professional superiority which contrasted quaintly with the careless garrulity of his ordinary conversation. His self-conceit was enormous, and, although a valuable adjunct in his *pose* before his patients, it raised a sort of hilarious resentment among his professional *confrères*, who saw through it. Dr. Brooksted-Hoare possessed a large practice as a specialist for the treatment of women and children. He was altogether a professional pet of society in his especial department. His fees were immense, but only commensurate with his consummate self-complacency. He delighted to talk of the duchesses and notables whom he counted among his patients. The pains and sufferings of Royalty were all subservient to his skill. If his communications concerning them were not always exactly correct, they at least served to extend his importance as a specialist.

"I have made a most careful examination in the case of—ahem!—her ladyship—the Countess of Endover—yes—aided by my friend Dr. Proctor here—who is, I believe, your usual family adviser —a most careful and thorough examination. I find —ahem!—I find that there is no possible chance of her ladyship ever becoming a mother. A mother— ahem!—in her present condition. I have, however, ascertained—ahem!—quite beyond the possibility of a doubt, that a trifling—let us say—ahem!—a very trivial operation—would remove this—this disability. There is a small ligament which interferes with the proper position of the organs relatively, which interrupts the—ahem!—the natural sequence of events. I cannot very well demonstrate this to the lay mind, but Dr. Proctor and myself are in accord that it could be easily and safely removed. Our dear young Countess is in every other way so beautifully and—ahem!—so perfectly formed that I have no doubt, if she were willing to submit to this, she would have no cause thereafter to disappoint her lord. Do I make myself clear? It is for her ladyship to decide—ahem!"

Here the little man stuck his hands under his coat tails as he balanced himself in front of the fire and reminded one strongly of a bantam cock which contemplated crowing.

Our own family doctor looked anxiously towards me. My husband and my papa looked at one another in mute astonishment.

"The necessities of the case would, of course, entail a little sacrifice of time and comfort on the part of her ladyship. There would be the usual antiseptics to administer, which Dr. Proctor would undertake of course—the slight operation to undergo—ahem!—let us say, a week's rest, and all would be in order again."

The Earl looked immensely relieved. He regarded me wistfully. Papa wore an expression of anxiety mingled with doubt. I put an end to the suspense.

"I am ready to undergo the operation as soon as the arrangements can be made. Tomorrow if you will; the sooner the better. I have made up my mind. I will take my chance."

My husband actually shed tears of delight. He pressed my hand. The two doctors beamed graciously upon me. Papa hid his emotion behind a well-affected compliment on my courage. Dr. Brooksted-Hoare hastened to reply.

"Be it so—tomorrow at noon—ahem!—I will be at your mansion. Oh, yes, I know the address. Leave all the arrangements to Dr. Proctor. He will, I know, have all in readiness."

The little medico made an entry in his notebook. Then he pompously bowed us all out.

A vision of disappointed sisters, of a cousin re-mitted to his pothouses and his scum of society, and his little bills, flashed across my placid vision as I took my seat in the carriage, none the easier for the disturbances caused by the exhaustive examination I had undergone.

I had now two great reasons to be satisfied with the resolution I had formed. The earlier intimation I had received from my medical friend was proved without doubt to be correct. The operation, I was informed by both physicians, had been perfectly successful.

"Dr. Proctor says I may sit up today, papa, and I may have what I like in the way of diet."

"I have sent for oysters, my dear Eveline, and Mrs. Lockett will send you up a roast grouse—also a custard pudding of her own especial make."

"How kind of you! Today I shall fare like a queen; but oysters, you know, dear papa, are supposed to stimulate other nerves than those of mere digestion."

"Yes, that is so. I believe I have felt the influence myself, especially when near my dear Eveline. No doubt they have a certain effect as an aphrodisiac. I believe it is on account of the large amount of phosphates they contain. Certain kinds of fish have the same result. The skate, that nutritious but much neglected flat fish, is one of them."

I could not help smiling at the serious professional air he assumed while thus lecturing. I let him see a twinkle in my eyes.

"You mustn't eat oysters, and you mustn't eat skate then, dear papa, when you come near your little Eveline. She has made certain very wise resolutions and she intends to keep them.

He drew a face of such abject dismay that I could not repress a little laugh at his expense.

"You are too cruel, Eveline, my dear child, but perhaps you act for the best. You have a will of your own which hitherto has always led you to avoid pitfalls."

"I did not mean that I would be so terribly severe as altogether to exclude those delicacies from my dear papa's dietary—only that—only—you see, papa—well! We must be careful how we handle things now."

"I have thought much on the same subject. I agree with you, my dear child."

"At the same time, my Charlemagne is a great conqueror. He cannot be expected to go altogether without the reward of his victories."

"I do not understand, my darling, quite what you mean."

"I will try to explain myself, dear papa. When the Emperor Charlemagne first indulged in the luxury of a debauch with his young daughters, you may be sure he was not long in arriving at a complete enjoyment of their charms. Then came a time when the pleasures of dalliance succeeded to the hot lust of passionate desire. No doubt those dutiful recipients of the great man's favours were early indoctrinated in all those auxiliary delights which go to make up the full pleasure of sensual gratification. Do you follow me, dear papa?"

He nodded, drew his chair closer to my bed, and I saw my opportunity. I was not slow to take advantage of it. I only dreaded his terrible disappointment.

"We must be careful. I have fully determined

there shall be a direct heir to the Earldom of Endover. I believe in myself. In so doing I already win half the battle. But I will have no weak or ailing offspring of a race which has grovelled in all the vices of the Georgian period, whose blood is as putrid as their morals are degenerate."

"My dear Eveline! Are you not a little hard on the Endovers?"

"Hard on them! If you only knew all I have learnt concerning them! The men, I mean—the father—the grandfather—the progenitors of this noble, unadulterated family. Why, had the grandfather of my husband not had the good fortune to have hit upon an American millionaire and married the pork slaughterer's vulgar daughter, there would not have been an acre left, nor a hearth to warm the vapid blood of his son, much less his grandson. No, papa, if I bear a child to succeed to the title and the estates, at least he shall be of strong, sound English blood. You may leave the rest to your little Eveline."

"By God! You are right, my child! I have unbounded confidence in you. But how will you compass all this? How carry out your idea?"

"As I said before, dear papa, leave all to me. I believe I shall succeed in all. I have faith in myself —we shall see. I am going down to Chitterlings. Endover goes with me. We are to have a second honeymoon, he says. There will be at least the *horns* of a new moon for *him*, and very little honey for me—the less the better."

"You frighten me, Eveline. I trust all may turn out as you hope."

I indulged in a little quiet laugh. I put forward

my lips for a kiss. He bent over me; our lips met. For a second my tongue touched his. His eyes lighted up with passion.

"You must not let me change my position, dear papa. Pull up your chair closer yet—so, that will do."

I gently thrust my right hand from out of the side of the bed. I had arranged a little *divertissement* for him, which I knew would exactly meet the exigencies of the case. A beautiful white kid glove covered my hand and half my arm, fitting like my own skin. On my wrist sparkled a lovely diamond bracelet, his own gift. He looked down. He beheld the snake-like advance of the little gloved hand, the glistening sheen of the perfumed glove itself.

"Oh, Eveline! All that for me? How deliciously inviting is that beautiful little hand."

He seized it—he covered it with hot kisses.

"We must be careful, dear papa, *how we handle things now.* Come—let me handle yours. Do you understand better now? Let me give my dear papa all the pleasure my active little fingers can bestow. I am to remain still, but Dr. Proctor says I may use my hands and arms. I want to avail myself of his kind permission. How stiff it is already! How delicious to feel its long white shaft. Oh! How I long to kiss it! But no! I want—I want to see all your sweet sperm come out. I want to bathe my new glove in it. Let me have this pleasure, dear papa!"

I knew him so well. I was quite aware of his peculiar lechery. I grasped his erected member. He leant over me. I whispered the old indecencies in his ear—the old invitations in so many crude expressions. I bade him not to spare my nice new glove.

He flushed—his lips grew dry and hot. The door
was locked—no one had a right to disturb us. I
slipped my nimble fingers up and down his darling
weapon. I squeezed it. I bore back the loose skin.

"Oh! My child—oh! Ah! You give me an ecstasy of pleasure!"

"Is that nice, dear? You wicked papa! You will
spoil my beautiful new glove! You will be coming
directly—I know you will. You cannot help it—
there! Do I rub this big thing as you like! Oh! How
red the top is now! What a contrast with the satin
white of my glove! Oh! A little drop already!
Quite a beautiful pearl! Oh, papa! There will be a
quantity, will there not?"

He breathed hard and bore up towards me. He
held back his clothes to avoid the consequences of
his discharge. I had my kerchief ready. My hand
rapidly manipulated his lovely member. How I
doted on the big, impudently obtrusive thing as I
shook it up and down! His delight was evident; enjoyment gave expression in his hard stentorian res-
piration, his open mouth, his upturned eyes. I knew
by all the usual symptoms he was on the verge of
his climax. It arrived. He straightened himself out.
I grasped my victim firmly. He discharged. The hot
thick semen came slopping over my hand. My glove
slipped about in the steaming overflow. He pushed
upwards to meet my rapid movements until he had
emitted the last drops. Then he sank back exhausted in his seat.

"Go at once and get a glass of wine, dear papa.
I must not have you reduced so much again for a
long while to come."

There is no change so beneficial for a convalescent as the sweet country air of the Lake district. The bracing breezes of Chitterlings would, I hoped, do much for me. Perhaps I expected their influence to be seconded by other and more potent agents. This may well have been. The Earl was with me. Endover was in his gayest humour. The day had been a long and fatiguing one. I begged him to excuse me. I retired early. I told him I felt worn out with fatigue. He wished to rejoin me in my chamber. I begged him to be reasonable. I was so tired. Tomorrow—yes, tomorrow night he should share my bed. My loving arms should reward him for all his forbearance. Yes! We would celebrate our new and second honeymoon. There should be no reason to complain of the coldness of his little wife.

I lay that night awake. I recalled in my mind the many instances of the Earl's indifference; his utter neglect when first, after so brief a period, he had treated me, his wife, as he had so many other women before me when the novelty of possession had worn off. I felt a disgust, a loathing I could not shake off. I thought of his low *amours,* of all I had heard, of what I knew only too well were his present associations. I remembered the pitiful history which poor Mrs. Hodge had revealed. As I did so, a thought came to my mind with the picture of her tearful earnest face. Did she contemplate a secret and a terrible retribution? Was she capable in her apparent simplicity of so double a scheme? I should know more tomorrow. I would satisfy myself ere I went further in the matter I had in hand.

Poor Mrs. Hodge! Simple Mrs. Hodge! What a cruel fate had left its stain and its memory with her! Only saved from the mire of moral degradation—from absolute destitution—by her strong unscrupulous common sense, she had made her escape in a marriage which, if it was not one of absolutely deep affection, afforded her at once a protection and a home. To her ignorant nature, born and bred among the peasantry of the estate—imbued only with the lowest perceptions of the moral sense, she looked upon her rustic spouse principally as a fine animal who had been the means of giving her two equally fine children and who was a sober and suitable companion in her quiet home. Like a certain class of dependents becoming fast extinct, her destinies were bound up in those of the great family in whose service, and under whose tenure, she and her progenitors had been born and brought up. They made themselves and their interests one with the noble house they served and in reality looked to the prosperity of their lord as a necessary adjunct to their own.

Mrs. Hodge was delighted to see me. We had frequently met since my first and memorable visit. The anxiety of the good woman on the subject we had discussed had by no means subsided, but she had abstained from any very pointed references thereto, merely contenting herself with a sigh and shrug of her broad shoulders, as if to deplore the fact and my want of appreciation of her views on the subject.

On this occasion she was particularly communicative.

"Ah, my lady, those big towns like Liverpool and London; the smoke and the fogs, and the bad air are not doin' your ladyship any good. If I may make so bold, your ladyship is thinner and paler than when you went away."

"You are right, Mrs. Hodge. I have not been very well."

"Nothing like the fresh air here, my lady. In a week you would be a different creature."

"I wish I was a different creature, indeed I do! I am not satisfied with myself, Mrs. Hodge."

"I don't wonder at it. Why, how can you be? And it's not all your own fault either. Ah! Dear me— dear me—what one has to put up with? Now my Jock—why Lor' bless you, my lady, there's no holdin' of him when he's on!"

She had sunk her voice to a mere whisper. She shut the door of the lodge. She came back and placed herself on her knees before me. It was her favourite attitude. There was something comically irresistible in the semipleading position she assumed. I laughed softly.

"Why, Mrs. Hodge, your Jock must be a terrible fellow indeed by your description. I should not care to be in your place."

"Wouldn't you, my lady? Sometimes I think you would though. He's not much to look at: only an honest plainspoken ad, but he's true as steel, and— and he can hold his tongue. He's as silent as the night. That's what he is! Don't tell me your ladyship is content. I've told you already what I think. It ain't in nature—a beautiful sweet young creature like your ladyship and wedded to—to—"

"Oh, Mrs. Hodge! What's done can't be undone, you know!"

"No, but it can be amended! Do you think I'd waste all my young days if I was in *your* place? Not I!"

"What would you do, Mrs. Hodge?"

"What would I do? Well, if I found my husband was no husband to me, but had deceived me into thinking him *a man*, I'd get one in his place. That's what I'd do! So should you, my lady!"

She hobbled up close to me in her excitement. Her volubility seemed to carry her away. She laid her hands caressingly upon my knees. She brought her face closer. She felt more confident—she grew bolder as she saw me smile. I laid my hand softly on hers. She was about to speak again. I motioned her to remain silent.

"I will not disguise it from you. I do not attempt to deny my great disappointment. That which you related to me on the occasion of my first coming here, Mrs. Hodge, made a great impression on me. I am young. As you say, I am in perfect health. You are a woman and you know what a woman's nature is. There should be no reason on my part why I am childless."

"No, I am sure of it, my lady. I know the cause. It is no fault of yours—why should you continue so? I should not be content in your place."

My blood rose to my face; my eyes flashed; I half rose. The good woman recoiled, half frightened. I was in very earnest now.

"*I will not be childless if it depends upon me to prevent it!*"

I clenched my hands. I stamped my foot imperiously—my breath came short and angrily. Mrs. Hodge clasped her hands together as she knelt.

"Oh, bless your ladyship for that! Now you speak like the great lady you are. Keep to that! Oh! Keep to that, my lady, and—and *try my Jock!*"

Chapter VII

The night came and also my lord. After a long drive across the country we had dined, or rather supped, about half past nine. The champagne had done its work with my husband who was sufficiently lively. As for myself I was too careful of the part I had to play to allow myself a liberty with the exhilarating beverage. I pass by all the details of that unpalatable nuptial couch. Suffice it to say my wiles succeeded in affording him a complete enjoyment of his marital privileges while my precautions rendered it perfectly impossible any consequences, such as he hoped for, could follow. The Earl left my bed charmed with my warmth and vivacity. He was equally proud of himself and of his virility.

I cannot say I shared his sentiments. His weak and languid attempts had only succeeded by my assistance, but they were sufficient to convince him of his prowess in the lists of love. The night passed for me almost without sleep. I was restless, excited, and uneasy.

The evening following we had arranged a dinner party. It was a hunting reunion. Only gentlemen were invited. I retired early. I left the men enjoying themselves over their wine and their cigars. I had been the only lady present. No doubt my absence was the signal for the real revelry to commence. I retired to my chamber pleading fatigue to my maid and, having dismissed her, locked myself in for the night.

My bedroom was upon the ground floor. Three long windows opened upon a wide verandah. One had only to step out to enjoy the scent of the roses. My object in doing so on this occasion was different. Just as the clock struck nine, I stood outside upon the tessellated pavement. Someone was crouching in the shadow of the wall. A whispered word, a cautious footfall on the lawn—I was by the side of Mrs. Hodge. I wrapped my long cloak around me closely. I drew over the hood. Silently I followed her across the dark lawn through the shrubbery, along the shadowy footpath under the double row of stately elms which bordered the avenue. Not a soul stirred here after dark, save only coming or departing guests. We kept on together in the deep shade of the spreading foliage. We reached the lodge in silence. I followed my conductress through the portal. She shut and barred the door.

A dim light was shed by a small lamp upon the table. Mrs. Hodge took me by the hand. She led me forward. We passed into the room on the right. I stood beside the bed. All had been arranged. I slipped off my cloak—my skirts. I stood in my *chemise de nuit*.

I had anticipated the adventure with eagerness. Every detail had been planned beforehand with scrupulous precision. My feelings were intensely excited. A restless longing for the embrace of a strong man had troubled my thoughts all day. I had been roused by the faint efforts to which I had submitted the previous night. I determined to surrender myself without reserve, at least on this occasion. The stake was immense; the game was well worth playing for. No gambler ever felt more enthusiasm as he staked his pile upon a single chance. I had brought all my wits to bear. There is an enormous power for good or bad in a strong will. I devoted mine with all my naturally strong energy to this object. The second title had too long lain dormant. There were the three sisters all secretly plotting—jealous of me from the first, and the dissolute cousin to whom the usurers were becoming more accommodating as time rolled on and brought no news to lessen his pretentions to the succession. Last, and by no means least, there was my natural womanly pride, the instinct of maternity unsatisfied—the galling feeling that I—Eveline—would eventually be supplanted in the enjoyment of the property for which I had risked so much—the jointure of the Countess of Endover.

Mrs. Hodge put her finger to her lips—she held the bedclothes open—I slipped backward into the feather bed. Two strong arms entwined themselves around my slender middle. They drew me down into contact with a man's hirsute body. I felt alarmed in spite of my resoultion.

"Oh, Mrs. Hodge! Pray do not leave me—oh, pray!"

"Hush! Hush—be silent—he's a lamb to what he is sometimes!"

I noticed the change in her intonation—the respectful distance, the conventional modes of address were gone. This was also part of the comedy.

A rush of hot desire passed through my nervous system as I felt the warmth and solidity of the male who held me. That it *was a male* there was not the slightest doubt. My back—my buttocks rested against his belly and thighs. Already his parts protruded viciously. His instrument began to assert its virility. I interposed my hand— "Oh!"

Mrs. Hodge was still beside the bed. I could just see her outline in the darkened room. She held my left hand. My right encountered a monstrous limb. My hand mechanically closed upon this object. It responded to my exciting caress. I felt a bush of curly hair—a muscular pair of thighs. I remained thus a few minutes—not a sound was heard. Then the right arm which had held me was softly unlaced. A large hand inspected my charms. My bosom—my belly—my mount, and, lastly, the central spot of man's desires. If my assailant's passion had been already roused, my own responded to it. A sudden movement served to turn me on my back. At the same moment, Mrs. Hodge assisted by a rapid jerk of my left arm. I raised my right to protect myself in a half real, half feigned effort of modesty. Immediately my bedfellow was upon me. In dragging me towards him downwards, my *chemise* had been turned up. My body lay naked to his attack. He was not slow to take advantage of the position. The fortress lay open. He had only to march through the portal.

"Oh, Mrs. Hodge! I—do not let him—pray—oh! Oh!"

There was no response from the good woman

who had not released my hand. Instantly I was
helplessly extended beneath the weight of a man's
naked body.

Under such circumstances a woman never com-
plains of the inconvenient pressure. It is true that
the elbows of the operator take on themselves a
certain part of the load. For all that the position
appears to be the normal one. It is certainly the best
—the one peculiarly adapted for the exchange and
enjoyment of those emotions which accompany the
act of copulation—those tender emanations of passion stimulated and excited to an almost insupportable strain—those outbursts of intense ecstasy
which are wrung from the yielding female form
vibrating beneath the efforts of a vigorous male.

I had seen Jock on several occasions when visit-
ing the lodge. Usually he made himself scarce by
slipping shyly away by the back door. I had rarely,
however, exchanged more than a simple salutation
with him. He struck me as a particularly fine young
man whose physiognomy displayed more intellec-
tuality than fell to the lot of the rustics around. His
wife took pleasure in repeating her commendation
of his intelligence, his industry, and his constant
endeavours to instruct himself in the principles and
practice of agriculture. He became thus an object
of interest to me, particularly after the extraordinary invitation the simple woman had extended to
me. In short, I had made my observations. I had
matured my decision.

If ever I was in a condition, after my forced abstinence, to fulfill the requirements of perfected
copulation, to relish the joys and participate in the
animal pleasure of the act, it was now. My feelings

were worked up to frenzy. I remember little of the scene that followed. I received the huge organ of virile manhood with a gasping sigh of wild delight—a little cry of mingled pain and pleasure. My assailant lost no time, his arms were around my light body, his own was in determined conjunction with mine. He seemed to be anxious to incorporate himself with me. He worked with vigour. He did not spare me. He seemed incapable of controlling his emotions. Mrs. Hodge remained beside me. A few whispered words of encouragement came from her parted lips as the significant sounds and movements progressed beneath her. Then there came a time when I held my breath, when the long pent-up forces of nature seemed about to give way. Suddenly I knew the climax had been reached—the end attained. I received a copious outpouring of nature's prolific balm. Then my companion lay still as death, save for the fluttering of his breath upon my neck.

I draw discreetly the veil over the remainder of that night's pleasure. It was already late when, guided by my faithful conductress, I again found myself within the precincts of my own chamber. I enjoyed the long slumber of satisfied nature. I woke in the broad sunlight to a new sensation—a new hope.

"My sweet Eveline is looking all the better for her stay in the delicious air of Cumberland. I quite envy you that lovely little paradise you have there."

"Indeed, papa, I feel much stronger. It is the air, as you say, which has done me so much good. I have, I am sure, derived much benefit from my visit there. Endover has gone to his moor again."

"You have not forgotten your promise, my dear child. We were to repeat our experiences of the peephole. Will you join me there this afternoon? I have arranged something for your gratification."

"Do tell me what the nature of it is, dear papa."

"Well, it is a rather peculiar affair in which the actors will have no knowledge of the presence of witnesses whatever."

"And we two are to be the witnesses? Oh, that will be lovely!"

"Yes, my dear, there are two convenient apertures through which we can enjoy together the interview which will take place. I have reason to believe it will be of exceptional interest to us both '

"You quite raise my curiosity, dear papa. Do tell me—what is the affair to be like?"

"I must first say that it is not the ordinary thing at all. It appears that a certain gentleman, whose name and personality are both unknown to me, takes a woman to this place. I am told by my informant who conducts this very private establishment that she is rather young—in fact a mere girl, although a very charming and beautiful one. It also appears that the gentleman is suspected of a close connection with this young woman. We shall probably know more by and by. Anyhow it is not the business of my informant to trouble herself about such trifles. She is discretion itself."

He well knew my perversion—my passion all in accord with his own. It was evidently his desire to

play upon it—to afford another practical example
of the amiable weakness so lightly recorded by Voltaire in the case of the great Charlemagne.

"Do you mean to say, dear papa, that the gentleman is a near relation? That it is—in fact—a—a
case of *incest*?"

"I believe it is, Eveline, from all I have been
told."

"Oh, how delicious! Yes, certainly we must see
that."

"You charming darling! How our views con-
join! How closely our tastes—our passions coin-
cide! Listen, my child, while I tell you more of this
subject which engrosses us both."

"The crime, if crime it be, is as the world—at
least as the Biblical account of it. Did not the children of Adam and Eve, brothers and sisters, copu-
late and procreate? The Bible is full of instances of
this original and entrancing weakness. Not to quote
the example of Lot, the brother-in-law of Abra-
ham, whose two young daughters, for want of a
male, as the version goes, but in reality from a real
lascivious passion to play with a parental sugar-
stick, made their father jolly with the fermented
juice of the grape. They then excited him to such an
extent that the vigorous parent lay with them both
and all three united in a copulative orgy.

"King David's favourite son, Amnon, was possessed of so absorbing a passion for his sister, Ta-
mar, that nothing short of violating her could satisfy his virile passion. Only picture that scene—the
brother exalted by uncontrollable lust, seizing upon
his beautiful sister as she struggled before him,
and then revelling in her virgin charms. Not that

the virgin so much dreaded the act itself, but she feared the foolish position in which she would be placed, and suggested that her father, King David, would not deny them their little irregularity if his consent were asked. Do not newspapers of our own times frequently give us lecherous details of these convenient family relations of fathers with their daughters, of brothers with their sisters, and of mothers with their sons?"

Chapter IX

That same afternoon papa and I duly ensconced ourselves in the snug little closet on the left in the narrow passage which led to the chamber I already knew.

We had not long to wait. Our door was bolted— the two apertures were uncorked. We had found that each commanded a most complete view of the bedroom. Our heads were not six inches apart. We had chairs on which to sit with soft cushions upon them. I noticed that the legs of these seats were covered with india-rubber pads, so that no sound would be audible if they were moved. They were the caps or cups which are supplied for sticks and crutches. A soft carpet covered the floor and a padded rest was fixed above each peephole upon which to lay the forehead. Everything was luxuriously complete. Presently I heard the sound of footsteps in the corridor. The door of the bedroom opened. A voice in gentle accents murmured: "This way, please!" The door was closed again after giving ingress to two individuals. Then there was silence—

profound, but for the gentle breathing of papa behind me.

The first who came under my view was a short, thickset man of some five and forty years of age. His hair was already turning grey; his closely cut beard and heavy moustache were of the same grizzly shade. His features struck me as being ordinary without vulgarity, and he possessed a look of ardent sensuality which, to my practised eye, there was no possibility of mistaking.

The second comer interested me more. She was a young lady—a mere girl whose age could not have exceeded from sixteen to seventeen years of age. Indeed, from the very youthful face and unformed bust she might well have been a year younger. She was far from being either full-grown or fully developed. What, however, struck me most was her extreme beauty. She had a skin like alabaster, white and soft. She was fair and plump for a girl of her age. Her features were regular and good and bore a close resemblance to those of her companion. I noticed that, dressed in the usual girlish fashion of her age, she had very short skirts and wore socks so that her calves were without stockings, showing the naked legs above the tops of her perfectly fitting, high, and delicate little kid boots.

Having carefully bolted the door, the man threw himself upon a lounge. The girl set herself, with the curiosity of a child, to examine and take note of the apartment. He watched her every movement as a cat studies a mouse. I thought I already detected a flash of obscene desire in his liquid eye as he rapidly scrutinised every change of position. Then he threw off his coat, opened his waistcoat, deposited his watch and chain on the adjoining table, and removed his necktie and shirt collar.

"Do you see her boots?" whispered a voice at my ear. "What nice legs she has! What is he going to do, I wonder? She's very small."

"Yes, and so pretty too! Do you notice the likeness, dear papa?"

We could distinctly hear every word they spoke.

"Come here, Lucy!"

The girl obeyed with an air of indifference which appeared to me to hide a certain amount of fear. The man put her upon his knee.

"When did I do it last?"

The girl blushed scarlet.

"It was Wednesday, a week ago—the day mother went to Liverpool."

"What did I promise you this time, if you were good."

"You said you would give me a new photographic album and a whole pound of chocolate *fondants.*"

"What—all that! Well, I suppose I must be as good as my word. Now then, Lucy, let's see if you are getting to be a young woman."

"Oh! I wish I was already a grown-up young woman!"

"It will all come in time—you are getting on fast."

While this edifying conversation was progressing, the man had let the young lady slip from his knee. She stood between his legs. His left arm encircled her tapered waist. His right played with her ankles, her calves, and her knees. Then he ad-

anced his eager hand a little further. Suddenly he
ent forward and pressed his lips to hers with a
ervent embrace which spoke volumes to us witnesses. He sucked long and ardent kisses from her
with the bestial avidity of a satyr.

"Who told you about kissing, Lucy?"

"That girl at school. She said the men knew best
how to kiss."

"She was right, dear girl! What else did she
say?"

"Oh, I don't know—but she said men liked to
feel the girls about—well—you know—under their
clothes."

"Yes, I think she was right, dear child! So they
do!"

Suiting the action to the word, he slipped his
hand further up between the girl's thighs. His eyes
glowed—his lips parted.

"Oh, there it is! What a nice little slit it is!"

"Oh, father! Don't! That hurts! Pray, don't!"

We looked at one another for a moment. The
secret was out.

"Give me your hand, Lucy. Put it there—do you
feel that?"

"Oh yes, I do! I know—you told me about it."

"What did I tell you it was? What did I say you
might call it?"

"I remember! You told me last time. You said it
was *a prick*!"

The man had been loosening his clothes. He held
the girl's hand close to him as they continued—

"What did that girl at the school tell you it was
called?"

"She said some other name. I think she said it

was a *diddle*. It was when she pointed to the statue
of Mercury on the stairs. But it was not at all like
yours. It was very small and hung down. Yours is
always upright, father—and oh, so big!"

He drew aside his shirt. He exposed his naked
member with the young woman's hand in contact.

"Isn't that nice, Lucy—oh so nice! We are all
right and quite alone here. You have only to be
quite quiet and play with my prick."

"Yes, I know. Now mother's at Liverpool, we
shall not be found out. Oh, my! If I was! How she
would beat me! But—but—you won't forget the
album, will you, father! I'm promised several pho-
tos to put in it already."

"No, my darling, certainly not. But come, take
off your clothes. I want to see you naked. I want to
see all your pretty things."

"Oh, father! Must I take them *all* off?"

"All except your *chemise*. Of course not your
boots. They are too smart to lose sight of."

As the pretty girl stripped, I feasted my eyes on
the lascivious exhibition. She was as fair as one of
Watteau's beauties and far more comely. A lovely
little Venus, with limbs like the most delicate ivory.
The man sat at his ease contemplating the process
of disentanglement from the manifold tapes and
laces which hindered the operation. His member
was exposed in its erected state beneath our full
gaze. He had evidently no shame, but on the contrary showed rather a Satanic delight in all the indecency he perpetrated.

"Ah, that's right! Now come here, Lucy! What
a delicious little slit! Let me feel it! How soft and

warm it is—how my fingers slip in between the pretty lips. You must never let the boys touch it. You must always keep it for me."

"Mother says some day I'll have more hair on it."

"Yes, I dare say, unless you let me take care of it for you. But Lucy, my prick wants to be kissed."

The girl went down on her knees. She clasped the man's member, a large and long one, in both hands, and imprinted a fervent kiss on the livid gland. He pushed it forward towards her.

"Now suck it a little, Lucy! Think of the chocolate!"

The young lass opened her lips. The man pushed forward. The big head entered Lucy's mouth; she sucked to order.

"Oh, that *is* nice! That's *delicious*—stop now! I must suck your slit. Put your feet on the sofa. Bend over my head—so!"

The satyr held the delicate girl close to him. He parted the rosy lips of her peach-like slit with his fingers, then he applied his eager face, covering her belly and beautiful mount with humid kisses. Finally, he sucked her parts until he appeared to have exhausted his breath. Lucy seemed to feel no particular sympathy with her parent's toying, but rather to be inspired by a certain obedience, which, no doubt, she connected with the promised reward. Then, hot from his obscene caress, he sat up.

"That was a real treat to me, Lucy! Now I want you to turn round and round slowly that I may see how nice you look naked."

The fair girl obeyed, slowly rotating, posturing, and posing her exquisitely graceful and youthful

form beneath the bestial gaze of her excited pro-
genitor. As for the man, he sat upon the edge of
the lounge, his legs wide apart, his shirt drawn up,
his member, red-topped and erect, curving its length
backwards towards his navel as if confident of the
pleasures yet in store for it. Then he rose and,
catching the little sylph in his arms, carried her un-
resisting to the ample bed.

"Look, look, Eveline! Do you see? Do you think
he is going to put his member into her? It looks
like it."

As cautiously, I rejoined:

"Yes, papa, it looks like it! What a beautiful
girl! What a fine thing he has! I should like his
thing, papa! Would you like her?"

I gently lowered my hand. I clasped his limb,
loose already from the confinement of his trousers.

"Oh! How stiff you are, dear papa! This erotic
scene is almost too much for you. Pray keep calm!
Let us look on and watch them further."

The girl was on the bed; the man was kneeling
over her naked form.

"You won't hurt me again like last time, will
you?"

"Of course not, Lucy! Only hold still; put your
pretty legs apart! Now raise your knees up—so! I
must lie down on your soft little belly and feel how
warm it is!"

"Oh! But you are pushing it into me! It's—it's—
oh, my! It's too big! Oh, father, pray don't—you
hurt!"

"Be quiet, I say, you young she-devil! You were
not making all that noise when I caught you with
young Symes."

"Oh, oh, no! But his thing was not near so big as yours, and he was ever so gentle."

"Well! If he could have you, so can I! Lie still, I say! It's going in now—there! It's half in already! How tight you are, Lucy—you young harlot! I'll tell your mother if you cry out! Lie still, I tell you! There! There—now you've got it! Oh—ugh! How nice it is! Oh! Jig—jig—joss!"

The man began to move up and down. Lucy took a big mouthful of the bedclothes and half shut her pretty eyes.

"Oh, father! It's too far in! You hurt—"

"Nonsense, Lucy, you must have it all! I'm too stiff to stop now! Hold up! Let me put my hands under your bottom. That's right. Now I can get in better! Oh, my—it's lovely!"

The girl groaned. The lascivious parent commenced to move up and down with a regular cadence. It was easy to see he was in absolute possession. From our hiding place we could see his weapon moving in and out between the girl's plump young thighs I began insensibly working papa's limb in my warm hand as we looked on. The man stopped occasionally as if to prolong and linger over his pleasure. The girl lay utterly passive, her little hand convulsively clutching the sheet as if to fortify her to bear the process of the disproportionate coitus with less suffering. Suddenly her companion retook himself to his libidinous exercise. A few rapid jerks—a thrusting, straining movement upon his little victim—and it was easy to see his climax was at hand. It came. He fell with a gasping cry upon Lucy's rosy little form and lay bereft of all motion save the hoarse breathing with which he accompanied the overflow of his nature.

"He has done! He has discharged right into her!" whispered dear papa.

My hand grasped the erected staff—it pushed itself forward. I worked it quickly, decisively. A plentiful stream of hot sperm gushed over my tightly fitting kid glove. Papa sighed deliciously. His head reclined on my shoulder. He had succumbed to the excitement of the scene.

The voices of the strange couple in the bedroom at length aroused us both.

"I want to know what else that girl at the school told you, Lucy. Didn't she say she had two brothers? Now don't hide anything from me, my girl. You know I'll not tell mother, and you had better tell me all about it."

"Well, so I will, father, if you won't be cross. Amy says she has two brothers, both older than her, and that they taught her all she knows about—about diddles—and things."

"I suppose they had nice little games between all three?"

"Yes, but not at first. It was her younger brother, Fred, who began it, she says. He got her into the wood behind their house. They live in the country, you know—and there he pulled up her clothes and made her let him put his fingers to her slit. Then he showed her his thing and she found it got so stiff and big when she touched it! After a time, the elder brother found them out and he wanted to play at it too."

"Well, Lucy, and then, I suppose, they began in earnest?"

"Yes, they did. The elder brother had a much

larger diddle than Fred. He was seventeen. One day he got Amy down in a quiet corner of their garden, and I do believe he would have pushed it quite into her little pussy, but it came on to rain, and while they were sheltering in the greenhouse the gardener caught them. Amy says she is sure he saw what they were doing. Alexander was the name of her big brother and he ran away, but the gardener stopped her. He explained to her why Alex could not push his diddle into her slit. He said that she had an egg there like all very young girls, and that she ought to have that egg broken, and that she would be quite a woman and able to play with the boys and even with the men. She was very much obliged to him for explaining all about it to her. She told me she felt very grateful to him so that when he offered to break the egg for her she thought how kind it was of him. She told me that the gardener locked the door of the greenhouse and put her on some hay in a wheelbarrow. Then he let down his trousers and showed her his diddle—"

"You mean his prick—don't you, Lucy?"

"Yes, it must have been his prick—like yours. Well, he let it out for her to look at, she said. 'Oh, such a whopper! And all red at the top!' He took her in his arms and pulled up her clothes. Then he pushed his diddle—I mean his prick—up between her thighs and right into her little slit. Amy says he was not long doing it but that it hurt dreadfully— only she is sure that he broke the egg because she felt the yolk all running down her legs when he had done."

During this edifying history, papa and I had found it very difficult to restrain our risible tender-cies; we were quite relieved when the tender parent began once more to tumble and caress his charming daughter.

Her naive and innocent story had evidently had its effect, for his limb stood up wickedly in front of him as he pulled the girl roughly from the bed. He passed his lewd hands all over her Hebe-like figure. He was especially attracted by her rosy buttocks. Bending her face-downwards on the side of the bed, he pressed himself against her back. We saw his rampant member protruding beneath her soft little belly. Then he adjusted its nut to the pretty slit. Slowly and carefully he conducted his outrageous assault, till at last he contrived to sheath the greater part of the instrument in her vagina. Regardless then of the girl's complaints, he pushed in until the spasmodic vibrations of his loins told that his climax had been attained. Whether he had broken an egg or no, we had no means of ascertaining; certain it was, however, that poor Lucy's legs were covered with something which might have passed for a very pale yolk.

Chapter IX

Lord Endover was away still on his moor in the
North. I was again at Chitterlings. It is true the
fine air had done me good, but my residence had
not been productive of unmixed advantages.

On the contrary, I suffered from a nausea for
which I could only account in one way. The maids
in the laundry I thought eyed me as I passed. I even
caught two of them exchanging remarks which evidently concerned me. The old housekeeper took an
unusual interest in my movements. I thought she
looked upon me with a more patronising smile than
ever. What did it all mean? True, there was an
irregularity on my part—a certain period had
passed—I knew there was an overlong extension of
that interval which we are falsely taught became
the mitigated inheritance of Mother Eve The truth
I think only very gradually dawned upon me—I
own I was frightened as doubt became certainty,
so that one morning I sat down at my writing table
—I penned these lines to the Earl:

You have so often and so pointedly asked for
news—news which might very naturally be joyful to

us both, and I have so often had to disappoint you
that I tremble and hesitate on the present occasion
lest I may raise hopes only to have the mortifica-
tion of dispelling them in a subsequent letter. It will
however, I know, be a source of keen satisfaction to
you, my dear husband, to hear that I have the
strongest possible reasons for believing that your
wishes are likely to be gratified. That in fact I am
in a condition, at length, to become a mother. So
you see, gallant man, that you are a dangerous bedfellow. How shall I forgive you for the mischief you
have wrought?

My letter brought a prompt reply. The Earl
followed. The local medical attendant was con-
sulted. It was soon an open secret that the Countess
of Endover was likely—after all—to provide an
heir, or at least an heiress, to the noble Earl, her
husband. At first, the news was only whispered
through the house. It spread to the domain. It
reached the country town. It leaked out in a hundred
different little undercurrents. At last it fell with a
crash upon the expectant cousin and the three sisters of the Earl. They fairly groaned in vexation.
Then they fell one upon another. At length all three
turned round on the unhappy cousin. What might
have happened I know not, but fortunately a paragraph in *Society Peeps* made the matter no longer a
source of private inquiry. The necessity for the exercise of a dignity they really did not possess
obliged them to show a bold front. They received
the sarcastic congratulations of the crowd with
calm. If they inwardly raged at the disappointment, they were too well bred to let it appear.

The only one who could not be persuaded to

open her lips to the outside public, or to show any particular interest in the event, was Mrs. Hodge, but she returned the warm pressure of my hand with a satisfied shake of the head, accompanied by an expression of stolid conviction which was irresistibly comic, as she whispered softly: "I knowed it, I did! Your ladyship did right *to try my Jock!*"

"Ah, my dear Lady Endover, I am so very glad to see you! You do me too much honour. And your excellent papa, Lord L—— also! Well! So you have come to hear all the interesting facts—all the truths, and I fear—between ourselves—a fair, or unfair, proportion of lies also—at Bow Street. You will both stay and take a chop with me when the court rises—a *loin* chop, of course! Not a *chump* chop. Ah! You are both so good—how jolly! So glad to see you again! Here, Williams, go off to Mrs. W—— at once and get six best loin chops. What! Not eat *two*? Well to be sure! But your unexpected visit has given me quite an extra appetite."

"Really, Sir Langham, it is deliciously refreshing to see you so sprightly and gay—it does one's heart good."

"Ah, my dear young lady—you are too kind! Pardon me—I mean Lady Endover. I don't think there is much crime on the list today. Some of the ordinary kind—a wife pounded to death—a case or two of bigamy. Ah, Lady Endover, if they were all like you, we should hear no more of bigamy. That is—well—it depends of course—on—who

was first—ha, ha! I'm a sad dog! You must excuse
me. Lord L—— knows we were both boys once.
Then there's a sad case—a young fellow charged
with forgery. Then—let me see—oh—now that
won't do for you. It's a nasty case, but it won't
take long. My clerk tells me the evidence is very
strong and I think the culprit will plead guilty. You
must not be in court while that is on. I'll tell them
to put it first on the list. It's a way I have sometimes just to disappoint that objectionable class of
fashionables who come down here for such gar-
bage as this."

Sir Langham Beamer drew papa a little aside—
putting a fat finger in a buttonhole of his coat.
Then he whispered hoarsely—so hoarsely that I
heard all plainly:

"Case of indecent exposure—fellow has been at
it for months. His plan was to stand at the entrance to a yard in a quiet street and then when a
chance offered, he lugged out his—you know—and
wagged it at any likely woman who passed."

"Did he really? How dreadful!"

"Oh, we have lots of that kind of thing here.
Why, only last year I had a really serious case before me and sent it for trial. It was a woman who
strapped an unfortunate fellow down and then deliberately amputated his—well, his—you know—
the whole bag of tricks. The man died, so there
was no difficulty in the case, which went to the
Assizes as murder."

"I remember that case. The wretched woman
got twenty years penal servitude."

"When are we to go in, Sir Langham? I thought
the court was open."

"So it is—the chief clerk is hearing the night charges; they will not interest you much. There is a case, Lady Endover, I want to dispose of, and then you shall both come and sit by me."

Just then the door of the magistrate's private room opened. A buzz of voices sounded across the corridor. A police sergeant whispered to the dear old man and Sir Langham betook himself away with a courtly apology for his absence.

A short ten minutes passed. Then we were summoned to take our seats. Just as we passed into the Police Court, a man was leaving the dock. A warder held the iron gate open for him to pass down the steps which led to the cells below. He stared vacantly into my face. All power of recognition had passed out of that blurred, besotted gaze. As I looked, my mind went back to the timber yard and the man in the cloak. It was undoubtedly he.

"A very bad case. He's one of those fellows who are old stagers at the game. He pleaded guilty and got six months—lucky for him! He'd have had two years or more if he'd been sent to the Assizes."

It was a police sergeant. He spoke to Lord L——.

While we were still in the throng, another voice whispered close to my ear:

"From all rowdy cousins, scheming hags, and wicked spinsters—good Lord deliver us!"

Almost before I could rejoin an "Amen," the voice continued, but in a tone utterly different in its respectful intoration to the strong nasal drawl in which this invocation had been whispered:

"You have saved that man eighteen months of imprisonment."

"How so? What can I have had to do with it?"

I turned. It was a tall man in a baker's fustian suit. I knew the voice—the figure. It was Dragon.

"Just this. The chief clerk advised the solicitor —the solicitor advised his client. He pleaded guilty to save the time of the Court. He enabled the magistrate to convict him instead of sending him for trial. He could certainly have had two years as a previous offender at the Old Bailey. What brings your ladyship here?"

"If you will be at D—— Street today at six o'clock, I will tell you. I want you to execute a confidential commission for me—for the benefit of another."

"Your ladyship honours me too much. Always at your service."

I must not allow myself to forget that these notes, written only for my own perusal and reference—which no one else will ever read or see— save him I have designated as the custodian—do not contain more than rudimentary sketches of my intimacy with many of the actors therein. I care nothing for any critic, no such will ever have access to these pages. I am equally oblivious to the opinion of the public, who only know me as—*what I am not*.

My time came at last. All that wealth can do to minimise the agony of maternity I had in profusion. My child was born in the night. Next morning, Endover was ringing with the welcome news that there was at last a male heir to the Earldom

and estates. Little Lord Chucklington—the second
title had been lying dormant—lay crowing and
kicking in the nurse's lap. How I took him to my
bosom—how I had refused all anaesthetics; how I
discounted all idea of a substitute for his own
mother's breast; how he thrived and waxed a big
and healthy boy—all these things are matters of
history now. The Earl of Endover was enraptured.
I was an angel. Little Lord Chucklington was a
"cupid," and the experienced nurse nearly drove
my husband off his head with joy when she remarked that his infant Lordship was the "very
spit of himself." Everyone followed suit—congratulations poured in. The village was illuminated
that night. Bands played, drums banged, and trum-
pets rang out as the revellers dispersed only at a
late hour, sending the faint echoes of their joy on
the wings of the wind to my delighted ears in the
distant castle.

Eveline had arrived at the zenith of her ambi-
tion, but at what a sacrifice! My figure—that
fresh, youthful beauty which drove men mad with
desire to revel in it—was gone forever. As time
went on, I discovered another change—a transformation which only dawned upon me by slow
degrees. What may have been its cause will ever
remain a mystery—it is a fact, however, that all
sexual instinct, all desire, had departed from me
forever. Possibly—most probably—some derange-
ment of nervous tissue had taken place in parturi-
tion. It must be still only matter for conjecture. I
never disclosed the fact to anyone. From that time
forward I have devoted my life to my beautiful
boy.

I have yet a few notes to jot down here.

Dragon has always been my true and trusty friend. He is head of a department at New Scotland Yard.

Mr. Josiah and Mrs. Hodge have emigrated to Canada. They possess a huge farm on the western prairies. They are rich in the possession of five sons, the elder of whom are the mainstay of their parents in their agricultural industry. Mr. Hodge is reported wealthy, and all they touch is said to turn to money. Once a year a letter comes—always in the constrained, illiterate handwriting of bonny Mrs. Hodge, dutifully assuring me of their happiness. This is as regularly followed by the advent of certain hams and cheese with which my household is regaled.

A certain tall and fair-haired young medical practitioner one day received a letter informing him that if he chose to make application for a valuable appointment under the Charity Commissioners he was *more than likely* to obtain it. He did so —he succeeded. His services justified the selection. A second stroke of good luck fell in his way. Another and even more desirable appointment followed. His keen and correct power of diagnosis was soon known and appreciated. His able treatment of his patients brought him renown.

Dr. Brooksted-Hoare did not live to obtain the Baronetcy he coveted. His death left a vacancy in the ranks of those members of his profession who, as specialists, devote their talents to the treatment of the diseases of women and children. The opening was immediately taken advantage of by the same fair-haired aspirant to medical fame, Dr.

A——. He had found time to work for and obtain his "M.D. Lond.," and was informed in a certain mysterious manner that the lease of Dr. Brooksted-Hoare's house could be had by him for the asking at a merely nominal rent. He took the hint—also the lease. The aged Duchess of M—— sent for him one day. On the broad flight of stairs which led from the entrance hall, Dr. A——, as he descended, heard a visitor announced.

"The Countess of Endover. Will your ladyship please to pass this way."

A moment later a lady passed him going up. In her hand was the hand of a little boy, bright as an angel, a great favourite with her Grace. For a second, the lady's glance and that of the physician met. A civil inclination of the head, and she had gone. The doctor staggered against the wall. He seized the silken cord of the balustrade or he would have fallen. That which he divined when he reached his new home in the fashionable West had opened his eyes. He knew now, as he buried his honest, kindly face in the cushioned chair and allowed full vent to his tears of thankfulness and gratitude, *who* his benefactress had been and that the world was not all quite one of lust and selfishness.

FINIS

STAR Books are obtainable from many bookseller and newsagents. If you have any difficulty please sen purchase price plus postage on the scale below to:-

> **Star Cash Sales**
> **P.O. Box 11**
> **Falmouth**
> **Cornwall**

OR

> **Star Book Service,**
> **G.P.O. Box 29,**
> **Douglas,**
> **Isle of Man,**
> **British Isles.**

While every effort is made to keep prices low, it is sometimes necessary to increase prices at short notice. Star Books reserve the right to show new retail prices on covers which may differ from those advertised in the text or elsewhere.

Postage and Packing Rate
UK: 45p for the first book, 20p for the second book and 14p for each additional book ordered to a maximum charge of £1.63. BFPO and EIRE: 45p for the first book, 20p for the second book, 14p per copy for the next 7 books thereafter 8p per book. Overseas: 75p for the first book and 21p per copy for each additional book.

STAR BOOKS BESTSELLERS

FICTION

WAR BRIDES	*Lois Battle*	£2.50 ☐
AGAINST ALL GODS	*Ashley Carter*	£1.95 ☐
THE STUD	*Jackie Collins*	£1.75 ☐
SLINKY JANE	*Catherine Cookson*	£1.35 ☐
THE OFFICERS' WIVES	*Thomas Fleming*	£2.75 ☐
THE CARDINAL SINS	*Andrew M. Greeley*	£1.95 ☐
WHISPERS	*Dean R. Koontz*	£1.95 ☐
LOVE BITES	*Molly Parkin*	£1.60 ☐
GHOSTS OF AFRICA	*William Stevenson*	£1.95 ☐

NON-FICTION

BLIND AMBITION	*John Dean*	£1.50 ☐
DEATH TRIALS	*Elwyn Jones*	£1.25 ☐
A WOMAN SPEAKS	*Anais Nin*	£1.60 ☐
I CAN HELP YOUR GAME	*Lee Trevino*	£1.60 ☐
TODAY'S THE DAY	*Jeremy Beadle*	£2.95 ☐

BIOGRAPHY

IT'S A FUNNY GAME	*Brian Johnston*	£1.95 ☐
WOODY ALLEN	*Gerald McKnight*	£1.75 ☐
PRINCESS GRACE	*Gwen Robyns*	£1.75 ☐
STEVE OVETT	*Simon Turnbull*	£1.80 ☐
EDDIE: MY LIFE, MY LOVES	*Eddie Fisher*	£2.50 ☐

STAR Books are obtainable from many booksellers and newsagents. If you have any difficulty tick the titles you want and fill in the form below.

Name_____

Address_____

_____

Send to: Star Books Cash Sales, P.O. Box 11, Falmouth, Cornwall. TR10 9EN.

Please send a cheque or postal order to the value of the cover price plus:
UK: 45p for the first book, 20p for the second book and 14p for each additional book ordered to the maximum charge of £1.63.

BFPO and EIRE: 45p for the first book, 20p for the second book, 14p per copy for the next 7 books, thereafter 8p per book.

OVERSEAS: 75p for the first book and 21p per copy for each additional book.

While every effort is made to keep prices low, it is sometimes necessary to increase prices at short notice. Star Books reserve the right to show new retail prices on covers which may differ from those advertised in the text or elsewhere.

STAR BOOKS BESTSELLERS

THRILLERS

OUTRAGE	*Henry Denker*	£1.95 ☐
FLIGHT 902 IS DOWN	*H Fisherman &*	£1.95 ☐
	B. Schiff	
TRAITOR'S EXIT	*John Gardner*	£1.60 ☐
ATOM BOMB ANGEL	*Peter James*	£1.95 ☐
HAMMERED GOLD	*W.O. Johnson*	£1.95 ☐
DEBT OF HONOUR	*Adam Kennedy*	£1.95 ☐
THE FIRST DEADLY SIN	*Laurence Sanders*	£2.60 ☐
KING OF MONEY	*Jeremy Scott*	£1.95 ☐
DOG SOLDIERS	*Robert Stone*	£1.95 ☐

CHILLERS

SLUGS	*Shaun Hutson*	£1.60 ☐
THE SENTINEL	*Jeffrey Konvitz*	£1.65 ☐
OUIJA	*Andrew Laurance*	£1.50 ☐
HALLOWEEN III	*Jack Martin*	£1.80 ☐
PLAGUE	*Graham Masterton*	£1.80 ☐
MANITOU	*Graham Masterton*	£1.50 ☐
SATAN'S LOVE CHILD	*Brian McNaughton*	£1.35 ☐
DEAD AND BURIED	*Chelsea Quinn Yarbo*	£1.75 ☐

STAR Books are obtainable from many booksellers and newsagents. If you have any difficulty tick the titles you want and fill in the form below.

Name_____

Address_____

_____

Send to: Star Books Cash Sales, P.O. Box 11, Falmouth, Cornwall. TR10 9EN.

Please send a cheque or postal order to the value of the cover price plus:
UK: 45p for the first book, 20p for the second book and 14p for each additional book ordered to the maximum charge of £1.63.

BFPO and EIRE: 45p for the first book, 20p for the second book, 14p per copy for the next 7 books, thereafter 8p per book.

OVERSEAS: 75p for the first book and 21p per copy for each additional book.

While every effort is made to keep prices low, it is sometimes necessary to increase prices at short notice. Star Books reserve the right to show new retail prices on covers which may differ from those advertised in the text or elsewhere.